Outlaws

Ilene T. Goldman

October

Hood coughed the cold out of his lungs and curled tighter, as close to fetal position as his stiff creaky joints could manage. The street was quiet—or as close to quiet as it ever got at night—and his home sweet alley was dark and almost still. Not so much as a snore or a snuffle from his merry band of roommates. Only the usual rats and other vermin scurried in the shadows. Tonight, at least, Hood's mind recognized them for what they were.

With a grunt, Hood twisted to check the sky. The moon was high, partially hidden by clouds. Still a ways to go before dawn. He missed being able to sleep straight through til sunrise. Hadn't done that since . . . before 'Nam.

He pulled his trash bag jacket down over his bent knees and folded his arms against his chest. The walls enclosing the dumpster usually provided some insulation. The walls, the plastic bags, his friends' body heat should have been enough to keep Hood warm.

But nothing was usual tonight.

The chill bled through the bricks and bags like they weren't even there. Even the paved ground felt colder and harder than normal. Despite being huddled together, Hood and his Merry Men couldn't get warm enough to sleep well. With a shiver, he cursed the frigid October night.

He directed a few curses at the weathermen too. The Chicken Shack and the coffee shop played different channels, but both weathermen had predicted a frosty fall. And they were right. When the hell did that ever happen? They were even calling for snow on Halloween.

Snow.

On Halloween.

He'd never get used to that, no matter how many times it happened.

And it sure as hell didn't take a weatherman to figure out that a fall this cold foretold a long, hard winter. Maybe it was time to have Bernie haul those old sleeping bags out of the Chicken Shack's crawl space. It might even be time to turn night owl—sleep during the day so they could stay warm walking around at night. It was a bit early in the season for that, but Mother Nature ran on her own schedule.

Still, Hood had survived hard winters before. So had John. It was young Rojo and Much he worried about. Those boys only had one winter on the streets, and it had been a mild one.

A whimper drifted from below Hood's feet. Moments later came the sound of someone thrashing and then a whine. Had to be Much. That boy's demons were as big and mean as Hood's own—maybe worse, if that were possible. It was hard to tell, given how little Much ever said. Not that Hood himself was much of a talker.

Hood uncurled a leg and gave Much a gentle push. "Easy, boy," Hood whispered. "Just roll over, and it will go away."

The one practical instruction he'd gotten from that VA doc all those years ago: changing body position changed dreams. It took years of sleep-disturbed nights to master, but it proved to be the best medicine he ever got. It had kept him out of the damn booby hatch, that's for sure. Best of all, it didn't cost a dime.

A contented sigh and the shushing of plastic told him Much had taken the advice.

"Good boy," Hood whispered before curling up again inside his own trash bag jacket.

Boy. Rojo would call Hood out on that if he were awake. That boy—young man—carried a solid granite chip on his shoulder. It was one of the things Hood liked most about him, one of the things he'd recognized immediately when Tuck introduced the two young 'uns to the two old ones. Looking at Much and Rojo, Hood saw John and himself reflected back.

Rojo, like Hood, was short, dark, and quick to anger. Young Mitchell—Much—was quiet and thoughtful. Not as tall as John—no one was—but with that same long, lanky build and freckled fair complexion. If ever there were a poster child for corn-fed farm life, Much was it. As for his name, well, never had a nickname fit someone better. Mitchell never did say much at all.

Hood woke to the sumptuous smell of strong coffee.

"Thought you could use this." John stood over him, seeming even taller than his usual gargantuan self. That towering stature was how he'd earned the nickname "Little John" way back in their jungle days. Some guys had a funny sense of humor.

John's hand held a small paper cup from the fancy coffee place in the strip mall, the one that anchored the street-side end of the storefronts.

With a groan that became a long yawn, Hood pushed himself to a sitting position and grabbed the cup. The wispy white steam looked like the breath of life itself. Wrapping his hands around it, he closed his eyes and breathed deep, waking the crackle in his lungs. The warmth seeped into Hood's cold-stiffened hands. The ache in his fingers eased just a bit. He exhaled with relief.

When he opened his eyes, he noticed the others had matching cups. Much sat hunched over his, breathing in the steam. Rojo had his cup tipped at his mouth. Hood watched him take a big gulp.

"Not so fast, Red," Hood warned. "Better sip it slowly, make it last."

Rojo gasped and coughed.

Hood laughed. "Don't wanna burn yourself, either." He turned to John and raised his cup as if in a toast. "You been holding out on me?"

John chuckled, a sound more sarcastic than amused. "You got me. I'm a secret millionaire. Be nice, and I'll put you in the will." He turned serious. "I was up before the sun. I went to take care of business and found Chicken Shack Bernie loitering in the alley. He spotted us the cups of joe.

As a matter of fact, he insisted."

Hood had no difficulty reading between the lines of John's story. They'd been together more than half their lives. Bernie—manager of the Chicken Shack, a fellow veteran, and all around good egg—was worried about the Merry Men surviving the January-like night. He had stopped by specifically to check on them, even though it was his day off.

Ordinarily, Hood would call out the mollycoddling but starting an argument was not a good way to begin any day, especially one that began with free hot coffee. *Good* hot coffee, at that.

Instead, Hood raised his cup in a toast—a real one, this time. "To Chicken Shack Bernie. He ain't no chickenshit friend."

John raised his cup in response, followed quickly by Rojo and Much. The four men took their sizable sips simultaneously.

Mid-swallow, Hood fell into coughing fit.

"Careful, Boss!" Rojo called with a grin. "Don't wanna get burned!"

Hood opened his mouth to respond but was once again overcome with a series of hacking coughs.

Much's attention shot from his cup to Hood to John to Rojo then back to Hood again. "You okay, Boss?"

"Fine," Hood croaked, before descending into one more phlegmy cough. "You just take care of yourself, boy."

Much cringed and returned his stare to his cup, a pink burn on his cheeks.

John grimaced. "I don't know, Rob. I don't like the sound of that cough, either. Maybe—"

"No." Even hoarse, Hood's voice brooked no

argument.

"Don't be such a stubborn son of a bitch. You could at least let me finish the sentence."

Hood put his coffee cup on the ground, a few drops splashing over the side. His jaw squared, he concentrated his stare on John. "I *said* I'm fine. That means I. AM. FINE."

John met Hood's glare, his narrowed eyes calling the lie in Hood's words. They'd had this argument before. They would have it again. Friends didn't let friends live in denial. They called bullshit when they saw it, sometimes without words.

The rumble of engines in the strip mall parking lot and the squawking of the coffee shop drive-thru filled the silence. The staring contest continued. Four drive-thru customers later, Rojo and Much raised their eyebrows at each other and shrugged, the morning cold long forgotten.

"Hey!" Chicken Shack Bernie stepped into the enclosure entrance. Today, instead of his usual bowling-shirt-and-polyester-pants fast food uniform, he wore his usual weekend uniform: a ratty Bears sweatshirt, faded baggy jeans, and a beat-up pair of athletic shoes. A ball cap covered his short salt and pepper hair. From beneath the brim, he gave the scene a once-over. "Everything okay?"

"We're good." John pointed at the I VOTED sticker on Bernie's sweatshirt. "You do know today's not Election Day."

Bernie stood straighter and squared his shoulders. "What's your point? You got a problem with someone showing a little civic pride? Doing a little something called early voting?"

"Yeah? Who'd ya vote for?" Hood's question sounded more like a demand.

"I believe that's none of your business," Bernie answered with practiced nonchalance.

Hood stepped closer. "Who'd you vote for, Bern? Not that shit heel Gibson."

"What is it with you and the sheriff? He steal your girl or something?"

Hood narrowed his eyes. His anger hung between them, thickening the air like summer humidity. Mary Ann was nothing to joke about. "Who did you vote for, Bernie?"

Bernie shook his head. "No, sir. I'm not telling. We here in the good old US of A have this thing called a secret ballot—emphasis on the *secret*."

Fire burned in Hood's eyes.

After a heavy minute, Bernie stuffed his hands in his pocket and leaned forward, a roguish smile on his face. "I might be willing tell you who I did *not* vote for, if you asked nicely."

John snorted. Rojo and Much chuckled. Hood cursed under his breath and turned on his heel. Why give Bernie the satisfaction of seeing him smile?

"Not that it'll make any difference. Gibson's a shoe-in, no matter how many campaign signs you steal." Bernie nodded at the dumpster. Half a dozen blue campaign signs lay badly-hidden among the garbage, and that was just this week's haul. But Gibson had won the sheriff's office in a landslide. There was no reason to think his mayoral race would end any differently.

Hood scowled. "No way that bastard's ever gonna

be the boss of me."

Bernie cleared his throat. "So how about the coffee? Anyone need a refill?"

"Yeah, man." Rojo stood. "I could do with another."

John gestured for Rojo to stop. "No, we're fine. Thank you, anyway."

Rojo, trained to obey orders, did as he was told.

"Don't tell me you're too proud for seconds." Bernie took a step back and crossed his arms. "I thought we were friends. Friends treat friends to coffee. And maybe a muffin?"

John shook his head. "Not when that friend scrapes by on minimum wage."

Bernie dropped his arms. His voice grew louder, more irritable. He took a step toward John, emphasizing every word with a thrust of his pointed finger. "I'll have you know that as Chicken Shack manager, I make more than minimum wage. And no matter what I get paid, it's still more than any of you got. So let me buy you the damn refills."

With a *gotcha* grin, John shrugged and stepped aside for Rojo to pass. "If you say so."

"I do." Bernie turned to Hood, looking up, down, and up again. "I opened the back of the Shack. Your sleeping bags are in my office. Oh, and feel free to freshen up in the john."

There was no missing the gleam in Hood's eyes. "What exactly are you saying?"

Bernie gave an exaggerated sniff. "I'm not saying anything, except that the Shack's bathroom is open for whoever needs it, and there's toiletries in a bucket under the sink. Now," he gave a little wave, "let's go get that coffee."

Rojo grabbed Much by the shirtsleeve and pulled him along. "And muffins. You said muffins."

Bernie smiled and stepped in behind the boys, following them toward the coffee place. "I certainly did. You in the mood for bran or cinnamon?"

Much and Rojo shared a look before answering in unison. "Blueberry."

John watched the three men shuffle across the asphalt. Behind him, Hood coughed.

The day was sunny and bright, crisp but not unbearably cold. The Merry Men marched single file up the sidewalk on Yorkshire Road, Sherwood's main drag, the spine that connected the town's head to its ass. The route seemed flat and straight to those who traveled it by car, but the Men and others who traveled it on foot knew its every incline and decline, however slight they might be.

Yorkshire Road also served as the town's economic yardstick. Sherwood had originally developed around the rail line at its southern end. As it grew, it spread north. First, it stretched to the interstate, which replaced the railroad as the town's main freight route, and then beyond. The farther away one lived from those older parts of town, the greater one's wealth and status. The homeless shelter and The Moors, the shopping center that Hood and his men called home, sat in the borderlands between the working class and middle class sections of town—roughly the area that would be Sherwood's waist.

Today, the Merry Men had hoofed it a few miles south from their home, deeper into working class territory, what less imaginative types called "the wrong side of the tracks," to the Thrift 'N Gift. Now they were making their way back, with Hood in the lead, followed by John, then Rojo. Much trailed behind the others, weighed down and vision impeded by their thrift store haul: bags of blankets, sweats, socks, and jackets. The burden of being the youngest—and most timid—of the troop.

"How much do we have left?" John called over his shoulder.

Day laborers Rojo, Much, and John had worked nearly full-time the last few days installing storm windows, clearing gutters, raking leaves, installing Halloween decorations and displays. Even Hood, who panhandled by the interstate, had collected more than usual. With the promise of more work ahead, the men had decided to use their windfall to stock up for winter.

"Seventeen dollars and . . ." Rojo fingered the change in his palm. "Forty-six cents."

Conversation stalled as they reached the bus stop. A brightly colored piece of paper was loosely taped to the side of the bus shelter. The Merry Men watched as the breeze caught it and carried it away, an unnaturally yellow bird fluttering in the air.

John shrugged. "Hope that wasn't anything important."

The Men found Sadie huddled in the corner of the bus shelter's plastic bench, territory she'd claimed as her own years before. No one knew how many years— Sadie's story varied each time she told it—but long enough that she'd become a fixture in the community. Everyone knew Bus Stop Sadie. She was the one who'd taught Hood the ropes when he took up life on the streets a million years before.

Rojo dug through the bags in Much's arms. He pulled out a heavy wool sweater, gray wool scarf, thick wool socks, and heavy knitted mittens and held them up. Hood nodded and took the garments.

Gently, he laid the sweater over the dozing Sadie. It covered nearly her entire body. He wrapped the socks in the scarf and tucked them under her head like a pillow. Then he slid the mittens over her fists. He brushed Sadie's hair—a shade darker than the scarf she now rested on—off her face and kissed her forehead. "Sleep tight, Sadie-girl. Stay warm."

Sadie mumbled something unintelligible and snuggled deeper into her dreams. With the cold weather, she'd be up all night, walking around to keep warm. Always on her own, of course. It was safer that way—less likelihood of being hassled by the police, less likelihood of being harassed by men.

The Merry Men paused for a moment to watch Sadie sleep and then walked away. For the next block and a half, no one said a word, the silence filled by the rumble and rush of the traffic next to them.

As they passed the bank, with its clock that announced the time and temperature, Much spoke. He sounded hopeful, even through the muffling pile of bags balanced in his arms. "Hey, John, can we stop for burgers?"

Hood chuckled. "What? Bernie's chicken not good enough for you anymore?"

Much nestled his chin on the top of his oversized bundle. "Boss, if I eat any more chicken, I'm gonna grow feathers."

Hood's expression sharpened. "When you live rough, you take your meals where you can get them. You don't get to be picky."

"Yeah, I get it," Rojo chimed in. "Beggars can't be choosers, but—"

Hood spun around and took a menacing step toward the younger man. "Just because I panhandle, that don't mean I'm a beggar."

John put a restraining hand on Hood's chest.

Rojo stopped, a horror-struck look darkening his features. "No, that's not . . . Wait. What does that even mean?"

Hood squinted at Rojo. "It means, I don't badger people into giving. I just sit with my cup and wait for the spirit to move them."

Rojo took a deep breath. "Fine, but we have some coin now. We can be a little picky this once."

Hood spit on the sidewalk, turned on his heel, and resumed his stride. Shaking his head, he spoke to the sky. "These kids'll never get it."

He stopped and marched back, stopping a mere foot in front of Rojo. "What about tomorrow, huh? Or the day after that? Or next week? We spend that money now, what happens then? I'll tell ya—we won't have what we need to make it through the winter."

Much's bundles hit the ground with a series of thuds.

Rojo grabbed the fallen bags and piled them back in Much's arms, keeping a couple for himself. "Look, I get it. We're lucky to have Bernie. But it can't be good for him or his business to keep feeding us for next to nothing or just plain nothing."

Rojo's argument made sense to John. Heck, he'd tried to make a similar argument over the coffee. But Hood was right. If this winter proved as frozen and unforgiving as the fall suggested, they would need every penny for shelter. And there was Hood's cough, which was only getting worse. At some point, they would need to force some medicine down that stubborn SOB's throat, and meds cost money. The best thing they could do for their future selves was skip this meal.

John's stomach had other ideas, growling loud enough to give Much a fit of giggles. Even Hood cracked a smile. Maybe burgers weren't such a bad idea, after all.

"All right, boys. You win. We'll stop for burgers." He signaled to Hood to cross at the next corner. "But we order nothing that's not on the dollar menu, and no one spends more than three dollars, got it?"

"Got it," Rojo and Much answered together.

Minutes later, after a stop to distribute more winter gear, the men entered the parking lot of The Toasted Bun, savoring the fragrance of grills and grease. Rojo jogged ahead of the others. He reached for the door but stopped short of opening it. "What the fuck?"

The others followed the direction of Rojo's stare to a neon orange flyer taped in the restaurant window. "Don't feed the bums," he read. Designed to look like a sign at the zoo, the flyer's headline was accompanied by a drawing of a rat-like man in tattered clothes. Beneath the caricature, in smaller type, it read, "Feeding beggars only encourages their presence. Help keep our streets clean. Give to charity, not to vagrants." A drawing of a pointy crown decorated the bottom right corner.

"There's another one!" Much stood by the drive-thru entrance, pointing at a bright pink rectangle fluttering on the side of the menu board. He climbed through the planter to get a closer look before making his way back to the group. "It's the same."

"Screw 'em." Hood straightened his posture. With a wheezy deep breath, he yanked open the door and strode inside.

Rojo followed with a defiant "Yeah!"

Much looked at John, his question clear in his eyes.

John shrugged. "What the hell. The worst they could do is throw us out." The lie came far too smoothly, but no way was he telling Much that an arrest might lay in their future. The boy was nervous enough already.

Nervous without reason, it turned out. The Merry Men weren't the cleanest or the quietest in the burger joint, but their role as paying customers earned them service and a table. As far as John could tell, no one—not even the manager—gave them a second glance. The cashier never even looked up from the register.

The men carried their food—burgers, fries, and sodas all around—to a table in the back corner. Not one customer batted an eye, except for the couple who got up and moved two tables away.

Did anyone care about the flyers? Or were they invisible as the homeless people they condemned? John was starting to think like Much. He shook the questions out of his head and took a satisfying bite out of his cheeseburger.

An hour later, their hunger sated and the flyers

behind them, the men made their way back to their home behind The Moors. This time, they shared the burden of carrying and distributing the thrift store haul, which perhaps accounted for the extra spring in Much's step. Or maybe it was the laughter they shared as Rojo recounted an embarrassing tale of hot dogs, food poisoning, and his sister's confirmation dress.

Hood laughed himself into a coughing fit. Dropping his bags, he doubled over and pounded his chest. He sounded like he was going to spew out a lung. The others froze. John fingered the few dollars in his pocket—enough for a bottle of cough syrup.

But would cough syrup be enough to fix his brother-in-arms?

Hood pointed at John. "Don't even think about it," he croaked. "I'll be fine. Just gimme a minute."

John grimaced but nodded. When Hood descended into another round of hacking coughs, John turned and marched down the block, past Rojo, past Much, muttering the words *stubborn* and *bastard* and a few other barely-intelligible expletives in rapid succession. He stopped short at the pack of teens crossing the street—mid-block, of course, because why take the few extra steps needed to reach the corner and its protected crosswalk when you could dodge speeding cars for that surge of adrenaline? The afternoon clearly belonged to idiots.

John hunched his shoulders and pushed past the herd, storming forward until a yellow paper fluttering on a light pole caught his eye. He couldn't read the words, but there was no mistaking the human-rodent hybrid illustrating the center of the page. With a silent

"Fuck!," he tore down the flyer and crumpled it into a ball. Flinging it to the ground, he stomped back to Hood and the boys.

"Let's go." John moved past them without stopping.

Staring in disbelief, Much stammered, "But what about the rest—"

"We'll hand it out tomorrow. Or we'll give it to Tuck for the shelter." John's voice brooked no argument. The others grabbed the bags and followed behind, single-file, not talking or stopping until John did, which wasn't until the group entered the parking lot of The Moors.

"Much, go check Bernie's." John's voice was that of an officer giving orders to his grunts. "See if any of those flyers are hanging there. Rojo, you check the coffee place."

When the boys were out of earshot, Hood asked, "You wanna tell me what's going on?"

"I have a hunch."

John's hunch paid off. Both boys trotted back holding brightly-colored papers.

"Shee-it." Hood spoke the very word John was thinking. He grabbed the paper from Much's hand. "Bernie had this?"

Much let out a disappointed sigh. "On the front window."

Hood kicked his bags over to John and waved the offensive flyer in Rojo's face. "Bernie's no chickenshit friend, eh? Let's see what our buddy has to say for himself now." The Men marched across the parking lot, a gang looking for a fight.

Bernie held up a hand as soon as Hood stepped inside. "Don't say it! I had nothing do with it. I swear, and I can prove it." He disappeared in the direction of his office.

The Merry Men clustered around a table, their bags stacked on the chairs. John and Much fidgeted, while Hood and Rojo stood in taut angry silence—arms crossed and fists clenched.

Bernie returned and plopped a trash can on the table, the crumpled papers inside like discarded flowers. "I took them down as soon as they went up, but I couldn't keep up. Never seen such determined J.D.s."

"J.D.s?" John asked.

"Yeah. Bunch of teens put these up."

Those teens trying to cross the street! John described them to Bernie.

"Yeah, that's them." Bernie's face became pinched. "There's something else."

The men watched as Bernie pulled a paper turd out of the trash and smoothed it on the table. He pointed to the crown in the corner. "See that? That's the logo of Kingston Enterprises. My landlord."

Not just Bernie's either. Bruce Kingston was the biggest landowner in Nottingham County, and his Enterprises, the county's largest business.

"Fucking fat cat." Hood kicked the nearest chair. Rojo leaped out of its path. The chair hit the wall with a *bang*.

CHAPTER THREE

Rojo smoothed the bright orange flyer and pressed it against the wall of the dumpster enclosures the cold of the bricks chilling his hand. With his other, he waved for the duct tape, but Much—the keeper of the tape—didn't notice. He was too busy watching a couple of squirrels spar farther down the back wall of the alley.

"Yo! A little help here!" Rojo kicked at Much's shin.

Much jumped. "Dude!"

"Don't make me come over there," John warned in his best dad voice.

"Why are you hanging up that insulting piece of trash anyway?" Hood wanted to know. "You some kind of . . ." He snapped his fingers. "What's the word?"

"Masochist." Leave it to John to know.

"Yeah, *masochist*. You a masochist, Red?"

"So what if I am?" Rojo paused before turning to John. "What's a masochist?"

Hood chuckled.

With a smile, John said, "Son, if you have to ask, you don't want to know." His smile faded. With a crinkle in his brow, John waved at the pile of balled-up flyers at Rojo's feet. "Why *are* you hanging those pieces of trash?"

Rojo didn't even blink. "Insulation."

Hood leaned forward. "Say what?"

"Insulation. These bricks get pretty drafty. Hang a few of these up, no more draft." Rojo shrugged and got back to work.

Behind him, Much bit back a smile—but seconds later, his left eye began to twitch. His face turned red, and he fell into a raging case of giggles.

Hood grinned and shook his head. "Boy, you had me going. Now why're you really putting them up?"

"Seriously?"

"Nah, for kicks."

Rojo stopped and turned to Hood. Holding his boss's gaze and with an absolute straight face, he pointed at the orange paper. "Know your enemy. That's the first rule of war, right? Well, here's our enemy. If we're gonna survive, we need to keep him in our sights."

Hood and John exchanged a look before giving approving nods. "Fair enough," the bigger man said.

Rojo returned to his poster-hanging, Much to watching the squirrels. The four men shared a companionable silence until Hood spat, loud and large.

"Nah, that ain't fair enough." Hood stood. "Yeah, we need to know who the enemy is, but we don't need a stinking flyer to tell us. What we need is to take the fight to him." He reached over and grabbed a pink flyer. "Whaddaya think this'll do to Sadie? We have Bernie and our jobs to get us through. Tuck, if we really get in a pinch. Who does Sadie have? Who fights for her?"

Hood was right. A few bus stop regulars gave Sadie leftovers or half a sandwich every now and again. A few more dropped their pocket change in her plastic cup. It was never much, but Sadie managed to scrape by. Bernie wasn't intimidated by the flyers. Sadie's supporters, though, acted out of convenience more than conviction. They wouldn't be as steadfast if—when—circumstances made it less convenient.

Rojo and Much turned and gave their leader their full attention.

"A best defense is a good offense, right?" Hood paced the enclosure, hands clasped behind his back, finding his rhythm. General Patton would have been proud. "We sit here and wait for the enemy to come to us, we're behind before the battle even starts. It's people like Sadie who pay the highest price. So, let's not wait. Let's go get him."

"How, Boss?" Rojo asked.

At the same time, Much asked, "Who?"

Rojo pointed to the crown on the corner of the flyer. "We already know who. Bernie told us. Kingston Enterprises."

"Right," Hood said, with a satisfied nod.

John leaned against the dumpster and crossed his arms. "That still leaves Red's question. How?"

"Working on that."

Much stared at the flyers hanging on the bricks, rippling in the breeze. Much's face brightened. "We do what they did."

"You wanna hang flyers?" Rojo's voice dripped with dislike.

"No." Much yanked one of the posters off the bricks and waved it. "They hung these things on *our* turf. They tagged the places we hang out."

Rojo got it first. "Yeah, so we tag them, right?"

"Right."

"Tag?" Hood sounded doubtful. "Like the game?"

Rojo slapped him on the shoulder. "No, old man. Street art."

John and Hood both wrinkled their brows.

Rojo sighed. "Graffiti, you geezers. You do know what graffiti is, dontcha?"

Hood squinted at the young man. After a heavy moment, he nodded. "Graffiti, I can do. Count me in, boys."

"So what do we need?" John asked. Always the practical one.

"Spray paint," Rojo and Much answered in chorus.

Hood grinned. A sparkle lit his eyes. "Make it the ugliest color you can find."

"Better stop here," John told Bernie. The Merry Men had asked their Chicken Shack buddy for his landlord's address, but Bernie had insisted on providing the wheels for the operation. Now, at John's instructions, he was dropping off the gang three long blocks from the sprawling campus that Kingston Enterprises called home.

He swung his pick-up truck into the gas station and pulled around to the back. "I'll keep the engine running."

John offered his hand. "We appreciate the offer, but you shouldn't stick around. Things go pear-shaped, you scram."

"Like hell," Bernie answered with a smile.

Hood and the boys crawled over each other to get

out of the cramped quarters in the back of the cab. Each banged on the side of the truck in thanks. Bernie sent them off with a wave.

Crouching low, the four Merry Men made their way across the landscaped buffer between the gas station and its neighboring office park. Three jogged. Hood shuffled. They followed the buffer behind the office park to the edge of the Kingston Enterprises complex. Screened by a lilac hedge, the men stood and regrouped, each pulling a can of spray paint from his jacket pocket—another gift from Bernie.

Rojo shook his, the ball inside clanging loudly. "So we each take a wall and—"

"Nah," Hood cut him off. "Too risky."

"We go in pairs," John said. "One paints. The other acts as look-out."

Much nodded in agreement.

"Well, then, let's go!" Rojo grabbed Much by the arm and took off. They stopped at the building's side door. Doors, actually. The entrance was a set of tinted glass double-doors with a black frame and fancy tinted windows on either side. The perfect canvas for the hideous yellow-green color Rojo had chosen.

As Rojo studied his workspace, Hood and John moved past him to the front of the building. Hood had insisted from the beginning that he be the one to "decorate" Kingston's front entrance. "Go get 'em, Boss!" Rojo called to their backs. Then he shook his can and sprayed the first drops of neon green revenge.

Much was putting the finishing touches on his own handiwork when the ruckus started. Loud voices drew him and Rojo to the front of the building, where Hood and John were locked in verbal combat with a big-bellied uniformed rent-a-cop and a turd in a suit. Judging by the embroidered crown on the turd's silk scarf, it had to be none other than Bruce Kingston himself.

"We're just exercising a little freedom of speech," Hood shot at the security guard. "Ain't no crime."

"What you are doing is vandalism." Kingston enunciated every syllable. "That *is* a crime." He pointed at Hood's artwork. "And *that* is slander. Also a crime. Which is why the police are on their way and your ass is going to jail." Kingston pulled out his phone and dialed.

Rojo followed the direction Kingston had pointed. In bright orange paint, across the front entrance of Kingston Enterprises, was a giant caricature of Bruce Kingston, complete with a crown and a rodent-like face, a mirror of the image on the flyers. Emblazoned beneath the portrait were the words, "NO VERMIN ALLOWED."

Rojo snorted. To his right, he heard Much do the same.

The security guard whipped around in their direction. "You think this is funny? You'll see how funny it is when you're sitting in a tiny concrete cell with your buddies over here."

Hood and John took advantage of the divided attention and slid toward Rojo and Much. No sooner had the guard uttered the word *here*, then Hood shouted, "RUN!"

All four Merry Men sprinted for the hedges, the security guard on their heels, Kingston screaming into his phone in the distance. Rojo's ears filled with the sound of his own thudding heart, Hood's wheezing breaths, and the pounding of the guard's boots on the pavement. The pounding grew closer. Rojo put all he had into his stride, not daring to look around at the others. Looking slowed you down. He'd learned that the hard way.

He vaulted over the shrubs, stumbling when his feet didn't land quite right. A hand grabbed him and pulled him forward. Much.

"Come on, Red." No, not Much. John.

A few steps later, Rojo moved past the big man.

The pounding steps and huffing and puffing of the security guard seemed more distant. Or maybe that was wishful thinking. Gulping air, Rojo pressed on. Halfway behind the office park. Almost there. Much sprinted past him. Damn farm boy. He always was a better runner than Rojo.

Bernie's headlights blinked through the shrubs. Rojo kept his eyes focused on them.

Much reached Bernie's truck first and threw himself into the backseat. Rojo followed a few steps behind. They watched as John charged out of the office park and onto the gas station pavement.

"C'mon, c'mon," they muttered, tapping their feet.

John stopped. Rojo stopped breathing. What was the big man doing?

Wait. Where was Hood?

John waved, motioning for someone behind him to hurry: Hood. Had to be.

Where the hell was that old man?

Rojo squinted. Hood couldn't be that far behind. Sure, he wasn't the healthiest of the Merry Men—not with that cough, but he couldn't be in *that* bad of shape. Could he?

As if in answer, Hood stumbled out from behind the shrubbery, clearly struggling for air. The security guard burst out of the landscaping only steps behind, his face red and pouring sweat.

Rojo hopped out of the truck. The guard grabbed Hood by the jacket. Rojo took off, knocking the rent-a-cop to the ground with a flying tackle. He felt, more than saw, Hood crawl away. With one hand on the guard's chest, he raised the other in a fist.

"Red! Let him go!" John's voice echoed across the lot.

Rojo turned and saw a figure picking its way through the brush. Kingston. With a shout, Rojo shoved the security guard hard against the pavement, jumped to his feet, and ran for the truck. He threw himself in the back of the cab, landing squarely on Much's lap.

John grabbed Hood and practically dragged him to the truck. He tossed the panting Hood into the front seat and jumped into the back next to the boys. "Floor it!"

Bernie hit the gas before John had the door closed, the truck squealing around the side of the gas station's quick mart. Rojo's last glimpse was the security guard rubbing his head, while Kingston screamed into his phone. His words echoed in Rojo's head long after they were out of earshot: "You're the goddamn sheriff! If you truly want to be mayor, you damn well better do something about these thugs!" Rojo prayed the rest of that conversation didn't include Bernie's license plate number.

No one spoke. Rojo was sure they were all doing

what he was: watching for flashing lights.

When they pulled into The Moors's parking lot without incident, the air in the cab instantly felt lighter. One by one, the Merry Men climbed out of Bernie's truck. Rojo gave Bernie a fist bump in thanks, and they watched Bernie drive back out onto Yorkshire Road.

Much bounced on his heels, a big smile on his face. "That was fun. We should do that again."

Hood flung an arm around Much's shoulders. "You want a fight, kid? Good. 'Cause we just declared war."

November

The wind sliced through the alley, stabbing sharp cold deep into Rojo's bones. Wasn't *March* supposed to be the month that came in like a lion? What was November trying to prove?

Rojo's four layers of clothes, trash-bag jacket, and hand-me-down sleeping bag did almost nothing to keep him warm, even within the protected walls of the dumpster enclosure. The paper "insulation" he'd taped up was equally worthless. Many of the flyers had blown off, scattering the alley like confetti. The few that remained, although steadfast and stubborn, were more like gauze than fleece. Rojo might as well have been naked in the middle of the parking lot.

Maybe he should crawl into the dumpster. Let the garbage insulate him against the frosty temps.

No, that would require moving, and being inside the sleeping bag was better than being outside. Worse than that, if he climbed in there with the garbage, the others would never let him hear the end of it. Never.

Rojo curled tighter, willing his mind somewhere else, somewhere Jack Frost didn't hang. Mind over matter. Warm thoughts would warm his body. Even a flashback to the hot Iraqi desert would be welcome. Instead, his dreams found coffee, his hands wrapped around a Big Gulp-sized cup filled to the brim with a dark steaming brew. So much better than Iraq.

Heat seeped through the styrofoam, defrosting Rojo's fingers. He inhaled deeply, the warmth filling his nostrils, flowing down into his chest. This was no mess hall swill. Beneath the familiar bitter aroma, there was something else—something warm, something rich. Cinnamon? He took another whiff. Yep, cinnamon. Flavored coffee in real life was a waste, but in his dreams? Rojo licked his lips and sighed, his shoulders relaxing, his mind slipping another step deeper into sleep.

Much's whimpers reached him even there, but the Much of his dream wasn't the veteran sleeping restlessly beside him—it was the Much of the barracks at the FOB in Iraq. The Much who silently cried himself to sleep after that kid's death, the Much who blamed himself for what happened to that boy.

Rojo's jaw clenched at the memory, his hands curled into fists. It wasn't Much's damn fault, but nothing Rojo or that journo or their CO said had any effect. Even the shrink who did those useless discharge interviews hadn't had any luck—and she was a professional. Tonight, as they slept the sleep of the free, Much was anything but. Rojo's buddy was trapped, reliving that mission, seeing that boy die in the crossfire over and over again, convinced it was his bullet that killed him. Goddamn it.

Rojo flipped himself over and tried to find the coffee dream again. Coffee beat Iraq every day. He'd almost made it when the voices pulled him out. Distant at first, on the edges of Rojo's consciousness. The voices—male, unfamiliar—grew louder as the cobwebs of sleep faded. His sleep-laden brain couldn't process the words, but it recognized the tone. Someone was giving orders. Do this. Do that. Go there. Come here. *Stand straight, Marine! Forward march, Marine! Faster, Marine!*

Rojo had enough of that shit.

He shot up, jaw and fists clenched. He blinked.

This wasn't Iraq or Afghanistan. He wasn't in a tent or a hut on any FOB. He glanced left and right, down and around. Much, Hood, and John slept around him, pushed up against each other and the walls of the dumpster enclosure. Rojo exhaled. He was home.

A calm, authoritative voice rang from outside the enclosure. "There's a burned out metal can over here. They can't be far."

Rojo untangled himself from his sleeping bag and smoothed his trash bag jacket as quietly as he could manage. Standing on his toes, he peeked over the bricks. Two men were walking down the alley. Both wore sheriff uniforms. One carried a flashlight; the other, a nightstick. The deputy with the nightstick looked like Much might in another twenty-five years, if Much got off the street and lived a life of comfort and plenty. The other could have passed for his son. A new recruit, perhaps. Behind them, at the end of the alley, their car blocked any escape. A glance to the left, and Rojo saw another sheriff's car blocking the passage. He couldn't make out a face, but he could see the silhouette of someone sitting behind the wheel.

Rojo's hackles rose. He knew an invasion when he saw one. The cold vanished. All Rojo felt now was the tight nervous tension that came before a battle.

Without taking his eyes off the intruders advancing down the alley, Rojo nudged Much with his foot. He looked down only long enough to signal Much's silence and point toward John. Then he returned his gaze to the deputies while Much woke the other Merry Men.

He felt John step up next to him, felt the big man's body tense in anticipation. A moment later, Hood sputtered, "What the—?"

Before anyone could say anything else, Hood stepped out of their protected position and confronted the deputies. "Can I help you gentlemen?"

The older deputy—the one with the nightstick—stepped forward, his body braced for a confrontation. The younger deputy speed-walked past his partner, slipping his flashlight into his belt, and offered Hood his hand. "Sir. I'm Freed. That's Dubrowski. You are . . . ?"

"Hood." Hood shook Freed's hand, his expression pure skepticism. Dubrowski, meanwhile, had put away his nightstick. He stood back from his partner, arms crossed, clearly waiting to give the younger deputy the old I-told-you-so.

Which just left the shadow man in the car. Who the hell was *he*?

"Mr. Hood—"

"No mister, son. Just Hood." For once, Hood almost sounded patient.

"Sir—Hood—we've had some complaints. About you and your friends here." Freed gestured toward the Merry Men, all of whom were peeking over the wall of the dumpster enclosure like three Kilroys. At Freed's words, they stepped out and stood shoulder to shoulder, a defensive line between the invaders and the patch of ground where they slept.

"Complaints, eh?" Hood raised an eyebrow at his friends, his expression knowing and sly. "Who from?"

Freed's pause was slight, but Rojo and the Merry Men heard it loud and clear. "Um, the m—"

Dubrowski threw Freed a cautionary glance. "You know we can't tell you that."

Hood ignored the older deputy. "The m—? The merchants? Is that who you were going to say?" Hood waved at the back of the strip mall. "These merchants here. The merchants who share their food with us, who invite us to use their johns, who sell us their coffee, who stow our gear. Those merchants?"

Freed suddenly looked like a teenager caught in a lie. Behind him, Dubrowski shook his head. Someone was getting a spanking when they got back to the station house.

Hood stepped closer to Freed. Even though Hood was a couple of inches shorter, he seemed to tower over the younger man. "Sorry, son. I'm not buying it. The merchants here know us. They're our friends. If they wanted us gone, they'd give us the old heave-ho themselves. And they'd be a whole lot nicer about it than your friend here."

Dubrowski's left hand found his nightstick again and gripped it tightly. His right moved to his holster. His eyes never left Hood. Rojo caught the movement and elbowed Much. Without speaking, the boys stepped closer to their leader. At the other end of the alley, a car door opened.

Freed sighed and shrugged. "I don't know what to tell you." Rojo's CO had said and done the same thing in conversations with Iraqi locals; the young deputy was trying to de-escalate the situation. Would Hood let him? Would Dubrowski? Some dogs never let go of the bone.

"We got a complaint that a group of homeless were disrupting business here," Freed continued. "And—"

"A complaint? One complaint?" Hood nodded toward the car with the mystery inhabitant. "This is a heck of a lot of manpower for one measly complaint."

"Sir, if you'd let me—"

"Finish? Son, there's no need. It's crystal clear you're following orders. Your boss the sheriff sent you to clean house."

Hood studied Freed and nodded. "And you're not entirely comfortable with that, are you?"

Freed shifted his feet.

Hood had his answer. He winked back at his men. Nope, there would be no de-escalation here. "That's what I thought. Well, you can tell your boss—"

"You tell your boss he has no jurisdiction here."

Everyone turned to John.

"Excuse me?" The voice was more sharp than questioning.

The Merry Men turned in the voice's direction. Sheriff Gary Gibson—occupant of the car behind them—slammed his car door shut with a flourish.

John took a position on Hood's left. "I said, *Sheriff*, you have no jurisdiction here."

Gibson took the bait. "See that's where you're wrong. The sheriff is the highest law enforcement in Nottingham County. This strip mall is in Nottingham County."

"Therefore," Dubrowski spat, "our jurisdiction."

"Nope." John's tone was clipped, the word barely a full syllable.

"Nope?" Gibson drew out the question.

Hood pinched his lips and rocked back on his heels.

This is gonna be good, Rojo realized.

"Nope." John spoke with assurance. He even seemed to stand a little taller, if that were possible. "You want to know why? Two reasons. First, this strip mall is in the city of Sherwood. The *incorporated* city of Sherwood. As sheriff, you only have jurisdiction over unincorporated areas. You're grasping for power you don't have."

Freed looked wide-eyed at Dubrowski, who shushed his younger partner with another shake of his head.

Oh, yeah. Rojo bit back a smile. *Good doesn't even begin to describe it.*

John took a step in Gibson's direction. He added another finger to his countdown. "Second, being homeless is not a crime. So you and your minions trying to clear us out? That's not law enforcement, because there's no law to enforce."

"Well, listen to the professional." Dubrowski stopped short when Gibson held up his hand.

"Law enforcement officers are responsible for more than just enforcing laws." Gibson sounded like he was talking to a kindergartener. "We are also responsible for maintaining public order—"

"Law & Order?" Rojo called. "Isn't that a TV show?"

John responded with a shush, but Rojo glimpsed the hint of a smile. John took another step forward. "And then there's the castle doctrine. Do I need to explain that too?"

Gibson responded with clenched jaws and a harsh stare, but not Dubrowski, whose voice oozed disdain. "Castle, huh? Looks more like a dumpster to me."

John ignored the bait. "The point is, Sheriff, we're not going anywhere."

"But *you* are," Hood said, stepping next to John.

Without a word, Rojo and Much joined the line formed by Hood and John. While the older men faced Sheriff Gibson, the boys faced down the sheriff's lackeys, Freed and Dubrowski. All four Merry Men folded their arms and set their jaws.

Freed blinked first. If Rojo had to guess, he'd say the young deputy didn't like the math of the situation. Freed goggled at Gibson like a lost puppy. "Sir?"

Dubrowski and Gibson remained still, their expressions frozen in disdain.

The air was so thick, Rojo almost stopped breathing. The muscles in his arms and legs tingled with anticipation.

"Gentlemen, let's go." Gibson's order sounded like a suggestion, but the look in his eyes brooked no disagreement.

Freed moved first, taking backward steps toward his car. Without a word, Dubrowski turned and followed him.

Gibson stepped up to Hood, bending slightly, leaning close—a move clearly meant to intimidate Hood. "This isn't over."

Hood didn't blink. "Tell Mary Ann I said hello."

Gibson's eyes filled with rage at his wife's name in Hood's mouth. His glare stayed on Hood until he was back in his car.

The Merry Men watched and waited as the sheriff's car roared to life and rolled way.

Hood nodded with satisfaction. "I believe *that* is what's known as a tactical retreat."

CHAPTER FIVE

John sorted the money the Merry Men had dropped on the table. The pile of coins and bills looked impressive but didn't add up to much. They never did. Without turning to Hood, he asked, "You know they're coming back, don't you?"

The group sat huddled around a corner table in the Chicken Shack, rehashing their encounter with Sheriff Gibson and his minions only hours earlier. Somewhere in the back, Bernie was preparing their orders—and, knowing him, probably something extra, too. The odor of frying oil permeated the air. The television hanging in one corner played the news on mute; the other one, a sports channel, also muted. Other than a gaggle of teenagers sitting by the front window, the motley crew had the just-opened restaurant to themselves.

"What do you mean?" Much asked. "They have no jurisdiction here. John said."

Rojo answered. "We embarrassed them. Called them out. They're not gonna forget that." He leaned forward. "What was Gibson doing there in the first place? Since when does the boss sheriff go out on a trash run?"

"Simple," John said. "The election is only a couple of days away. Gibson needs to show he's tough on crime."

"Show who? No one else was there."

Hood grimaced. "Trust me, if he'd won, we'd be the stars of last night's news."

Much was wide-eyed. "But why us? We're not criminals."

Hood shook his head. When he spoke, he did so quietly but forcefully, his words heavy with experience. "That's not how the normies see us. We live on the street. We have our own rules, our own community. To most people, especially people like that rich bastard Kingston, that makes us criminals. Outlaws. It don't matter what the law books say."

John and Rojo nodded in agreement. In the corner, the teens laughed at their own joke.

Much started to ask another question but stopped when he saw Bernie carrying two trays stacked with food. The others followed his gaze.

"Now that's what I'm talkin' about!" Hood rubbed his hands together as Bernie set out two buckets of chicken, a plate of corn on the cob, tubs of cole slaw and macaroni and cheese, and a stack of yeast rolls.

Much licked his lips, his eyes widening as he surveyed the feast laid out before him. Rojo reached for an ear of corn with one hand and for a drumstick with the other. Without ceremony, he laid into the corn.

Bernie looked pointedly at Rojo. "I'd tell you to dig in, boys, but you beat me to it."

Rojo grinned, butter dripping down his chin.

"So I'll just say 'bon appetit,' and let you get to it."

John grabbed a roll and followed Bernie to the counter. Much watched John try to push money into Bernie's hand. He saw Bernie push the bills away and shake his head. Then Bernie reached behind the counter and grabbed a stack of extra-large soft drink cups. He took the money, dropped it in the top cup, and gave the stack to John. Shaking his head, John ambled back to the table muttering about free food and going out of business.

The teenagers left without ceremony, leaving their table piled with detritus. Much couldn't help staring. He'd always been taught to clean up after himself, to leave no trace. It didn't matter whether he was hiking in the forest preserve or playing in Grandma's basement. Leaving behind a mess like that? His foot twitched at the thought.

John distributed the cups, and one by one the men filled them at the self-serve machine. Much, though, took a detour, scooping the abandoned mess into the trash and wiping down the table with some spare napkins. Only when the table was spic and span did he fill his own cup and join the rest of the Merry Men. As Much slid into his chair, the kid working the counter gave him a nod of thanks.

The table grew silent but for the buzzing of the fluorescent lights overhead and the *oohs* and *aahs* of the hungry men. Minutes later, Hood sighed and pushed away his plate. "Mmm, mmm, mmmm."

Much put down his roll. "So, John, how'd you know all that jurisdiction mumbo jumbo?"

Hood looked at John, then Much, and then John again. "You gonna answer that, or should I?"

John shrugged and took another bite of cole slaw.

Hood planted both hands on the table and grinned. After a dramatic pause, he said, "John here studied to be a scumbag lah-yer."

Rojo dropped his corn cob. Wide-eyed, he turned to John. "Naw, really? You? A lawyer?"

John breathed deep. "It was a long time ago, a whole other lifetime."

"What does that mean?" Much asked.

"It means there's nothing more to say."

Much recoiled as if he'd been slapped.

"Dude." Rojo spoke in low, hurt tones. "No need to be rude about it."

The air at the table thickened. After a few heavy seconds of silence, John raised his hands in surrender. "No rudeness intended." He caught Hood's stare.

Hood raised an eyebrow. "Well? You gonna tell 'em?"

"We're family, John," Much chimed in. "Family don't keep secrets."

John sighed and took another bite of slaw. "Fine. Short version: I went to college, pre-law, majored in political science."

"What happened?" Much pressed.

John dropped his fork. "The war."

Much's face fell. The men all stared at their plates.

"Well, aren't you a bunch of Dispirited Dans." Bernie stood at the end of the table, a plate of cupcakes perched on his right hand. "Something wrong with the grub?"

Almost in unison, the Merry Men shook their heads and protested.

"Then what? There's more than crumbs on those plates, and that's not like you bunch."

Hood banged his drink cup on the table, a few drops of root beer splashing onto the surface. "Maybe it's cause we're not as welcome here as we used to be."

Bernie set the sweet treats on the table. "Oh, yeah?"

"Yeah, Boss," Rojo added. "We've always been welcome here. Right, Bern?"

"Damn straight."

"I'm not talking about Bern, specifically." Hood crossed his arms and leaned back in his chair. "I'm talking about this whole center. About our home out back. And the new vermin it seems to be attracting."

John sighed before catching Bernie up. "The sheriff and his minions were here hassling us this morning."

"Why?"

"They said the merchants complained about us," Much replied, a slight whine in his voice.

Bernie shook his head. "That doesn't sound right, but I'll ask around." He walked a few steps toward the counter, stopped, and turned around. "You know, rumor has it the landlord wants to sell our little piece of heaven, and from what I've heard, he and the sheriff are like this." Bernie crossed his fingers.

Rojo slapped the table three times in quick succession. "That's it!"

The others swung their attention from Bernie to Rojo, confusion and interest written all over their faces.

Rojo pushed away the plates in front of him. "When we went tearing out of Kingston's, I heard him screaming into the phone. Something about taking care of us thugs if the other dude wanted to be mayor. How much you want to bet the other dude was Gibson?"

John whistled low. "That would explain the sheriff's little visit."

"Well," Bernie said, "whoever's behind this, Red's right: I'm on your side."

The Merry Men finished the remnants of their meal in silence.

Bellies full, the four men took their time walking around the building to their nest in the alley. Rojo stopped two doors down from the Chicken Shack, in front of a nail salon whose window advertised manis, pedis, and something called gel nails. He spun on his heel to face the others. "Maybe we should clear out of here for a while. Find somewhere else to sleep."

Hood shook his head, a sure sign of disapproval. "Never took you to be one who'd run from a fight, Red."

Rojo's whole bearing stiffened. "I'm not. This isn't about the sheriffs." He paused. "Okay. It's not *all* about the sheriffs. It's about the cold too."

"What? You don't like sleeping under the stars? We got sleeping bags and layers of clothes to keep us warm, and if that's not enough, we climb into the dumpster and sleep there. Use the garbage to keep us cozy. And if that's not enough, we start sleeping days and—"

Rojo shook his head so hard it looked like it might snap off. "Boss, with all due respect, uh-uh. We nearly froze to death the last few nights. And you got that cough you don't want to admit—"

"What cough? You heard me cough today?"

Rojo refused the bait. "The point is, the dumpster's not gonna be enough. We need to be indoors, someplace with *heat*."

Two steps behind Hood, Much nodded like a bobble-head doll.

Hood looked ready to spit. John put a hand on his arm, leading Hood and the others away from the nail salon window, where an audience was starting to gather. He stopped in front of the vacant storefront that used to be a mattress store. "I'm not arguing with you, Red, but how are we going to pay for all that indoor heat?"

"We got that money Bernie wouldn't take," Much said in his usual quiet tone. "And I got another thirty bucks in my sock."

"I've got about that, too," Rojo added. "That's at least a couple of nights at that no-tell motel by the highway, with some left over."

"And then what?" Hood asked. "You've used up your stash before the worst of winter gets here. You boys got a lot to learn about living rough."

"We made it through last winter," Much said.

Hood poked Much's shoulder. "Last winter was barely a winter. And you survived because me and John took you under our wing."

Hood was right about last winter—Much and Rojo's first on the street—but Rojo was equally right about this winter. Much thought maybe John saw that, too, but Hood was the one who needed convincing. If nothing else, the past year had taught Much that the Merry Men always followed Hood's lead, even when Hood was wrong or didn't know where he was going.

Rojo stepped between Much and Hood. "Look, I'm not saying we get a room and hibernate for the entire winter. We keep working. This time of year, Much and

I get jobs almost every day putting up storm windows, raking leaves. Someone's always coming into the House & Home parking lot looking for a pair of hands for some project or another."

"We make more than enough each day to pay for a motel room," Much added over Rojo's shoulder. "And if you and John join us, we—"

"No thanks, son," Hood said. "I'm fine doing what I'm doing."

Rojo glanced at John, who gave a slight shake of his head. Rojo plowed ahead anyway. "Boss, you're the proudest man I know. How is it that you're so content panhandling by the interstate? I mean, doesn't that feel like charity? Wouldn't you rather *earn* the money?"

Hood met Rojo's eyes. His voice, for once, was calm and patient. "Son, it ain't charity. I *bled* for this country. I sacrificed *everything* that mattered to me, only to come home and be hated and ignored and spit on. What you call panhandling, I call collecting my due."

The men fell silent. Much swallowed the lump in his throat, the one that formed when Hood admitted to feeling ignored, the one that lodged there when Much resisted the urge to say, "Me, too." He didn't have to look at the others to know that they were wrestling with the same feeling. Feeling ignored was par for the course in their world. So was ignoring feelings. Like the feeling that maybe Hood's bravado was a rickety bridge over a deep crevasse.

Much pushed the thought away. Picking through Hood's brain pan wasn't about to keep any of them warm. He trudged behind the others as they all resumed the path back to their dumpster enclosure.

Rounding the corner, the men came to sudden stop. The dumpster enclosure door was closed. Had they left it that way? Usually they left it open, both as a courtesy to the stores and to minimize their presence.

But their stuff was stowed behind the dumpster.

Rojo sprinted ahead. He grabbed the handle, leaned to yank the door open, and stopped. He pointed at the padlock wrapped around the door handle. "What the fuck is that?"

Hood snorted. "Revenge."

CHAPTER SIX

The chatter of the radio filled the shelter's small backroom office, but to Reverend Michael "Tuck" Tucker, it was nothing more than white noise. He didn't need the weatherman to tell him about the record November temps. He didn't need the news reader to tell him about the PR campaign against Sherwood's homeless population. He didn't need the meteorologist to explain why this winter would be so much more severe than previous years. Shelter attendance did all of that. The first week of November and the dorms were almost at capacity. Soup kitchen demand had grown by even bigger bounds. Breakfast lines now routinely stretched out of the building and into the parking lot. It wouldn't be long before they reached the street.

Tuck sighed. He glanced through the numbers on his budget spreadsheet one more time before clicking SAVE and closing the file. He turned to the papers on his desk, October's accumulated invoices and receipts. He didn't need to add them up to know the shelter's monthly allowance was already blown. He tidied the stack and pushed it aside. If he could find the money, he wouldn't have to decide which bills to pay and which to skip.

He pressed his hand to his forehead. Where to find the money? That was the question, the one that threatened to push his receding hairline even further back. December would bring a flurry of Christmas donations. Those funds might cover November's deficit, but December and January would dig new and deeper holes. And none of that would pay October's bills. He needed money *now*. Could he ask—no, beg—his donors to give more, sooner? Why did it feel like he always had his hand out? They sure as heck never taught that in seminary.

"Knock, knock."

Mary Ann Gibson stood in the doorway, the hall light behind her giving her a celestial glow.

Tuck waved her in. "Lady Marian!"

The nickname had started as a joke, but Tuck spoke the name with respect. Back in the Bad Old Days, Hood's squad had earned the moniker "The Merry Men" and their patch of jungle, "Sherwood Forest." It made sense that Hood's girlfriend would become Maid Marian. In those days, nearly everyone in the squadron had a crush on Hood's girl back home: Mary Ann. Her photos and letters sustained not only her boyfriend, but his squad-mates as well. Frankie—one of the ones who never made it back—had even written a poem about her. Something about her eyes being the color of the summer sky and just as bright. Looking at Mary Ann now, all these decades later, Tuck saw that description still held true. Sure, her long brown hair was now gray and cut shorter, but for Tuck, that gave Hood's ex-girlfriend a measure of elegance. If anything, she shined brighter today than she had way back then.

Mary Ann responded with a curtsy. She

straightened and set two over-stuffed grocery bags on Tuck's desk. "I come bearing gifts. The Armchair Angels have been working their magic."

"Let's see what we've got." Tuck pawed through the bags, marveling once again at the talent of this volunteer army. What began six years ago with two bored elderly widows had blossomed into an award-winning senior service organization. Every year, the Armchair Angels knitted, crocheted, and quilted mountains of socks, mitten, scarves, hats, and blankets for the shelter. Shelter volunteers wrapped the donations and placed them under the Christmas tree. On Christmas morning, everyone staying at the shelter—young, old, and in-between—received a gift.

"Ellie said that's just batch one. There's more on the way."

"How much more?" Tuck asked, wide-eyed.

"I'm sure as much as they can manage. Why? What's going on?" Mary Ann dropped into the chair next to Tuck's desk.

"The usual. Figuring out how to rob Peter to pay Paul."

"If it's so usual, why the extra-grumpy look?"

"Because . . ." Tuck sighed, trying to reign in his run-away worry. "Because the *usual* gets worse every year. The number of people coming through our doors increases, and the number of dollars we have to care for them decreases. I just—"

"You just what?"

Tuck fiddled with a pencil, twirling it in his fingers, tapping it on his desk. "I hate that I'm even thinking the thought, but we might have to forgo the Christmas gifts this year and sell the Armchair Angel donations instead. Otherwise, I don't know if I can keep the doors open. It's a struggle to break even in a good month, but this month, with the wacky winter-like weather, our attendance is way above average." He threw the pencil down. "Long story short, we're already up to our eyebrows in red ink, and the month's barely a week old. And next month? Or the month after? January's always our hardest month of the year, and this January promises to be the hardest in a while. There's no way we'll make it."

Dropping his head into his hands, Tuck's shoulders sank in defeat. Mary Ann said nothing, for which Tuck was grateful. Even her kindest words would sound condescending to his discouraged ears.

Mary Ann put her hand on Tuck's arm. "What can I do?"

Tuck dropped his hands and took a deep breath. "Buy us a winning lottery ticket?"

Mary Ann chuckled. "I would if I could."

"I know." Tuck pulled a child's mitten out of an Armchair Angels' bag. He stared at it, his expression, his shoulders, his whole body drooped. "I hate to sell these."

"Don't. Those gifts mean so much to the residents here, especially the kids. Surely there's another way? Something else you can do?"

Tuck traced the pattern on the mitten. "Like what?"

Mary Ann searched the carpet for inspiration. She found it in the trashcan stashed next to Tuck's desk. "Can't you do what the Knights of Columbus do? You know, stand at intersections and collect money in jugs."

"Boots and Buckets. We have one of those scheduled for the spring. I could try to move it up, but permits are involved. You know how those wheels of bureaucracy are."

"Sounds like you could use a connection in the mayor's office."

"Or the city clerk's office."

Mary Ann's silence caught Tuck short. His gaze snapped from the mitten to his guest. She stared at him with that expression, the one his mother used to give him when he'd forgotten to clean his room or take out the trash. It hit him in a flash. "That's right!" He dropped the mitten, stood, and held out his hand. "Congratulations, Mrs. Mayor."

Among the news reports he'd half tuned out that morning was Sheriff Gary Gibson's victory in Sherwood's mayoral election. That made Mary Ann the First-Lady-Elect of Sherwood. Tuck finally had a friend in a high place.

Mary Ann shook Tuck's hand, and he dropped back into his chair. "So, I don't suppose we'll be seeing that much of you from here on out."

"Why on Earth would you think that?" Mary Ann's voice carried a tinge of anger, like she was scolding an errant child who didn't quite understand what he'd done wrong.

Tuck winced. "Well, you'll have all those official responsibilities and commitments now. I don't want to get caught short-handed. In case you haven't noticed, you're kind of essential around here."

Mary Ann had shown up at the shelter's front door within days of its opening, rolled up her sleeves, and done what needed doing. Her reassuring presence had become as constant and familiar to the waves of homeless who rolled through as Tuck was. Most volunteers moved on after a couple of years. Mary Ann had stuck around for more than a decade. Sure, she had a naturally giving nature—it was that same quality that had driven her to become a nurse—but Tuck thought maybe there was something more going on. A belief reinforced by her frequent questions about Hood.

Maybe she did all this because it made her feel closer to her first love.

Mary Ann grabbed the mitten off Tuck's desk and slapped his arm with it. "Stop right there. I found time to volunteer here when I worked full-time at the hospital. I can certainly find time to volunteer here and still fulfill any part-time responsibilities I have as the mayor's *wife*."

There was something about the way she said that last word, like it was a burden or insult or something. Tuck couldn't quite pinpoint it.

She slid back in her chair and sat up straighter. "I may even be able to help in new ways, with my new connections."

"Like expediting a Boots and Buckets permit."

Mary Ann gave a single nod. "Exactly."

Tuck should have felt relief at the offer, but the weight in his belly grew heavier instead. He couldn't ask Mary Ann to dirty her hands, not even a little bit. "No," he finally said. "No special favors."

"But—"

Tuck gave the stop signal. "No."

"You have to let me do *something*." Mary Ann's eyes lit up. "Hold that thought. I'll be right back."

She trotted out of Tuck's office, returning a minute or so later, her purse in hand. She pulled out her checkbook. While fishing for a pen, she asked, "How much do you need?"

Something that Hood once said echoed in Tuck's head. Tuck had been recounting Gibson's campaign visit to the shelter. Hood went on a rampage: "That asshole spreads shit and calls it polish. Any money he gives is covered in it. You take it, you're just as dirty as he is."

At the time, Tuck had told Hood that he couldn't afford to be picky, that he would accept any donation, but now faced with the possibility, he couldn't go through with it. Hood was right: Gibson's dirt got everywhere. He reached over and pushed her checkbook closed. "More than you can afford."

"Bullshit. You have no idea what I can afford."

Tuck sat up. It always came as a shock when Mary Ann cursed, even though he knew full well she could talk blue with the best of them. "Okay, more than you can give without your husband noticing."

Mary Ann's eyes narrowed. Her jaw squared. "I have my own money, you know. I don't need to ask my husband's permission for every cent I spend."

Tuck held up his hands in surrender. "Fair enough. And I do appreciate the gesture. But you do enough around here already. I can't accept your money too."

"Swallow your damn pride and let me help."

"Mary Ann—"

She cut him off with a stare as steely as any of Hood's.

Tuck bit his cheek, swallowing his urge to smile. When he could manage a straight face, he put on his counseling voice. "All right, you want to help. Let's see what kind of compromise we can make."

Mary Ann nodded. "Okay. Tell me what the shelter needs."

"Money. Lots of it."

Mary Ann paused. Tuck could see her wheels turning. "You won't accept my money, so how about this: when I was at the hospital, I wrote grants to get funding for special programs. What if I do the same for the shelter? I can write a pretty mean grant proposal, if I do say so myself."

"I like the way you think. It's a deal."

"Excellent. We're halfway there."

Tuck arched his eyebrow. "Halfway?"

"Grants take time, and you need help *now*. So, other than money, what do you need? What will help you get the shelter through the month?"

Tuck considered his wish list, sorting needs and wants and prioritizing individual needs.

Food. Since those damn posters when up around time, more and more people were finding their way to the soup kitchen.

Hands. Another employee or three would really help the place run more smoothly, allow them to give residents the attention they deserved.

No, employees cost too much. *Volunteers* are what he needed. An army of them—and not just the Thanksgiving Day do-gooders, although their help was much appreciated. He needed an army as loyal and dedicated as Mary Ann and the Armchair Angels.

He shared all of this with Mary Ann, who dutifully took notes on her phone.

"Well," she said, "I have a pretty big megaphone now. Let me see what I can do with it."

CHAPTER SEVEN

Mary Ann dropped the tea bag into her mug and poured the boiling water over it. While the tea steeped, she studied the pattern in the tile backsplash, tracing a path as if it were a maze. The blue and yellow tiles, hand-painted in Mexico, had been part of a surprise kitchen remodel about ten years back. An anniversary gift from Gary, but also an amends of sorts after months of her nagging and complaining about his double shifts. He'd installed the backsplash himself, which was why the tiles were not quite equally spaced or exactly lined up. That was part of their charm. The memory made her smile. Sometimes she missed the good old days of their marriage.

Her tea now dark brown but not quite black, Mary Ann pulled out the tea bag and squeezed it damp. She poured in a spot of milk, grabbed the mug and the newspaper Gary had left on the counter, and moved into the dining room.

Settled in the chair at the head of the table, she blew on her tea and took a sip while scanning the paper's headlines. More shootings in Chicago. Another county property tax hike. The governor at odds with the state legislature. Same stuff, different day.

She flipped the paper to see what it said below the fold. With any luck, a blurb based on her press release would be there. She'd worded it cleverly, she thought, calling for a "Season of Service in Sherwood." She put down her mug, raised it, and put it down again.

Picking up the paper with both hands, she read the headline two more times. DON'T FEED THE HOMELESS, TOWN COUNCIL SAYS.

So much for her press release.

Surely this was one of those misleading headlines, one that told half the story or just plain got the story wrong. What did they call it? Clickbait. Maybe that's all this was.

But no, the headline got it exactly right. Mary Ann read on, the lines on her face deepening. With every column inch, her grip on the tea mug tightened until her knuckles were ghostly white. With each paragraph, the room's temperature dropped another degree.

In response to public outcry . . .

Public outcry? What public outcry? Not those hideous flyers, surely?

. . . the Sherwood Town Council voted to outlaw the feeding of the homeless inside town limits. . . .

"So they're supposed to starve?" Mary Ann threw down the paper. Clenching her teeth, she blinked back angry tears. Tea abandoned, she picked up the article again. Surely there was some catch, some amelioration.

"Other cities have already passed laws to this effect," senior council member Walter Hagen *said.*

"That doesn't make it right, Walter, and you know it," Mary Ann said to her empty dining room.

But Walter, it seemed, had more to add. *"Street feeding may be an act of kindness,"* the article quoted him as saying, *"but it's a kindness that kills. It's enabling, and it keeps the homeless away from programs that can help them. It keeps them homeless.*

"But if we eliminate street feeding, force these people to seek food in indoor spaces at shelters and churches and other registered charitable organizations, we can get them into the system. We can provide them with the support services they need."

His use of the word *registered* did not escape Mary Ann's notice, but his "get them into the system" really rankled. She slammed the paper down on the table. "Did you ever think that maybe these people want no part of your system, Walter? Or that maybe your precious system is what pushed them onto the streets in the first place?"

With a big sigh, she picked the paper up again and found the page where the story continued. The whole piece was a car wreck she couldn't look away from.

The article ended quickly, simply noting that anyone caught feeding street people would be ticketed and fined. As if that somehow made it okay. As if criminalizing compassion was justifiable as long as the punishment was light enough. As if charity was ever a crime.

Mary Ann reached for her phone. She needed the straight scoop, but from someone with a sympathetic ear. She scrolled through her contacts and found Eleanor Hoyt, a junior member of the town council. Eleanor was in her forties, younger than Mary Ann, but with a fire for social justice that Mary Ann admired. In short, Eleanor Hoyt was the anti-Walter Hagen.

That proved to be a dead end. Eleanor wasn't

answering her phone. Mary Ann left a noncommittal voicemail, hoping her tone was matter-of-fact enough to hide her disappointment.

Who next?

Gary?

No. As sheriff, he had to uphold the new law and help the Sherwood Police Department enforce it. Unloading on him would only put him in a difficult and uncomfortable position. Unless he actually agreed with the policy?

He might. Mary Ann had always admired Gary's dedication to public service—it was one of the things that drew her to him all those years ago, when he was an earnest young beat cop and she was an equally earnest E.R. nurse—but his politics had always leaned right, while hers leaned left. Not to mention, Walter Hagen had been a vocal supporter of Gary's campaign for mayor. No, better not to approach her husband about this.

She picked up the paper again, hoping the words might rearrange themselves into something more positive. They were just as discouraging the second time around.

What about Tuck? The shelter was barely scraping by as it was. Now the Town Council expected it to— what did Walter call it?—"provide social services" to even more people, and everyone knew damn well that the Walter Hagens of the world, and their town councils, had no intention of giving the shelter or any other social service organization any more resources to help meet that growing need.

And Rob, John, and the boys. Would they survive without handouts?

Mary Ann threw down the paper one last time. She needed to find some answers.

She drove to The Moors on automatic, oblivious to the changing scenery as she traveled from one side of the proverbial tracks to the other. It was John's shoulder she needed now. He had a knack for talking sense, and sense was exactly what she needed.

She purchased large coffees for the gang and walked around back—only to find the alley empty.

She started to turn around when a shiny block on the dumpster enclosure caught her eye. She stepped closer. Was that a *padlock*? Since when were garbage bins padlocked? Maybe the Men did it to protect their stuff?

Something wasn't right, but damned if Mary Ann could figure out what.

Back at her car, Mary Ann couldn't shake that twitch of wrongdoing. Another thing John could help her make sense of, if she could find him.

A visit to the House & Home parking lot, where Rojo and Much were trolling for work, led to a drive down Yorkshire Road. John and Hood, it seemed, were making rounds, checking on the regulars, making sure everyone had food and warmth. She found them at a bus stop, chatting amiably with a gray-haired woman whose face was a road map of hardship. Mary Ann could see that same map being drawn on Hood's face. The boy she'd fallen in love with was long gone, but that didn't stop her missing him. Sometimes so much she ached.

She pulled alongside the curb and rolled down a window. "Anyone up for a cup of coffee?"

Hood turned his head in Mary Ann's direction, but gave no further acknowledgement. John, however, smiled, waved, and strolled over. Hood turned his attention back to the woman, their body language making them seem like son and mother.

John slid into the front passenger seat and picked up one of the coffee cups. "Cold coffee? Really?"

"If you were where you were *supposed* to be, they wouldn't be cold."

"And where was that?"

Mary Ann nodded at the drink in John's hand. "Your home sweet alley."

John noticed the name on the coffee cups. "Right. Well, we're not there anymore. Obviously. We've, uh, holed up for the winter."

"A bit early for that, isn't it?"

John took a swig from his cup. "Tell that to Mother Nature."

"That padlock on the dumpster have anything to do with it?"

"You mean the padlock your husband put there? Yeah, that was part of it."

Mary Ann froze. Gary? "Why would he do that?" she asked in a gasp.

"You'd have to ask him."

She would. This one, she absolutely would.

Mary Ann exhaled loudly. She'd come to John for solace, not another dilemma. Now she was adding to his pile of woes. She hated bearing bad news. It had been her least favorite part of nursing, her least favorite part of life. No matter how much practice she had, her stomach still did somersaults every time. Today was no different. Her brain struggled to put the words in the right order.

She put her hand on John's arm. "I hate to ask this, but have you seen today's paper?"

"Can't say as I have."

Mary Ann smirked at the sound of Hood's voice coming out of John's mouth, but the smile quickly vanished. "The town council passed this new law. It's horrible."

"How horrible?"

Her gaze focused on Hood, who was sharing a bagel with his friend, hand feeding her piece by piece. She'd forgotten how gentle he could be. It wasn't a side he let show very often. Seeing it now tugged at her heart. She swallowed hard. "It is now officially illegal in Sherwood, Illinois, to feed homeless people."

John cursed. "What does that mean? Is Tuck in trouble?"

"No, the shelter's okay. Soup kitchens are okay. All charitable institutions are. Well, 'registered' ones are, whatever that means."

She nodded toward the duo in the bus shelter. "The city outlawed street feeding. At least that's what the article called it. Apparently, being a charitable individual is a crime." Mary Ann couldn't keep the bitterness out of her voice.

She watched John's mind spin. First those vile flyers. Then the padlock on the closest thing they had to a home. Now the town council did this. She could practically see the rug being yanked out from under his feet. How could he *not* feel like the universe was out to get him? "This is going to hurt you and the boys, isn't it?"

John looked out the window. "Not as much as it's going to hurt others. Not as much as it's going to hurt Sadie." He turned back to Mary Ann. "This new law, do you know the ins and outs?"

"A little. It's a ticketable offense. Punishment is a fine. Don't know how much." Any amount would be unreasonable, but Mary Ann kept that to herself.

John's brow creased. Mary Ann could see his brain turning this over, mulling possibilities, weighing consequences. "So if a person gives their leftovers to one of us, they'll get a ticket and a fine."

"That's how I understand it."

"What if it's a restaurant? Say, for the sake of argument, the Chicken Shack. Let's say their manager gave us a bucket of chicken from the day's leftovers. What would happen to them? Would they be fined too?"

"If it were up to me, no."

John gave a sad smile. "If it were up to you, a whole lot of things would be different. The world would be a kinder, gentler place."

Mary Ann conceded the point. "I suspect, though, that they too would be fined."

John clicked his tongue. "Well, then, I hope Bernie's got enough in his swear jar. And that the other Sherwoodians who help us do too."

CHAPTER EIGHT

Veterans Day broke sunny and above freezing, much to the relief of the Merry Men and the rest of Sherwood's homeless. Hood, John, and the boys spent the day indoors anyway, crammed into Tuck's office at the back of the shelter. Some traditions couldn't be broken—no matter how nice the weather. Veterans Day was one of them.

Every year since they came home, Hood, John, and Tuck gathered on November 11th to toast their comrades and reminisce on their war years. Beginning last year, Rojo and Much joined in the observance, which had become finely tuned over the decades: beer in plastic cups, pepperoni pizza on paper plates, and war movies. This year's playlist included *The Deer Hunter*, *Apocalypse Now*, and *Platoon*. Tuck had offered to include *Hurt Locker*, but Rojo nixed the idea. His experiences, and Much's, were still too raw to consider that film—or any other about the wars in Iraq and Afghanistan—entertainment. Even movies like *Three Kings*, about the brief and nearly-forgotten Gulf War, hit too close to home.

For a few minutes, the tiny office bustled with activity. The boys pushed the chairs and desk out of the way, the chairs against the back wall and the desk against the side. John taped paper over the small back window, a task he was awarded solely on the basis of his height. Then John and Rojo retrieved the TV/VCR cart from shelter storage, the squeaky wheels echoing down the hall as they pushed it toward the office. Meanwhile Tuck dug the tapes out of the back of the bottom drawer in his filing cabinet, and Much arranged the refreshments on Tuck's relocated desk. Hood taste-tested behind him.

Once everything was in its proper place, John slid the first tape—*The Deer Hunter*—into the machine. With the FBI warning glowing from the screen, Much distributed a cup of beer to each man, and they all stood in a circle.

Hood cleared his throat and held up his drink for the first toast. "To Frankie, Joey, and Dix—fallen but not forgotten."

"And Aron and Tyrone," Rojo added. He and the others raised their cups and bowed their heads.

Tuck offered a small prayer, which the Merry Men answered with a quiet "Amen."

The film's opening credits began to roll, the first notes of the score signaling the men to grab their slices and find their seats. The room fell silent as the tanker truck wound its way through town.

Right about the time the buddies were being warned not to get their asses shot off, the film cut out, the screen filling with static. The VCR made an odd screeching noise, as if it were screaming in pain.

John and Rojo jumped to their feet. One in front of the machines and one in back, they tinkered with the plugs and cords, but to no avail. John ejected the tape. As he pulled it out of the VCR, the film unspooled in a tangled mess. He traced the tangle back into the machine, where the film was knotted around the

VCR's innards. He held up the snarled remains. "Sorry, gang. It looks like movie day is a bust."

Tuck paled. "I don't suppose any of you know how to fix something like that?"

"Sure, you just need a pencil." Hood chuckled at his own joke.

Rojo, on the other hand, sounded genuinely contrite. "Sorry, Rev. I don't think anyone could resuscitate this beast. Might be time for Blu-rays."

"What the hell is a blue ray?" Hood punctuated his question with a swig of beer.

"It's a disc, boss, like a DVD."

"So go get one. They got one of those rental machines over at the gas station, don't they?"

"Yeah, there is, but we'd need a special player—and you can't get those from the rental machine."

Tuck sighed. "Any idea what one of those players would cost?"

To a man, the others shook their heads. Their response hit Tuck where it hurt the most.

"We can still watch the tube." Rojo grabbed the clicker and flipped through the channels, stopping at an old war movie starring John Wayne.

After a few minutes, Hood and Tuck were calling for something different.

"But . . . but it's the Duke," Rojo protested. "It's un-American to turn off the Duke."

Hood threw his empty beer cup at Rojo.

John reached up and paged through the channels. "Give an old man a break, Red."

Much pointed at the television. "Wait! Stop! Isn't that Miz Mary Ann?"

The room fell silent again, but for the sound of the television.

"And look! There's her husband."

Mayor-Elect Gibson, in full sheriff's regalia, stood behind a microphone and in front of a row of large waving flags. Between him and the flags sat a row of folding chairs, Mary Ann in one, the outgoing mayor and town council members in others. The rest of the chairs were occupied by a young man in dress blues and people who must have been his family. Gibson gestured in the young man's direction.

"What the—?" John increased the volume.

" . . . debt of gratitude to PFC Chandler and the other young men and women from our community who answered the call to service," Gibson was saying. "They represent the best of what it means to be American, willing to lay down their lives so that we may be free."

"Well, ain't that cheery." Only Hood could make *cheery* sound like a curse word.

"Thank you, PFC Chandler, for your service, and thank you, Chandler family, for your sacrifice. Welcome home, soldier, welcome home." Gibson paused while the crowd applauded.

Rojo pointed at the television. "Where do you think that is?"

Tuck leaned forward, squinting at the screen. "Looks like the park next to the library."

By now, all of the Merry Men were glued to the set. Such welcome home ceremonies were not unheard of. From what the boys had said, John was pretty sure Much had one. But there was something off about this one. John just couldn't put his finger on what.

"You think he's okay?" Much asked.

Hood snorted. His snort was followed by cough, though not as body-wracking as the fits he'd had days earlier. "Mayor Sheriff? Not a chance. Look at all those fake medals he's wearing."

"No, the PFC. The one who came home. Do you think he's okay?"

"What do you mean, son?" Tuck's voice was low with concern.

All eyes were on Much, who took a deep breath before speaking. "I mean, he's so calm sitting there with all those people and flags and cameras and noise . . ." Much swallowed hard, his eyes wide with wonder and fear. "How does he do that?"

"Aw, man, that don't mean nothing," Rojo said. "Maybe crowds aren't his thing, you know? Maybe it's flashing lights or fireworks or barking dogs. Maybe it's quiet that gets to him. But something does. Something in him is cracked. That's just how things are. You don't take a tour through hell and come back whole."

"But what if was just one tour? I mean, I was still okay after my first tour. So were you. It took two others to—"

"Man, no one does just one tour these days. You know that."

"Yeah, I know." Much's voice was soft, his expression all wounded puppy. His shoulders sagged. "But still—"

Tuck put his hand on Much's shin. "Enough with the whys and what-ifs, son. You'll only drive yourself crazy."

"Er," Rojo added with a grin. "Crazy-er."

Hood *tsked*. Much cracked a smile, but it wasn't enough to erase the fear and worry in his eyes. John shook his head, and they all turned back to the TV.

The camera was focused on an easel, a red cloth thrown over the back of it and what looked like an elevation sketch propped up on the tray. John couldn't quite make out the details of the image. Gibson, still at the microphone, pointed at the display. John shushed the room and increased the volume on the set, stopping just before it hit maximum decibels.

Gibson's voice filled the small office. ". . . remind us of the price of freedom. This new Veterans Walk will do that, with each brick honoring a service member who has roots in our community. The fine people at the county historical society have compiled a roster of Sherwood veterans from the Civil War to the Korean conflict. We are grateful to Bruce Kingston and Kingston Enterprises for funding each of those bricks. Families and friends of those who served in our nation's more recent conflicts—from Vietnam to Iraq and Afghanistan—may purchase bricks for their own beloved."

Rojo dug in his pockets. Tossing some change on his paper plate, he asked, "What do you think? Is that enough to get us a brick?"

John and Hood snorted in unison. Tuck and Much answered with smiles.

On the television, Gibson gestured again in PFC Chandler's direction. "So often we take for granted the presence of these heroes in our community."

Hood pounded his leg. "Damn straight."

"When the Veterans Walk opens this summer," Gibson continued, "let it become a place of contemplation. As we walk the path, as we read the bricks, let us remember the sacrifices made by those it honors and let it remind us to treat the veterans among us with the honor and respect they so rightly deserve."

Gibson stepped back from the microphone, acknowledging the crowd's applause by waving with both hands, as if this were a whistle stop on his campaign. Did he realize that he'd already won the election? Or was he just a sucker for an audience and accolades? Behind him, Mary Ann and the Chandlers clapped politely.

In Tuck's office, John studied the Merry Men's reactions. None were positive. Hood looked homicidal; Rojo, judging by his clench fists, wanted to hit something. Much looked like he'd been punched in the gut. Only Tuck managed to keep his expression almost neutral.

Rojo found the words first. The more he spoke, the louder he became. "Honor and respect, huh? Locking us out of our home? Making it illegal for our friends to feed us? That's what you call honor and respect? I think you need a new dictionary, sir, because that's sure as hell not what I consider honor and respect."

"Me, either!" Much chimed in.

"Amen," Tuck muttered just loud enough for John to hear.

Hood opened his mouth to speak but coughed instead—a deep phlegmy cough that sounded like he was about to spew a lung. When he regained himself, he spoke hoarsely. "We should teach him a lesson. Teach him what today really means."

The others nodded, Rojo especially vigorously.

"What did you have in mind?" John sounded more worried than curious.

Hood drained his new cup of beer. "What? I gotta come up with everything?"

Rojo clapped his hand over Much's mouth. Much always struggled to recognize rhetorical questions.

Much ripped Rojo's hand away. "Wait."

He crawled across the floor, stretching to reach his backpack under Tuck's desk. Leaning against the desk, he dug through the bag, tossing out a crumpled t-shirt, a pair of socks, a comb. He pulled out a can of spray paint, leftover from their Kingston Enterprises adventure. He shook it. It was half-full—still good for something. "How about this?"

One by one, the Merry Men grinned.

CHAPTER NINE

The graffiti story led all the local news broadcasts. Along the path of what was to become Sherwood's Veterans Walk, someone had scrawled "Never Forget" and five names. The names Francis Toretto, Joseph Harrington, and Dixon Carter were each accompanied by a Vietnamese place name. The others—Aron Zapata and Tyrone Wells—bore the names Kandahar and Ramadi. Every news clip included a soundbite of Sheriff Gary Gibson saying that as well-intentioned as the graffiti might be, it was still vandalism, and its perpetrators would be caught and prosecuted to the fullest extent of the law.

Hood raised his flask in toast to Gibson's image on the television. "I'd like to see you try, you bastard."

The Merry Men were back in their room at the motel, a little hungover from their Veterans Day shenanigans but otherwise not much worse for wear. John, Rojo, and Much sat on one bed, counting out the group's daily earnings. Hood sat on the other, having already tossed his meager collection of small bills at the boys. The television had been playing as background noise until Gibson appeared. As usual, his appearance caught everyone's attention.

The newsreader concluded the story by noting that Mayor-Elect Gary Gibson was hosting a Thanksgiving luncheon for his campaign staff and supporters.

"Wonder if any of them are homeless." Rojo's voice dripped with sarcasm.

Much wasn't alone in his confusion. John and Hood looked equally baffled.

"The Sheriff would be breaking the law," Rojo explained. "He'd have to be arrested."

Hood chuckled. "I'd pay to see that."

"Who wouldn't?" Rojo shot back.

The news broadcast concluded with a story about the increased demand at soup kitchens for the upcoming holiday. John shook his head. "Of course there's increased demand. The damn law won't let regular folks feed the needy. Where else are they going to go?"

"You think Reverend Tuck is ready?" Much asked.

"He's as ready as he can be," John said with a shrug.

"Which is a fancy way of saying no," Hood said.

Much picked up a handful of bills. "We should help."

"I appreciate the sentiment, boy," Hood answered, "but there ain't no way Tuck will take it. He's too proud. Besides, we're gonna need that dough. Won't be long till the work dries up. The longer we can stretch our funds, the better. Especially if Jack Frost is sticking around for an extended visit."

Much deflated. His big heart struggled to accept Hood's logic. The Merry Men were fortunate, more than anyone else who lived on the streets of Sherwood, more than anyone who depended on Reverend Tucker's hospitality. Hood was right—they didn't have a lot—but it was wrong not to share what little they did have. It was wrong not to give back.

Rojo scooted to the edge of the bed, leaning

forward as if he were in huddle. "So we don't give money."

"You want to help serve?" John asked.

"Sort of. I want to provide the food." Rojo planted his feet solidly on the floor and stared intently at Hood.

Hood returned the stare. "You want to steal the food from Gibson's luncheon."

"And give it to the shelter."

"Then what?" John asked. "Tuck gets questioned and maybe even arrested for theft? We can't do that to him."

"So we give it out ourselves," Much said. "Like we did with the clothes from the thrift store."

"Not bad." Hood folded his legs back onto the bed, his face bright. "Not bad."

The others gathered around him and began to plan.

Saturday was cold and cloudy, with the threat of rain hanging over Sherwood. Rain would complicate the Merry Men's plans, but they decided to move forward anyway—Much out of guilt, Hood out of sheer cussedness.

It wasn't difficult to learn the luncheon's time and location. Gibson's need for public accolades meant he had publicized his benevolence far and wide. The difficulty was in getting from the motel to the Sherwood Inn and Suites, from the depths of one side of town to the far reaches of the other. The men had purposely left Tuck and Bernie out of the loop, which meant no wheels, so it was foot and bus the whole way. By the time they disembarked four blocks from the hotel, Hood's face was flushed and his breathing ragged.

"Are you sure you want to do this?" John asked. The low tone of his voice made it clear he wanted the answer to be "no."

Hood shook off John's concern with a wave of his middle finger.

They trudged the last half mile to the hotel in silence. Traffic here was lighter. Fewer residents per square mile meant fewer cars on the streets. The men fell into a single line in descending order of age—Hood, John, Rojo, Much—a reflex from their days in uniform. At the edge of the hotel parking lot, Hood held up his fist, and they all stopped. The Inn and Suites rose in front of them, a six-story white-brick building with a portico that extended across a circular driveway and sculpted walkway. Cars pulled into the drive one after the other, each vehicle fancier than the one before it. The people who stepped out of the cars? They were dressed to the nines, as Much's grandma would say. Every one in his or her Sunday best.

A florists' truck drove past the men and swung behind the building. Hood pointed, and the men followed the same path.

The back of the hotel was alive with activity. The hotel's service doors were propped open to welcome the delivery trucks. Workers scurried from the trucks, through the doors, and back again. Hood smiled. The flurry of movement was just the cover they needed.

At John's nod, Much and Rojo pulled empty paper bags from their backpacks. They unfolded and opened the bags to disguise the lack of contents and distributed them among the Merry Men. Carrying the bags and walking at a forced nonchalant pace, the Merry Men made their way into the hotel, nodding and smiling at each worker they passed.

They continued the charade once they were inside, weaving their way through the bustle of hotel staff in the hallway to the kitchen.

At an intersection, Hood stopped short, John almost bumping into him.

"What the—?" Rojo hissed. "Keep moving, or we'll get caught."

But Hood's attention was to the left, down the hall toward the lobby. Amid the well-dressed minglers stood a woman in a blue floral dress, her gray hair curled at chin level.

Mary Ann.

Of course she was here. She was married to the luncheon's host. It was her job to smile, shake hands, and play the gracious hostess.

Mary Ann took a step back and laughed, turning her head ever-so-slightly as she did. If she turned her head so much as a fraction more . . .

"Shit." Rojo jumped forward, landing with a twist on the other side of the intersection.

John gave a push, and Hood stumbled forward. The spell was broken. Much hurried to catch up, and all four Merry Men speed-walked toward the kitchen.

The activity in the kitchen made the movement in the hallways seem like slow-motion. Much had expected the kitchen to smell good. It was, after all, where the food was cooked. Instead, it overwhelmed his senses: the constant movement, the shouting of directions, the mingling of so many different scents. His head started to swim. He ducked back in the hall, closed his eyes, and took a deep breath.

When he opened his eyes, he noticed the open door opposite. It led into some kind of supply room and a stash of white chef's jackets. He grabbed four and hurried back to his friends, shoving one at each Merry Man. "Here. Put these on."

Two of the four metal carts lined up along the kitchen wall had food on them: baskets of rolls on one, Caprese salads on the other.

The Merry Men slipped into their jackets and sidled closer to the carts. Someone behind them clapped his hands. They froze.

"I'm sorry to interrupt." Gary Gibson stood in the doorway. He wore a black suit with an American flag lapel pin, his shoes mirror-shiny, his hair as dark as his suit. Much could have sworn Gibson's hair had been grayer on television.

The four Merry Men held their breath, dropping their gaze to their shoes, doing their best to hide in plain sight. Except Hood. He stared daggers at the sheriff. Thankfully, John's heavy hand on Hood's shoulder seemed to keep him in place.

"I just want to say thank you," Gibson said. "I know this luncheon means extra work, and I want you to know it's noticed and appreciated."

"Dude," Rojo whispered to no one in particular, "you already won the damn election. You can stop campaigning now."

Gibson moved around the room, shaking hands with each worker. Hood nodded at his men, and they wheeled the carts toward the door.

The wheels of the first cart thumped onto the hall carpet.

"Hey! Where are you taking those?" The voice was male and authoritative, but not Gibson's. The Merry Men kept moving, the stares of the kitchen staff burning on their backs.

"Excuse me! It's not time for those yet! COME BACK HERE!"

Gibson's voice overlapped with the first one. "I know those men! They're criminals! They have warrants for theft and vandalism. Get them!"

A split second of hesitation then a stampede of footsteps.

Hood broke into a run. The others followed suit. The carts clattered, the plates and baskets bouncing on the trays. People in the hallways hugged the walls. By the time the Merry Men reached the door to the back lot, Hood was wheezing loud enough to be heard down the block.

Rojo and Much shoved some bread baskets into their bags and pushed over the cart. John pushed over the second cart, spilling dozens of Caprese salads on the ground, and followed, dragging Hood with him.

Less than a block later, they heard sirens. Gibson had called in the cavalry. The men changed course, zigzagging behind buildings and through landscaping, avoiding the sidewalks and sightlines to the street.

They couldn't run all the way back. Hood would never make it that far. Already, he was red and sweaty and wheezing. Much doubted Hood would make it to the next block. But Hood always did. Still, a few blocks was far different from a few miles. They couldn't afford to stop and wait for a bus. They'd be too easy to spot. The cops would pick them up in no time.

Rojo made a sharp left down an empty street, blocks ahead of the bus route they'd taken hours earlier. The others followed. Hood's wheezing gave way to thready gasps as step by step, he fell farther behind. John, ever watchful of his best buddy, doubled back and threw a supportive arm around his friend.

Two blocks later, Rojo made another left, essentially guiding the Merry Men into a U-turn. The men stayed low, using the cars parked curbside as cover. The sirens continued in the opposite direction, growing fainter by the minute.

The men slowed, as much in deference of Hood as out of a feeling of safety. Three blocks later, they reached a bus shelter. John practically carried Hood into it. If anyone need to sprawl on a bench, it was the old man.

Except there was no bench. Not a usable one, anyway. Instead of a wide flat bench one could sit on, the space was now occupied by a narrow angled bench with raised dividers. There was no lying down on that.

Hood collapsed against the side of shelter, under a poster advertising the friendly service and no fees at a local bank. "Hey, Red." His words came between heavy breaths. He pointed at the bag of bread. "Sadie gets first dibs."

"Of course." As if they would have considered anything different.

Rojo, meanwhile, pushed at the angled bench with his foot. He put the bag of bread on it. It slid off. Then he tried sitting on it. "What the fuck is this? How is anyone supposed to sit here?"

John answered. "My guess is, they're not."

Rojo stood with a grimace. "What's the point of that?"

"Maybe that explains it." Much pointed to a sign by the curb.

John stepped over to the sign, which was about the size of a parking regulations sign, and read it aloud. "For your safety and theirs, do not give to solicitors. Support a local charity instead. Those who need assistance call 815-555-1212. Sherwood cares."

"Sherwood cares? My ass." Hood's curse sent him into a fit of deep, racking coughs.

December

December broke mild. Compared to the sharp cold of late October and November, it felt almost spring-like. The Merry Men spent the daylight hours outdoors, once again hustling jobs in the parking lot of the House & Home store. The Merry Men minus one. Hood, as usual, preferred to panhandle by the interstate. Rojo still didn't understand how that could be more satisfying than honest manual labor, and he hoped he never would. Tuck stayed locked in his office at the shelter, crunching numbers, begging for pennies from strangers, stripping one saint to clothe another.

Rojo turned his face toward the sun. Too bad it wasn't warm enough to sleep outside; the motel walls were closing in. He shut his eyes, basking in the sun's light. The day had been slow. A trickle of cars had entered the parking lot, none in need of their services, but that wasn't unusual for a weekday this early in the month. Another couple of weeks and they'd have as much Christmas decoration work as they could handle. He supposed he should be worried—they needed the cash, after all—but a day lazing in the sun? Sometimes that was exactly what a body needed.

A nondescript sedan slowed to stop a bit ahead of where the Merry Men were sitting. John got up to investigate.

Much gave Rojo's shoulder a gentle push. "I'm hungry. How much we got left?"

After the failed Thanksgiving lunch raid, Rojo ended up the Merry Men's money-keeper. He didn't remember volunteering for the job, and John certainly never appointed him to the task. It just sort of fell to him by default, the same way taking care of Mama and his brothers and sisters fell to him after his father died. Maybe it was something about being the oldest child.

Much pushed him again. "C'mon, Red."

"Hold your horses." Rojo dug into his pockets. He counted out the findings in his palm. "Five dollars and thirty-two cents."

"That's it?"

"That's it."

The boys were silent for a moment.

"What could we get for that?" Much asked.

"A pack of gum if we're lucky." John dropped down next to Rojo. In answer to Rojo's raised eyebrow, he said, "A bust. Guy just wanted directions."

"You shoulda charged him for it."

"Next time, maybe I will."

Much brought them back on point. "Hey, guys, what are we gonna do about dinner?"

John's exhale sounded like defeat. "Bernie's. We got no other choice."

"But that new law—" Much was the first to revert to worry.

"We'll pay him." Rojo stood and zipped his jacket up to his neck. "We don't have much, but we can give him something. A couple of bucks." A squint from John and he reconsidered. "Okay, maybe just one.

The point is, we'd be customers, and he wouldn't be breaking the law."

Rojo's answer seemed to satisfy Much. He stood, and together the boys pulled John to his feet. John stretched his back with a grunt. Rojo swore he heard John's knees crack, too.

"Getting old sucks, boys," John said. "Don't do it."

Rojo slapped Much's back. "Sure thing, man. We'll get right on that."

The three men trod out of the parking lot and toward their old strip mall stomping grounds in companionable silence.

The bell on the Chicken Shack's door announced the Merry Men's arrival. The clock hadn't yet started creeping on the dinner hour, so the restaurant was largely empty but for the employees prepping for the evening rush.

"Well, lookee who it is!" Bernie emerged from behind the counter with his arms outstretched, his shoes squeaking on the linoleum floor. "The Lost Boys come back to roost."

Rojo clicked his heels twice. "There's no place like home."

"That's the Wizard of Oz," Much mumbled. "Lost Boys are Peter Pan."

"Technicalities," Rojo mumbled back.

After a bro-hug with John, Bernie stepped back and counted. "You seem to be missing one."

Rojo snorted.

"He's not missing," John said. "He needed some alone time."

"Right." Bernie clearly didn't believe John's answer.

Much's stomach growled at top volume.

Rojo grinned. "Think you could hook us up with some vittles, Bern?"

"Vittles? You've been hanging out with Reverend Tucker, haven't you?" Bernie waved the men to a table. "Take a seat, and I'll serve you a meal fit for a king."

John grabbed Bernie's arm. "We're not royalty, and we can't afford to be fed as if we were. Are we clear?"

Bernie yanked his arm back, his offense clear on his face. "Now you sound like your buddy Hood, proud and ashamed all at the same time. I thought you were better than that, John."

"It's that new law, Bernie," Much said. "We don't wanna get you in trouble."

"What? It's against the law for a man to make dinner for his friends?"

"When those friends are homeless, yeah." Rojo let his bitterness fill his voice.

"Well, if I may quote our dear absent Mr. Hood, fuck that." Bernie stomped toward the counter, stopping only to snap at his gape-mouthed employees. "Get back to work! Or I'll get you all toothbrushes and make you scrub the floor."

With Bernie in the kitchen slamming things around, Much turned to John. "Is that it?"

John shook his head. "How much we got again, Red? Lay it all out here."

Rojo spread their meager savings on the table and watched while John sorted it by denomination—coins here, dollar bills there. John studied the collection and then slid the two pennies into his palm. He walked toward the kitchen with the coins clenched in his fist.

"Giving him our two cents, eh?" Rojo called after him, laughing at his own bad joke. It did draw a smile from Much, though, which made it slightly less bad. Slightly.

At Rojo's urging, the men took their feast out back to the alley. It wasn't so much that he wanted to avoid drawing the attention of any customers, but that he wanted to spend as many minutes in the fresh air and open space as possible before being cooped up again. Oh, the things he did for Much. Cold as it was at night, he'd still have been happy to sleep under the stars again. He was sure Hood would too. But Much felt safer at the motel, insisted on going back as long as they had the money to afford it—which wasn't much longer, at the rate things were going. What kind of buddy denied even temporary solace to his friend?

Out of habit, Rojo went over to the dumpster enclosure and tugged on the padlock. It held. With a grumble, he smacked it—but it barely moved. As much as it kept them out, it also kept their precious few belongings in. Not to mention, it meant they no longer had anywhere to store their thrift store hauls, which meant they couldn't help all the people who depended on them. People like Sadie. If things didn't change soon, the Merry Men would end up just like her. Rojo took another swing at the padlock before heading back to the others.

Meanwhile, Much found some crates that weren't completely soaked with winter muck and set them as a makeshift dining table and chairs. It was almost civilized. The men tucked in without ceremony.

Rojo groaned with pleasure. Grease and salt and batter and yeast and cheese—Heaven in cheap plastic containers. He licked his lips and dug back in. This is what he missed. Fresh, hot, fried, fast food.

"Sorry, Mama," Rojo muttered before devouring another heaping spoonful of baked beans. Mama's pride and joy had always been her frijoles, the product of a gazillion ingredients and almost as many hours of cooking time—unless she'd started taking shortcuts, like Abuela had in her last years. Everyone pretended to ignore the cans in the garbage, and Abuela's cheatin' beans became a family joke. Did they still make that joke? Maybe he should call home and find out.

No, the last time he called home, it was ten minutes of listening to Mama fret and cry. Rojo shook off the bite of homesickness and shoveled another spoonful of Bernie's beans into his mouth. Yep, these beans were definitely nothing to joke about.

Much's lip-licking suggested he found the food equally rapturous. So did the speed with which he devoured the meal. Was he thinking of home too?

"Well, well, well, what have we here?" That sheriff Dubrowski stood behind John, thumbs hooked in his belt, diabolical pleasure in his tone. But his uniform wasn't from the Nottingham County Sheriff's Department. Now, he wore the blues of the Sherwood Police Department. Gibson's flunky apparently followed Gibson everywhere.

John held up a drumstick. "Officer, why don't you join us? There's plenty to go around."

Dubrowski patted his ample stomach. "No, thanks. Promised the wife I'd save my appetite."

Much coughed. "You're *married*?" His question earned him an elbow in the ribs from Rojo.

Dubrowski, ignoring the question, leaned over John's shoulder. "That looks like it's from the Chicken Shack. Am I right?"

"Boy," Rojo said with a knee slap, "nothing gets past you."

"Hmmm, I might have to check that out." Dubrowski gave a mock salute. "You boys have a good night."

Rojo shot John a worried glance. He was gratified to find a similar expression on John's face. They both turned, and together with Much, watched Dubrowski round the corner toward the front of the building.

Rojo shook his head. "That can't be good."

Another exchange of looks with John and the Men stood, abandoning their feast to feed their curiosity. Without speaking, they speed-walked to the Chicken Shack's back entrance.

Rojo eased open the door; John held it that way. Much leaned in close. Over the sounds of the customers, the fry oil, the cash register, and the teen girl working the counter, they heard Bernie greet Dubrowski.

"What can I get you, Officer?" Bernie asked.

"Some information."

"Sure. Anything you need."

"The three men eating out back in the alley—you know them?"

"Yeah. They're regulars."

Rojo recognized the false casualness in Bernie's

tone. The Merry Men weren't the only ones who smelled a rat—the kind that didn't share the alley they once called home.

"I don't suppose they paid for that food?"

"What kind of business do you think I run? Of course they paid for it. All my customers do."

"I don't suppose you've got the receipt," Dubrowski said after a pause.

Rojo could only imagine Bernie's expression. His own was a mixture of indignation and fear, a look he saw mirrored on John and Much's faces. Did Bernie have a receipt? He'd taken John's offering but did he ring up their meal at the register? Rojo hadn't noticed. If there was a receipt, did it show full payment or just the two-cent token John forced on him? Did any of that matter? Dubrowski'd had it in for the Merry Men since their confrontation in this very alley back in October. Receipt or not, Bernie was an easy target for the officer's revenge.

The cash register drawer dinged open.

"This all looks like some sort of code." Dubrowski spoke slowly. "Tell me what it all means."

Bernie pointed out the men's food items one by one: the chicken, rolls, beans, macaroni and cheese. "This number here is the subtotal. This one's the sales tax."

"And this one?"

"Friends and family discount."

"So these boys—are they friends or family?"

"They're brothers. Veterans, like me. So, yeah, I cut them a break when I can. Like I would for anyone else who's served. Including yourself."

Dubrowski cleared his throat. Rojo took that to mean Dubrowski hadn't been in the service. Figured.

"Okay, so leaving that aside, what's this number?"

"Store credit."

"And this one?"

"That last one is the balance due. As you can see, it was paid in full."

"A whole two cents."

"Yessir. You want to see the pennies?"

"Sir, could you come out from behind the counter?"

Bernie must have complied because the next words the Merry Men heard were Dubrowski's. "I am placing you under arrest for violating Sherwood city ordinance 13-015. You have the right to remain silent. You have the right to an attorney. If you cannot afford an attorney—"

The Merry Men eased the door shut. Much peered up at John. "What are we going to do?"

CHAPTER ELEVEN

Much kept one eye on the courthouse entrance and one on the plastic bottle he and Rojo were kicking back and forth. They'd fished the bottle out of a trashcan and brought it to the grassy island in the courthouse parking lot. On a day like this—slightly overcast and chilly—soccer seemed a much better way to spend the time than sitting and staring. Hood preferred the latter, perched on the island's curb, focused intently on the courthouse doors, cracking his knuckles one by one—left hand first then right hand then left again.

John was inside, a witness to Bernie's arraignment. Hood, having already mentioned the words *jail break*, had been persuaded to stay outside, lest he get their friend thrown in jail for a misdemeanor, fine-able offense—or worse, get himself thrown in jail for mouthing off. Rojo and Much were Hood's guards.

When the courthouse door opened, Much froze. The bottle hit him squarely in the forehead.

"Dude!" Rojo called. "Pay attention."

Much jabbed with his chin. "Look."

Hood shot to his feet. Bernie was starting down the courthouse steps, John looming behind him like the ghost of Christmas past. Soccer game forgotten, Rojo and Much followed Hood across the parking lot.

"Well?" Hood demanded.

Bernie waved a piece of paper. "Fined. $500."

"That's not bad," Much said. Then, seeing Bernie's expression, he added, "Is it?"

"C'mon, man," Rojo answered, his voice rife with injustice. "Even five dollars is too much. This whole situation is bullshit, and we all know it."

"I appreciate the support, Red." Bernie put a hand on Much's shoulder. "And no, $500 isn't a lot in the grand scheme of things."

John cleared his throat and rocked back on his heels. "But—"

Bernie sighed. "But . . . the judge doubled the fine. I really owe a thousand."

Rojo exploded. "That's not fair! He had no right—"

John held up his hand. "The judge had every right. Bernie here started spouting off about how the law was unjust and how we all have a duty, a *responsibility*, to disobey unjust laws."

And here they'd been so worried about Hood mouthing off. Rojo and Much gave side glances at their fearless leader, who crossed his arms. "Bern, you been reading Gandhi again?"

Bernie harrumphed.

"Bernie talked himself right into a contempt of court charge," John finished.

"So . . . the thousand bucks. You got that?" Much asked.

Bernie shook his head. "Nope. I could swing the five hundred. But not much more than that."

Hood held out his hand. "Bern, you ain't no chickenshit friend. And neither are we. You leave it to us. We'll get you that $500. Hell, we'll get you the full thousand if we can."

Rojo nodded. It was their fault Bernie was in this mess. It was only fair that they got him out of it.

Bernie's brow crinkled. "How?"

Hood shook his head. "Best you don't know."

Bernie studied each of the Merry Men. Each one shook his head. Mum was definitely the word.

They watched Bernie get in his truck and drive away before trudging back toward the motel.

"Boss," Rojo asked, "how are we gonna get Bernie that money?"

Hood clapped Rojo on the shoulder. "Beats the hell out of me. You got any ideas?"

The sky darkened as slightly overcast turned to gray and threatening. When sharp drops of cold wet began to pelt the Merry Men, they ducked into the nearest fast-food joint and splurged on 99-cent coffees. They took a table with a view of the rain, sitting in silence until Rojo nudged John's arm.

"Look." Rojo pointed at the television mounted in the corner of the restaurant. Usually, the set was tuned to a children's station. Today, it played the news.

The Men turned in time to see the chyron, "Police Report Rash of Catalytic Converter Thefts."

Rojo leaned in and lowered his voice. "Maybe that's what we should do."

"What?" Much asked.

"Steal catalytic converters. I've heard how it's done. Slide under the car, in and out in minutes."

"We do not steal." John's voice was low but absolute.

Much pursed his lips. "We stole those rolls."

"That was different."

"How?" Much and Rojo asked together.

John looked at Hood. Hood crossed his arms and smiled. "Don't look at me. You got yourself into this."

John shifted in his seat. "Well, we were trying to help people."

"And now we're trying to help Bernie," Rojo said.

John folded his hands on the table. "That was about embarrassing the sheriff too. But now, you want to steal from ordinary citizens, everyday joes—from people who struggle as much as we do just to get by. You want to take away something they worked their butts off to get? If we start doing that, what do you think will happen to the few people who help us? We have few enough friends as it is. We start stealing, and that number will drop to zero. Then we really will be screwed."

Rojo opened his mouth to argue and then closed it. His shoulders sagged. John wasn't wrong. It would be like stealing from Mama. Or Much's sister. Or Reverend Tucker. Rojo would die to protect any one of them.

He cast a glance at Much, who was lost in his coffee cup, guilt painted all over his face.

There had to be another way.

"What's going through that noggin of yours, son?" Hood's eyes were narrowed, as if he were using x-ray vision.

Rojo threw another gulp of coffee down his throat. Outside, the rain danced on the windows. "So we don't go after working folks. We stay away from the train station, the grocery stores. We go after the people who can afford it, who'll have the best insurance. The country club, that fancy steakhouse. You know, the people who already hate us, the ones who think we're vermin, the ones who pretend we don't exist. People like the sheriff and his friends."

Hood grinned. "Son, I like the way you think."

The parking lot of the Sherwood Country Club sat at the end of a long drive and, like that drive, it was bordered by trees—old, overgrown trees that created a wall between the country club and its golf course and the rabble who lived beyond it. As if that weren't enough, the club employed private security to keep the riffraff out of the parking lot and off the grounds. Every Merry Man knew the story of Mary Ann and her Toyota being called the "wrong sort" and chased out of the parking lot by the club's rent-a-cop. At a time when even the revered Augusta National was admitting women, the Sherwood Country Club remained a bastion of white men of a certain age and bank balance.

John was certain that simply walking past the club driveway would be an unforgivable offense, and here they were camped on the other side of the Wooded Wall. Most of them, anyway. Rojo had gone ahead to scout the premises—every mission needed recon. John prayed the excitable young man didn't do anything stupid. This whole escapade was risky enough. The last thing they needed was for Rojo to get caught—or assault a security guard.

A wolf-whistle signaled the all-clear. John, Much,

and Hood trod carefully through the trees, Hood's labored breathing drowning out the crunch of their footsteps. The man belonged in a doctor's office—or better yet, the hospital—but that was a fight for another day. Besides, if this went sideways—and there were a million ways it could—they'd all be in jail and Hood's healthcare problem would be solved.

They found the parking lot about half-full, surprising for a Thursday evening. Thankfully, security seemed to be off-duty, or maybe just inside sitting next to a blazing fire, sipping a fancy cup of coffee. As expected, the cars in the lot were all high-end: Lexus, Mercedes, even a Jaguar and a couple of Land Rovers. And one lovingly kept Mustang. A '67 Shelby Mustang, by the looks of it. Rojo stood next to it, caressing the hood with a rare gentleness.

"Not this one," Rojo said.

"'Course not." Hood's agreement sounded like a dismissal. "Classics like this don't have catalytic converters. Only cars built after '75 do."

Rojo and Much stared at Hood.

"What? I used to be a mechanic."

John chuckled. The boys rolled their eyes.

Hood walked up one row of cars and down the next, stopping behind a silver two-door. He pointed at the bumper and grinned. "This one."

Puzzled, John and the others swung around to join him. Emblazoned on the bumper was a red, white, and blue sticker with the words "Gibson for Mayor." Rojo pulled out the wrench he'd "borrowed" from Tuck's shelter—Tuck would have asked too many questions— and dropped under the car. Minutes later, he held out the catalytic converter.

Much grabbed it, and Rojo scooted out. "That's twenty bucks, easy!"

The men scanned the lot for other cars with Gibson stickers and liberated two more catalytic converters. Rojo was working on a fourth when a flashlight panned across the lot, passing and then returning to the red Acura.

"Hey, Mr. B! How'd you get out here before me?" A hefty male voice carried across the lot, punctuated by a few unhurried footsteps. "Hey!," he said, his tone changing. "You're not Mr. Babcock. Who are you? What're you doing with his car?"

Much hit the pavement first. John made it to his knee, pulling a wobbly Hood down with him.

"Don't try to hide. I know you're out there." Heavy footsteps—the guard was moving toward them—not at a run but fast enough.

"Damn it." Rojo scooted out from under the car, the half-detached catalytic converter hitting the ground with a clank.

"You have thirty seconds to show yourselves!"

"What do we do, Boss?" Much whispered, three converters cradled in his arms.

"Not a damn thing," Hood hissed.

"You're trespassing on private property!" the voice continued. "I'm calling the police, and you will be taken into custody and charged."

"C'mon." Rojo grabbed Much's sleeve. Staying low, they made for the woods. John followed, dragging Hood behind him.

"HEY!"

The guard spotted them and took off in chase, all

the while shouting impotent threats. The pounding of his steps felt like a hammer in John's head. He should have know this would go FUBAR. The Merry Men were many things, not all of them good, but they were most certainly not thieves. Not very good ones, anyway. They should have learned that from their bread run.

The men crashed into the woods. John heard the guard behind them, keeping his promise. "This is the Sherwood Country Club. We have four trespassers committing a possible theft in the parking lot. . . ."

Hood stumbled, each breath jolting and rattling. John pulled him behind a tree and whistled for the boys, gesturing for them to hold up. Rojo and Much dove behind a tree a few paces ahead but within John's line of sight, the sound of John's breathing and Hood's wheezing echoing in the woods. Like damn spotlights announcing their location. They had to keep moving.

Loud crunches announced the guard's entrance into the woods. John waved the boys forward. No reason for them all to get caught.

"These woods are country club property. You may think you're safe here, but you're still breaking the law. And I'm still going to have your ass." The guard spoke and moved with bravado.

John hauled Hood to his feet. "Let's go, buddy."

Hood swayed. Even the dim evening light, Hood looked eerily gray. There was no way he would make it across the Wooded Wall. He seemed to know it, too.

Hood looked up into the tree that towered above them. Pointing at a branch, he said between heavy, wheezy breaths, "Hoist me up. Rent-a-cop won't ever look over his head. Come get me in the morning."

The guard's footsteps grew closer.

John studied Hood and the tree branch. The guard might not find Hood up there, but Jack Frost would. No, if they were going to survive, it was going to be together. That's how they made it through 'Nam. That's how they made it through after-'Nam. That's how they'd make it through this. Besides, Marines never left a man behind. Never.

In one smooth motion, John bent, grabbed Hood's knees, and threw his friend over his shoulder.

Hood pounded weakly on the big man's back. "You son of a bitch! Put me down! I ain't no sack of flour!"

"Yeah, well, you're not a tree hugger, either. And I am *not* leaving you behind." John plunged forward, weaving among the trees. He didn't know when the guard's footsteps stopped, but by the time they exited the far side of the woods, the only footsteps he heard were his own.

John caught sight of the boys a block away. Rojo paced while Much stood opposite, the picture of stillness. Both were empty handed. Where the hell were the catalytic converters?

Much saw John and Hood first, his eyes widening at the sight of Hood slung over John's shoulder. Rojo paced a few more steps before stopping short. He turned slowly, following Much's gaze, and bit down hard on his lip.

John slid Hood to the ground, where Hood promptly kicked John in the shin—and wobbled.

Grabbing Hood's arm, Rojo said, "C'mon, Boss. There's a place to sit—"

"Let go of me!" Hood yanked his arm back and

stumbled. Rojo reached for Hood again and was answered with a swat. "I'm fine! See how well you move around after being hung upside down like a side of meat."

Rojo held up his hands in surrender, and Hood nodded. "That's more like it. So how'd we do?"

"Not so good, Boss." Much sounded cowed, almost embarrassed.

"What does that mean? I saw Red here take three of those puppies. I saw *you* carrying them. Where the hell are they?"

Much gave his answer to the sidewalk. "I, um, dropped 'em."

Hood's face livened with anger. Rojo hopped between him and Much. "It wasn't his fault, Boss. Those things are hell to run with."

Hood stared down Rojo for a long second. "Shit." He turned on his heel. "Shit. Shit. Shit. You know what this means, don't ya?" He took a menacing step toward Much. "Don't ya?"

Much, still using Rojo for cover, shook his head.

Hood threw a punch at the air. "Bernie's going to jail."

CHAPTER TWELVE

Tuck sat behind closed doors in his office, playing his weekly game of Russian roulette with the shelter's bank accounts. He picked up the next invoice. Would this be the one that put them in the red? The early December warm-up plus a wave of Thanksgiving donations had provided a small reprieve—emphasis on *small*—but that new city ordinance, the ban on feeding the homeless, had driven even more people to the shelter and its soup kitchen. And had the city ponied up any money to help pay for these services? Of course not!

Even Hood and the Merry Men had taken up residence, although Tuck suspected there was more to their story than they let on. He always figured it would take Hell freezing over to get Hood under this roof. Hell wasn't dripping with icicles just yet, but maybe a few snowflakes had started to fall—even if Hood did insist on sleeping outside by the back door and not inside with everyone else.

Shuffling and banging across the hall in the kitchen announced the beginning of the morning's breakfast service. At Tuck's insistence, the shelter provided the healthiest, heartiest meals it could afford. During the spring, summer, and fall, donations from local farmers helped fill the baskets and stretch the budget. But this was winter, when nothing grew but Tuck's gray hairs.

It wouldn't be much longer until cheap sugary cereals—the kind Tuck detested—were the only thing on the menu. Tuck closed out the register and rested his head in his hands.

"Knock, knock." Mary Ann's head peeked through the door. "Everything okay in here?"

Tuck pasted on a smile. "Why wouldn't they be?"

Mary Ann arched an eyebrow. Her no-nonsense stare was the best in the game. Legend had it that in her nursing days, she'd brought an overinflated nationally-recognized surgeon to his knees with just that stare. It had certainly put Hood in his place on more than one occasion.

Tuck, who was neither as inflated as the surgeon or as stubborn as Hood, crumbled. He shook his head. "Just the same ol', same ol'."

Mary Ann would not be dismissed. She dropped into the chair in front of Tuck's desk and crossed her legs. "Does this mean we're going to have that conversation again? The one where I take out my checkbook and you tell me you don't need my money, even though you really do?"

Tuck smiled, a blush creeping across his cheeks.

"So let's just skip to the part where you tell me what you need."

Tuck sighed. Once again, he needed everything. Money. Food. Volunteers.

A rap on the door interrupted his list-making. Much peered into the room and then held up a rolled-up sleeping bag. "Rev? Mind if we stash these here?"

Tuck waved his assent, and Much and Rojo stacked four sleeping bags in the corner. Nodding thanks, they left to grab breakfast, or so Tuck assumed.

Tuck waited until the door clicked shut. He stared at the bags, all four worn from use. These weren't the only four used the previous night. Almost a dozen more had been rolled out in the shelter's dining room, the only way to accommodate the overflow of recent weeks. "Beds," he finally said. "We need beds." He clicked his tongue. "Except we have no place to put them."

Mary Ann sat quietly, her mouth twisted and her forehead creased in thought. After a few moments, she stood. "Let's take a walk."

She led him down the hall, away from the organized chaos of the breakfast service, giving each shelter resident they passed a smile and a kind word. Tuck watched each one brighten at her touch. If ever there were one of God's angels on Earth . . .

Mary Ann stopped at the men's dorm. She and Tuck stood in the doorway and surveyed the room and its rows of cots, a few of which were still populated. Her tone was firm but gentle. "Excuse us, gentlemen. Could we have the room for a moment?"

The men obeyed without question, quickly and quietly filing past the angel and the reverend.

Mary Ann walked to the middle of the empty room, her shoes squeaking on the linoleum floor. Turning slowly, she studied each of the four walls. "What about bunk beds? We can put bunk beds along the walls and line up cots in the middle. When our population drops, we can put the cots in storage."

Her use of *we* didn't escape Tuck's notice. With anyone else he'd assume it was the royal *we*, but not with Mary Ann. She'd get down in the muck with him.

All he had to do was ask. Heck, she'd probably jump into the foxhole before he ever got a chance to form the question.

"I like the idea. But that many new bunkbeds? That will cost a small fortune."

Mary Ann gave him a sly smile. "Who said anything about buying them?"

"Huh?" The light bulb flipped on. "Ah, the boys."

"We need bunkbeds. They need work."

Tuck smiled. "A match made in Heaven."

They proceeded back to Tuck's office, a new skip in the reverend's step. They sketched out the three dorms, calculated the available space, and the number of bunkbeds that would fit. Tuck drew up a rough design—simple yet sturdy—and used that to devise a materials list.

"You know," he said, putting down his pencil, "we'll need pillows and bedding for all these beds, too."

"I bet our Armchair Angels could help with that."

"Let's hope you're right."

Tuck watched as John held open the shelter door for a young mother and her two young boys. The boys raced into the parking lot, playing their own version of tag, making up rules as they went along. Mom shuffled straight to a dirty Ford Explorer.

"Boys! School! Now!" Weariness underscored Mom's firm tone. The boys, though, didn't give her any trouble, clambering into the car while negotiating rules for a new game.

"We're seeing a lot of that," Tuck said, as the

Explorer rumbled to life and exited the parking lot. "Entire families forced out of their homes and onto the streets. It's a growing problem, one I never imagined when these doors opened. Back then, I thought—"

"All street people were like us?" John said.

Tuck gave a sad smile. "Something like that."

John flashed back to the nights the Merry Men spent crammed in the dumpster enclosure, the chill that never left their bones, the hunger that was never fully satisfied, the flask tucked in Hood's pocket, the cough that Hood could never quite kick. "Kids, man."

"The kids are the worst part. We're just not equipped to help them. We don't have a place for them to play or do homework or—"

John put a hand on Tuck's shoulder. "At least we can give them a place to sleep. Let's go see if the lumber's here."

They found the boys at the shelter's back door, deep in conversation with Mary Ann.

"Sorry, ma'am," Rojo was saying, "I just can't see it. You and Hood? No way."

Mary Ann smiled. "Why is that?"

"Because you're kind and gentle and sweet and he's . . . not." Rojo's face glowed a bright red. "I mean, he's angry and stubborn and sarcastic and—"

John chuckled. "You better stop there, Red. You'll never be able to talk your way out of the hole you're digging."

Rojo looked over John's shoulder at Tuck, who answered with a knowing shake of his head.

"It was a long time ago." Mary Ann sounded resigned. "Rob and I are very different people now."

"So what happened?"

Everyone stared at Much, who up until then had been little more than a silent bystander.

"And don't just say 'the war,'" Rojo added. "I'm sick of that shi—stuff. Sorry, ma'am."

"No apology necessary," Mary Ann answered. "I've cleaned up my fair share of shit. I've also been known to use the word myself on occasion."

John bit back a smile, while Tuck studied his shoes. Rojo would never forgive the laughter they were working so hard to suppress.

"To answer your question," Mary Ann continued, "I don't know *what* happened exactly, but the war had everything to do with it. One day, I got a Dear Jane letter postmarked Vietnam, and it was over."

"Wait." Rojo stood straighter. "*He* dumped *you*?"

Mary Ann nodded.

"Just like that?" Much asked.

"Just like that." Mary Ann snapped her fingers.

John and Tuck cleared their throats. Mary Ann made it sound so simple. Back in Vietnam, John had watched his friend wrestle a conscience like a black bear, watched Hood's letters home grow shorter and farther between as he tried to protect his shining girl from the darkness of war. Hood could never lie to Mary Ann, so he told her less and less. He waited longer and longer to open her letters, then even longer to answer them, until he finally stopped reading them altogether. Then came the ambush and Hood's final heart-wrenching letter.

John was with Hood after that ambush, as his

friend tried to compose that letter. He saw Hood crumple in agony as he wrote his goodbye. Hood hadn't blithely dismissed Mary Ann with that letter; he'd ripped out his own heart.

"To be fair," Tuck said, "there was nothing 'just' about it."

Mary Ann pursed her lips but accepted the chastisement. "No, there wasn't." She took a deep breath, clearly conflicted about what to say next and how. "I tried to mend fences when he came home, but the war had changed him. It took his light, his laughter, and put thick unscalable walls in their place. I couldn't find a way in. Then Rob reinforced those walls, added a moat and some alligators, and I had no choice but to keep my distance. But I know what's on the other side of those walls." She shared a flash of sadness, or maybe regret, with John and Tuck. "We all do. That's why we stay."

Rojo cleared his throat. "Speaking of Hood, where is our fearless leader?"

"Where do you think?" John answered.

"I thought you three were like the Musketeers—all for one, one for all, and all that crap. But he'd rather beg by the interstate than help his best buds?"

John and Tuck exchanged a glance and shrugged.

Rojo turned to Much. "Dude, promise you'll do me better than that."

Before Much could answer, the lumber delivery truck rounded the corner.

Tuck waved it down. "What say we get to work, eh, boys?"

Lumber unloaded and stacked, the three Merry Men got to work. Within minutes, the room echoed with the pounding of hammers and scratching of saws.

Another length cut, Much pulled down his face mask and wiped beads of sweat from his forehead. "Dude," he called to Rojo, "you know I've got your back."

Rojo acknowledged the sentiment with a nod.

Much put the mask back into place, grabbed another two by four, and sawed away.

They fell into a rhythm, their tools knocking out an irregular percussion beat. John sang out the first lines of "Doo-Wah-Diddy."

Rojo and Much stopped working, their faces scrunched with confusion. "You okay, Boss?" Rojo called. "You sound like you might be in pain."

"Very funny, Red." John punctuated his sentence with a thwack of his hammer. He swung the hammer again, trying to get back his rhythm. "GODDAMN . . . FUCK . . .FUCK . . FU—"

John's thumb exploded in pain. He bent and turned circles, clutching his injured hand, tears filling his eyes. Much dashed out of the room, Rojo to John's side. Much returned with a bag of ice and a motherly woman in tow.

"Mary Ann went with Reverend Tucker to get mattresses," she said. "I'm Patricia. Let's see what I can do."

She reached for John's hand. He flinched and pulled away. Rojo grabbed the ice and handed it to John, who placed it gingerly on his thumb.

"C'mon, dear, let's have a look."

John lifted the ice just enough to give her a peek.

His thumb was twice its normal size, glowing angry shades of purple and red.

Patricia grimaced. "I don't like that at all. We should get you to the hospital."

"No!" All three Merry Men shouted in unison.

Patricia jumped, her eyes wide with surprise.

John swallowed a lump of pain. With forced calm, he said, "I'm sure it looks worse than it is. I'll ice it for a while. I'll be fine." He didn't tell her that hospitals meant expenses, that they needed all their money for food and shelter. Even worse, a hospital meant social workers. It was better for everyone if they stayed off the official radar.

Patricia pursed her lips. "Well—" She extended the word an extra six syllables.

"Tell you what," Rojo interjected. "John will wait in the dining room, icing his thumb. When Mrs. Gibson gets back, he'll let her check it out. If she says he needs the hospital, he'll go." He narrowed his eyes at John. "Right?"

John grumbled agreement. His giant frame slumped as he trudged out of the room behind Patricia.

"I left him in here." Patricia's voice sounded hollow, like she was calling through a tunnel. Her next words came through loud and clear. "Dear lord, he snores like a bear!"

Sprawled in a folding chair, John stirred but kept his eyes closed, his feet propped up, and his head tilted back.

"Thank you, Pat," Mary Ann said. "The boys are

unloading the mattresses. Could you help them get everything set up?"

Footsteps exited the room. John felt a hand on his left shoulder.

"Okay, you big lug," Mary Ann whispered. "You can open your eyes now."

He opened one eye to see Mary Ann, her arms crossed, a bemused expression on her face. He opened the other eye and grinned.

She slapped his leg. "Sit up. Let's see what you did to that thumb."

John swung his feet off the chair, and Mary Ann plopped into the seat. She pushed the bag of what was now water off John's hand and pressed her finger gently on the swollen digit.

John flinched.

"Any chance I can talk you into getting this x-rayed?" Mary Ann continued to poke at John's thumb. Each poke provoked a torturous throb, but John managed to grunt an "unh-unh."

"Stubborn SOB, aren't you?" She released John's thumb and studied his eyes, which were glazed with pain. "Tough, too. I don't think your pupils could dilate any more. What are we going to do with you?"

"Kiss it all better?" John mustered a smile.

Mary Ann planted her hands on her knees and pushed herself up, giving John a saucy smile. "Nice try, soldier. I'm taken."

And now, so was John's usefulness.

CHAPTER THIRTEEN

The snow fell in heavy sheets, burying Sherwood under thick white blankets. Mary Ann sat nestled in her living room window seat, propped up by a mess of floral throw pillows, watching the winter storm. She snuggled deeper into her afghan and gave thanks that she was safely home.

She'd toyed with the idea of staying at the shelter. Her gut told her that's where she could do the most good, where she could keep her hands the busiest. After all, Tuck needed all the help he could get. Even with the new beds, it was going to be standing room only tonight. He'd pushed her out the door, though, as the first snowflakes fell. As she trudged across the parking lot, Patricia and the other volunteers rolled out sleeping bags in the dining room. Guilt gnawed at her the whole slippery drive home, but now—settled at home, her shoes off, her vision cleared—she was grateful Tuck sent her away. Because now she could do the real work of helping the shelter, the work she'd promised to do more than a month ago.

She reached for the folders stacked beside her on the floor. Each folder represented a sliver of hope—a grant application that, if won, could give new life to the shelter. She pulled out the first one and read it over. As she skimmed, she made notes: important milestone dates, details to include in the application, key points to emphasize. On a separate pad, she started list of information that she needed from Tuck.

She slid the annotated application back in its folder and started a second stack next to the first one. She picked up the next grant file and repeated the process.

The NOAA radio squawked to life. Mary Ann jumped, her pen scribbling a stray line down the length of the page.

"The National Weather Service in Chicago has issued a blizzard warning for Nottingham County, which is in effect from 5 p.m. Thursday to 1 p.m. Central Standard Time Friday," a monotone computerized voice announced.

One p.m. tomorrow? The storm was supposed to be over by midnight. Mary Ann sat straighter, giving the radio her full attention.

The warning droned on, *"Sustained winds with frequent gusts of 35 miles per hour or greater with heavy snow are expected to last until 4 a.m. Accumulations of 12 to 18 inches are expected, with drifts 5 to 6 feet high possible. The heaviest snow and strongest winds will occur after midnight into the early morning hours of Friday.*

"Falling and blowing snow with strong winds will create whiteout conditions, making travel extremely dangerous. Do not travel. If you must travel, have a winter survival kit with you. If you get stranded, stay with your vehicle."

Shit. Mary Ann shoved her papers to the floor. As much as she loved this house, it had a tendency to lose power during the gentlest of wind gusts. It didn't stand a chance in a blizzard. She pushed her fingers through her hair. "Okay, girl. You know what to do."

She swung herself off the bench and headed for the linen closet. Standing on her tiptoes and stretching, she reached for the heavy blankets on the top shelf. She managed to pinch a corner of one and pulled. The whole pile tumbled down on her head.

"Goddamn it." Mary Ann kicked away the blankets that had landed on her feet.

She surrendered to a wave of helplessness. It was only for a moment—she never allowed herself more— but in that moment, she missed Gary, resented his absence, envied his job and his commitment to it. Why wasn't he there with her? Why couldn't he be home to help her for a change?

Because the county was facing an emergency, and it was all hands on deck—that's why. Gary was spending the night at the county command center, helping to coordinate relief and emergency efforts— one of his last acts as sheriff before his mayoral inauguration. He'd tried to sound apologetic when he broke the news, like he always did, but Mary Ann knew how much he loved playing with logistics. If he'd stayed home, he would have driven her crazy with his Monday-morning quarterbacking.

Still, he could at least call home to check on her. He'd done that in the early days, during his late night and all-night shifts. The farther he'd moved up the food chain, though, the faster that fell by the wayside. She would just have to check in with him. Again.

He answered on the first ring. "Hey, honey, how you holding up?"

"I'm fine. I was just grabbing some blankets and a flashlight, in case the power goes out."

"That's why I love you. You're so independent, so prepared. A regular Boy Scout. But use the lantern instead of a flashlight. It'll give you more light. And don't forget to bring in a stack of firewood."

Mary Ann looked down at her socked feet and wiggled her toes. "The lantern's in the garage, isn't it?"

Gary answered with a grunt that Mary Ann took as a yes. The wood, of course, was out back, stacked against the side of the house. Silently, she cursed the need to pull on shoes. Aloud, she said, "How are things there? Everyone playing nice?"

"Things got a little tense when the storm became a blizzard. I heard at least one weatherman's name being taken in vain. But we've got plenty to keep us busy."

Mary Ann could practically hear his smile, which made her smile. "I'll let you get back to it then."

"I'm glad you're okay."

"Right back at ya, Mr. Mayor."

She stuffed the phone in her pocket and reached down to scoop up the blankets at her feet.

Blankets.

Tuck.

Oh, God, the shelter.

She shoved a blanket under her arm and pulled out her phone. Then she slipped it away again. What could she do? Offer to come over and help? Not with the storm wailing outside.

Tuck would decline the offer anyway, and calling now would only be a distraction. She'd check in tomorrow, when the blizzard had passed, and help Tuck assess any damage. Now it was time to batten down her own hatches.

She braved the wilds of the garage and side yard to

fetch the lantern and some firewood, the howling wind giving speed to her steps. Safely back in the house, she stacked the logs by the fireplace and set up the lantern on the side table next to the NOAA radio. Then she kicked off her shoes, brewed a pot of tea, and grabbed a favorite romance novel from her shelf. Back in the living room, she settled in the wingback chair, blanket on her lap, tea within easy reach. She pressed open her book but struggled to stay focused on the words.

She reread the same sentence eight times before giving in to her worry. As the wind roared outside, her thoughts finally gave in to what she'd been skirting: Hood, John, and the boys. They hadn't been at the shelter the last couple of days. Where could they possible be that could be safe? Warm? Outside, the wind began to whine.

On the other side of Sherwood, far down the economic yardstick of Yorkshire Road, the Merry Men were settled in their favorite no-tell motel. They'd vacated the shelter to, as Hood put it, make room for those who really needed it. The boys had gotten enough storm-prep work to cover the cost of the room for a couple of nights. Hood's panhandling had garnered enough for some food. The wad of dollars Mary Ann had slipped into John's pocket for the beds stretched all that even further.

The calm in their crowded new quarters belied the blizzard raging outside. Empty pizza boxes balanced precariously beside the trash can, which was filled to the brim with empty coffee cups. Hood lay sprawled on one of the room's two beds, snoring like the proverbial freight train—a sound that almost drowned out the howling wind outside. Rojo sat curled on the floor at the end of the bed, giggling. Whether he was giggling at Hood or the Will Ferrell movie on the television, Much couldn't tell. John reclined on the far bed, reading a paperback as thick as a textbook, his injured hand resting on a pile of pillows. Much himself sat by the window, hunched by the table lamp, whittling a piece of scrap lumber from the bunkbed project. The dim yellow light cast by the lamp forced Much to squint while he worked. When his eyes became achy, he gave them a break by gazing elsewhere in the room. This break, he focused on John. Specifically, the ridiculously thick paperback on the big man's lap. Much thought about what it would take to get him to read a book like that. He couldn't come up with bribe large enough.

"Hey, John, whatcha reading?"

John propped up the book so Much could read the cover. Stephen King. Well, at least it was someone Much had heard of.

"Where'd you get it?"

John answered without looking up, more than a hint of snark in his voice. "The shelter. They have a paperback trading shelf. You should try it sometime. I think I saw a couple of those comic books you boys like."

"Graphic novels," Much and Rojo corrected at once.

John ignored them, his attention not wavering from his book.

"How's the thumb?" Much asked.

John gave Much a thumb's up, which Much assumed meant "okay." The thumb didn't look okay, though, trapped in Mary Ann's makeshift splint and swaddled in rolls of gauze. Now that Much thought about it, it looked kind of like a bowling pin. He couldn't stop the smile.

"What?" John's stare was concentrated on Much.

Much shrugged. "Nothing."

"What are you doing over there, anyway?"

"SHHHH." Rojo pressed his finger to his lips. "I'm watching here. Besides, I don't think we wanna wake the sleeping bear." He gestured at Hood, but then noticed the wood in Much's hands. "Wait, what *are* you doing?"

Rojo stood, moving to get a closer look at Much's carving. He stumbled, picked up an empty whiskey bottle that must have fallen from Hood's hand. Shaking his head, he tossed it into the trash can.

"Holy crap, man!" Rojo grabbed the carving from Much. "That's awesome! What is that? A . . . a—"

"Stegosaurus," Much said.

Rojo traced the sculpted dinosaur, running his fingers along the dinosaur's roaring mouth and following the curved plates on its back all the way to the end of its spiked tail. He turned and held up the dino for John to see. "Look at this."

John set aside his book. "That's really good, kid. What's it for?"

Much's cheeks burned. "The shelter." With a stammer, he explained, "I thought the kids might like some toys for Christmas."

"*Some* toys? How many have you made?" Rojo asked.

Much handed over a pillowcase he'd borrowed from the shelter's linen closet. Rojo carried it to John's bed and dumped the contents: a Tyrannosaurus Rex, a triceratops, a horse, a rabbit, a couple of boats, and a seal that rocked when Rojo tapped its nose.

Rojo and John shook their heads, amazement written all over their faces.

"Kid, where'd you learn how to do this?"

"My Gramps," Much answered quietly. "He made all our toys."

Rojo and John kept shaking their heads.

"Shoot, son," John finally said. "You could sell these. Probably make a good living too. These could be your ticket off the street."

Much's lungs seized. His heart pounded. He stared at Rojo, his eyes wide and rabbit-like.

Rojo nodded. "Now why would he want to do that?"

The question hung in the air until all three guffawed. They returned to their individual pursuits while Hood, on the bed, snorted and shifted positions. Outside, the wind roared as it piled snow against the door.

CHAPTER FOURTEEN

Hood woke with a mouthful of cotton and a dull ache behind his eyes. As hangovers went, this wasn't even a 3.0 on the Richter scale—just enough pain to remind him he was alive. With a grunt and a wheeze, he rolled onto his side and found himself facing a lumpy pillowcase.

A few pats told him the pillowcase's contents were hard, but the shape didn't make any sense. He pushed himself to sitting position and reached inside. His hand came out holding a wood rabbit. He set it down and reached in again, this time pulling out a wooden car.

He overturned the case, dumping toy after toy onto the bed. A few clattered to the floor and onto a sleeping Much.

"Hey!" Much scooted to sitting position and gathered the fallen toys into his arms. "Watch it!"

Hood's eyes widened. Did meek little Much, the boy who never said boo, really just scold him? Maybe the kid was tougher than Hood gave him credit for. "You do these, kid?"

"Yeah, and it took me hours." Much's raised voice stirred Rojo and John awake.

Hood held up the toy car. "What're they for?"

"Christmas presents," Rojo chimed in. "For the kids at the shelter."

"They're not bad, kid." Hood tossed the car to Much. "But those kids need clothes more than they need toys."

Much drooped. "You're probably right. But toys are all I have to give."

Much and Rojo scooped the toys back into the pillowcase. The room fell silent except for the sounds of John in the bathroom and Hood's creaky stretches.

When John exited the john, Rojo dashed in.

"Y'know . . ." Hood spoke slowly, "we could get some clothes to give 'em."

"Give who?" John asked.

"The kids at the shelter. Much here'll give these toys. But the rest of us could get them some warm clothes."

John flashed back to the mother and kids he'd met. "What about the parents? They could use stuff too."

Hood gave a careless wave. "Sure, them too."

"With what? This?" John held up the crumpled singles he'd thrown on the night stand the previous day. "This won't even buy a pair of cheap underwear. And forget about us eating for at least a week."

Hood rolled his eyes. "I didn't say we'd *buy* the clothes. I said we'd *get* them."

John closed his eyes and breathed deep. "I'm not going to like this idea, am I?"

"Don't matter if you don't like it." Hood wiggled his thumb at John. "You ain't gonna be part of it."

"Part of what?" Rojo asked as he stepped into the room.

Much muttered, "Something about getting clothes for the shelter kids."

"Cool! Count me in."

Two days later, after the mountains of snow had been blown and plowed and sculpted and the parking lots and sidewalks made passable again, the Merry Men set off. John and Much headed straight to the shelter, pillowcase of toys slung over Much's shoulder like Santa's bundle. Hood and Rojo accompanied them for a few blocks before making a detour to complete Operation Clothing.

At any given time, there were half a dozen or more blue clothing donation bins scattered around Sherwood, usually tucked in the corners of strip mall parking lots. No one was really sure who owned the bins or where the clothing went once it was collected. The signage on the bins implied the contents went to charity, but Hood was damn certain that not so much as a sock had ever been given to any of Sherwood's needy. The time had come to change that.

Rojo and Hood found the first bin in the second strip mall they visited. Try as they might, they couldn't get through the piles of plowed snow stacked against it. Hood made a comment that if *they* couldn't get through it, certainly no nameless charity workers planned on doing so what was the point of putting the bin there in the first place?

They decided to move on, Rojo thinking that Hood shouldn't waste all his energy on one possibly empty bin when there were so many others. They made their way back to the sidewalk and trudged onward, hunched against the cold. A long block later, Rojo leaned close to Hood. "Boss, I think we're being followed."

Hood threw a glance over his shoulder. Spotting the cruiser took no effort at all—and not just because of the light traffic. The police car hung back in the right lane, moving slower than the few other cars on the road, a jungle cat stalking its prey.

Hood lowered his head and his voice, barely moving his lips as he told Rojo, "Keep walking."

At the next corner, Hood steered Rojo right and then across the street, into the Sugar N Spice donut shop. Hood flexed his tingly fingers, and Rojo dug into his pockets for a few of John's crumpled bills. While Hood took those bills to the counter, Rojo settled at a corner table, where they could see the street without being seen.

Sure enough, the cruiser had stopped—not in the parking lot but along the curb. A stakeout, if Rojo ever saw one. He tapped his foot and drummed his fingers on the table, beating out a quick, irregular rhythm.

Hood shuffled over with two small cups. He slid one across the table to Rojo, tossing change after it. The coins pinged on the table. Rojo sat ramrod straight, the picture of alertness.

"Down, Red." Hood dropped into his chair and took a long, slow sip from his cup. "Sixty-three cents ain't worth it." He took another sip. "Sit rep."

"Bogie at two o'clock. Parked on the street." Rojo leaned forward. "I can't tell if it's a Sherwood Police car or a sheriff."

Hood's face lit up. "Gibson?"

Rojo watched Hood's light dim when he said, "Nah. Not the man himself. Maybe one of his flunkies." Rojo squinted out the window. He could just make out the face behind the wheel. "Damn."

He plunked his cup on the table. "It's the main flunky, Dubrowski."

The two men drank their hot chocolates in silence, but Hood's wheels were turning. He ached to give Dubrowski a piece of his mind—well, his fists—but he had a mission to complete, one that left no room for personal vendettas.

One glimpse at Rojo told him the same tug-of-war was going on in the kid's head.

Hood snapped his fingers in Rojo's face. "Earth to Red. You with me, boy?"

Rojo blinked. "So what do we do, Boss?"

Hood turned and looked out the window again, his gaze focused on the sheriff's car. "We complete our mission."

"But Dubrowski—"

"Has no grounds to stop us if we're just walking down the street."

"He will when we crack open that box."

Hood's grin filled his face. "Then we'll just have to lose him, won't we?"

They finished their drinks and waited, hoping that Dubrowski would get called away. After an hour, they ran out of patience and luck. They bussed their table and snuck out the front door, using a group of college-age boys as cover.

By the end of the block, their shadow had found them again. Hood cursed under his breath and heard Rojo do the same. He forced himself to walk at a leisurely pace, as if he and Rojo were two gentle-men taking their—what were they called? —daily constitutionals.

They continued in this way for three more blocks, Hood tightening with tension with every step. Then Rojo nudged Hood with his elbow. "Up ahead and across the street, Boss."

Sure enough, a blue bin—a reasonably accessible one—stood in the parking lot of what used to be The Gourmet Grocer. With the store gone, the parking lot was empty. A perfect scenario if it weren't for their damn tail.

"We go past it and then turn around," Hood said. "We come at it from the back."

Rojo nodded before turning to the sky, as if offering a prayer.

They kept moving as they had before. A block past their target, they crossed the street, careful to obey the signals and use the crosswalk. They continued their casual pace. At the entrance to the Grocer's back alley, Hood gave a short whistle and the two men sprinted down the alley and dove into the snow piled behind the loading dock. Hood gave a ten count before peeking toward the street.

Dubrowski's cruiser blocked the alley's entrance. Hood ducked back down and held up his fist to silence Rojo. He closed his eyes and counted to thirty before peeking again. The cruiser was still there.

With a silent curse, Hood dropped to his ass and sat with his back against the loading dock. Cold seeped through the seat of his pants. Rojo dropped into position next to him. Not ideal conditions for waiting it out, but what other choice did they have? The two men dug a little nest for themselves, using the snow for cover. Hood rubbed his hands together to keep his blood flowing.

After a few eternal minutes and a jab of Hood's elbow, Rojo peered over the top of the loading dock. The cruiser was gone.

Rojo punched Hood's arm and jumped to his feet. Hood struggled to his. Shaking the stiffness from their legs, they proceeded in a half-crouch along the back of the building and around the corner. They stopped at the front of the building and studied the open parking lot between them and the clothing bin.

Because the storefront was vacant, the parking lot—like the back alley—hadn't been plowed. Rojo and Hood high-stepped across the parking lot, their heads on swivels, ready to dash if the police cruiser came back into sight.

When they got to the bin, they shook the snow out of their shoes and then dug to get to the door. Their hands wet and almost numb with cold, they paused to reheat their paws in their armpits.

Rojo grabbed the edge of the bin door with his fingers and pulled. The door didn't budge. "We need something to pry it open."

"No shit." Hood unzipped the top of his jacket and pulled out Much's knife. "Borrowed this, just in case."

"Alright," Rojo said slowly, "but if that knife bends or breaks . . ."

"All my fault," Hood assured him.

The knife wasn't long enough or strong enough to force open the door, but it worked like a charm to loosen the door's hinges.

"Yahtzee!" Hood cried when the door finally swung open.

The bin wasn't even half full, but it wasn't empty.

That's what mattered. The half dozen full, round plastic grocery bags looked promising, and so did the loose items mixed up with them. The two Merry Men pulled out the bags and started stuffing whatever stray garments they could fit into the bags as well.

"Well, well, well, what have we here?"

Rojo and Hood jumped, the bags landing with a *swish* in the snow. Where the hell had Gibson come from? The mayor-elect stood on the sidewalk, mere feet from the would-be burglars, his car idling behind him. For a long second, the only sounds were passing traffic and the clicks of Gibson's hazard lights.

Gibson stepped into the parking lot. "This wouldn't be a robbery, would it?"

Hood and Rojo stood straight. The cold that chilled their bones vanished, and a tightly-strung anxiety took its place.

Gibson circled them. His boots squished on the wet ground, a sound almost as annoying as his tutting. "How the mighty have fallen. The great Robert Hood reduced to petty theft. Isn't that rich?"

Rojo willed Hood to let it pass. Let Gibson have his fun and get on his way. Let him take the damn clothes, if he wanted. Let it go so they could get back to the others in two whole pieces.

"Or were you planning on sleeping in there, now that you've lost your beloved alley?" There was no mistaking the taunt in Gibson's voice.

"It wasn't lost," Hood growled. "It was stolen, and you're the bastard that stole it."

Gibson laughed. "I prefer to think of it as cleaning out the vermin."

"Vermin? Is that what we are? The people your

wife is dedicated to helping? What the *fuck* did she ever see in you?"

Gibson's face burned bright red. "How dare you talk about my wife that way! How dare you talk about her at all. You keep her name out of your filthy mouth."

Hood didn't blink. "Mary Ann *Wilson*." He placed particular emphasis on Mary Ann's maiden name. Then he grinned. "And she was mine long before she was yours."

Gibson raised his fist, clearly aiming for Hood's face. Rojo sprung before Gibson could swing, knocking the mayor-elect off his feet. Gibson's head hit the ground with a thud. Fearing Gibson was unconscious, Rojo glanced back over his shoulder. Hood was scooping up bags of clothes.

"Let's go, Red, before that asshole gets up and throws us in the clink."

January

CHAPTER FIFTEEN

"Damn it!" Tuck slammed the newspaper against the kitchen counter.

"Bad news?" Mary Ann asked from behind the pantry door. Her purse stashed, she grabbed a couple of mugs from the staff shelf.

"For some." Tuck dropped the paper. He ran his fingers through what was left of his hair. How to explain his anger without angering Mary Ann?

Closing his eyes, he took a deep breath, counting to five. He opened them to find Patricia peeking in the doorway, motherly concern filling her face and her voice. "Everything okay, Reverend?"

"Yes, Pat, everything's fine. Thank you." He waited for her to walk away. When her footsteps were beyond his hearing, he turned to Mary Ann. "That's one little white lie God will have to forgive."

Mary Ann poured coffee for the both of them. "Tell me."

Tuck leaned against the counter, but his posture was far from relaxed. "There was this bill before the town council, back before your husband was elected. We—me, Joe Huston from the Unitarian Universalist Church, Rabbi Knapp from Beth Sinai, a couple of social workers from the county—lobbied hard against it. The council voted it down. It was only a one-vote margin, but the bill didn't pass. That's what matters."

"Sounds like a victory."

"That's what I thought, too. Until I saw this." He tossed the newspaper in Mary Ann's direction. "The very legislation that was voted down three months ago, the newly inaugurated mayor issued as an executive order. It is now illegal to panhandle or solicit anywhere within the Sherwood town limits. Panhandlers can be banished from neighborhoods and even arrested if they're caught a second time."

Mary Ann skimmed the article, the crease in her brow deepening with each paragraph. "So what does this all mean? For you? For the shelter?"

Tuck shrugged. "I don't know exactly." Tuck started to sip his coffee but changed his mind. "No, that's not true. The very minimum, it will mean less money, since we can't do our Boots and Buckets drives anymore. Under the new law, that's soliciting."

Mary Ann bit her lip.

"What?"

"You, soliciting. It's a mental image I just . . . I can't . . . I'm sorry." Holding her hand up in apology, she guffawed.

Tuck's brain knotted with confusion. He watched Mary Ann descend into a fit of giggles—and got the joke. With a grin and bright red cheeks, he said, "Not that kind of soliciting, thank you very much. I *am* a man of the cloth."

Mary Ann fell into another giggle-fest.

Tuck crossed his arms and tried to look stern, but he couldn't hold back a smile. It took some effort, but he finally managed to get himself under control and soon after Mary Ann did the same.

"Seriously, though." Tuck wiped unshed tears from his eyes. "It's not just the shelter bank account that will suffer. We have residents here who make their livings panhandling. Not to mention one particularly ornery veteran we both know and love."

Mary Ann sighed. "Rob."

"The very same."

Mary Ann closed her eyes. Tuck could practically see the conflict playing across her face. Her husband, as one of his first acts as mayor, had issued a law that endangered her first and possibly one true love. Yet she had fallen in love with both men, so they must have something in common. Tuck was damned if knew what it was.

Mary Ann took a loud deep breath. "Okay. I'll see what I can do."

Tuck gave her a hug. "Just so we're clear: I'm not asking you to do anything. I'm not *expecting* you to do anything. It's okay if you do nothing."

"No, it's not okay to do nothing. Not when a law hurts people instead of protecting them." She patted Tuck's hand. "I'm not doing this for you. I'm doing this for myself. Because I need to." Through the kitchen doorway, she watched the shelter residents bus their breakfast trays and start out the door to start their days. "I'm doing this for them."

Mary Ann put down her cup, grabbed her coat from the hall tree, and walked out the front door behind a group of regulars.

A knot of worry settled in the pit of Tuck's stomach as he watched her go.

Being First Lady of Sherwood had its perks. Mary Ann sailed past the receptionist and into the suite of rooms that comprised the mayor's office. Gibson's administrative assistant, a young 20-something woman named Ashley, sat at her desk, engrossed in a phone call. Mary Ann waved but kept going, not knowing or caring if Ashley acknowledged her.

She swept into her husband's private office, a smile plastered on her face—the same smile she used when she needed him to clean out the garage or unclog the gutters. "Hi, honey!"

Gary Gibson's head snapped up. He blinked. His chief of staff, Peter LeClerk, standing next to his boss, did the same. Gibson recovered first.

"Sweetheart! What a surprise!" He moved out from behind his desk to give Mary Ann a peck on the cheek. "What brings you here?"

"What? A wife can't drop in on her husband just because?"

"A wife, yes. Of course." Gibson gave LeClerk a not-very-subtle nod to leave the room. Then he turned back to Mary Ann. With a smile that might have been sincere, he said, "But we all know you're more than just 'a wife,' eh?"

He guided Mary Ann to one of the wingback chairs opposite his desk. He took the other, settling into it like a therapist courting a patient. His posture didn't escape Mary Ann's notice. Her visit made him uncomfortable, or at least unnerved. Good. That gave her the advantage. She hated thinking about her spouse in those terms, as an enemy instead of an ally, but she couldn't help it. The Gary Gibson in that article, the Gary Gibson who issued that order, the Gary Gibson serving as mayor, was not a man she recognized anymore. Certainly not the kind, considerate beat cop she'd fallen in love with. Had that been a mirage, a mask she saw without ever noticing the man behind it?

"You're offended." Gary sounded contrite. "I'm sorry. It was just a joke. A bad one."

Mary Ann pursed her lips and nodded. Maybe it was that Bruce Kingston, the real estate mogul who owned half of Nottingham County and more than half of Sherwood and the largest donor to Gary's mayoral campaign. Now it seemed that Bruce owned her husband too—she saw it in the sexist jokes Gary suddenly made. He'd never told them before he started spending time with Kingston. Was that because he didn't approve of them, or had Bruce emboldened him to show his true colors?

"Look, I know you. Something's bothering you. It's in your eyes, and your shoulders, and the extra-straightness of your spine. What can I do? How can I help?" He put his hand on her knee. At last, Gary sounded and acted like the man she expected him to be.

Mary Ann's shoulders dropped, but only a bit. Her mind stayed sharp. "I saw something in the paper today. I wanted to ask you about it."

"It couldn't wait until dinner?"

Mary Ann tilted her head. "When was the last time you were home for dinner?"

Gary gave a small closed-lip smile. "True. I'm sorry about that. But you could have called."

"I wanted to make sure I had your full and

undivided attention—and you have a habit of multitasking when you're on the phone."

Gibson smiled, but his smile couldn't hide the tension that sat in his shoulders. Splaying his hands, he said, "I only have eyes—and ears—for you. Ask away."

Mary Ann cleared her throat. "The other night you said you had to work late because of some legislation that the town council had voted down."

"That's right."

"Was that the bill about panhandling? The one in today's paper?"

"Yes."

Mary Ann leaned forward. "But that bill was voted down before you were ever elected mayor."

Gibson sighed. "It was. But Walter Hagen reintroduced it, thinking some of the new council members would vote in favor. Walter was wrong."

Mary Ann inhaled deeply. "But you agreed with Walter, you disagreed with the council's vote, so you issued an executive order."

"I did."

"And that's legal? You can do that?"

Gary leaned back and crossed his legs. With an exaggerated nod, he said, "Yes, ma'am. That's the beauty of our system of checks and balances."

Mary Ann swallowed her hatred of her husband's campaigning voice. She'd perfected the skill months ago, and now it was second nature. "So what's the council's check on *you*? I mean, if they disagree with your order?"

"You came here for a civics lesson? Forgive me, but that's not the Mary Ann I know."

Mary Ann acknowledged the point with a harrumph. "Point taken, but I don't understand why. Why the order? Why outlaw panhandling? I can count the number of panhandlers I see in Sherwood on one hand and have fingers left over. They're not exactly a menace to society."

Gibson scooted his chair and clasped his hands around Mary Ann's. "Please don't take this the wrong way, but there's a lot in this town that you don't see. A lot that I saw, that my team saw, when I was sheriff. Stuff that I protect you from—"

Mary Ann pulled her hands away. "I see a lot more than you think I do. I volunteer at a homeless shelter, for crying out loud. I was an emergency room nurse for years before you and I ever met, so don't tell me I need protection. I can take care of myself, thank you very much."

"Of course you need to be protected. You're a woman. It's my job as your husband to protect you and my job as mayor to protect all the women of Sherwood. I'm just . . . I'm trying to keep the promises I made when I campaigned for this job."

Mary Ann pushed down the angry words that wanted to fly in retaliation. Right now, Tuck needed her to stay focused. The fight against Gary's sexism could wait until later. She exhaled. "I'm not saying you're right, because you're not, but what about the charities who collect donations at traffic lights? The firemen with their Fill the Boot campaign, the Knights of Columbus with their buckets, the Salvation Army with their bell ringers? Your order defines that as solicitation, which means they can't hold those fundraising drives anymore. That's hundreds of dollars, maybe thousands, of lost income. That doesn't seem fair."

Gibson bit his lip. Rubbing his knees, he said, "You're right. That isn't fair. Maybe we didn't think this through all the way."

We? He was the one who issued the order; he was the mayor. The buck stopped with him. At least, it was supposed to.

"No, you didn't. And that's going to cost people their lives."

Gibson stood and moved back behind his desk, gesturing toward the door. "Tell you what, I'll talk this over with the team, and we'll see what we can do. We certainly don't want to punish the do-gooders in this world. The order doesn't take effect until February 1st. We have some time to change it, if we need to."

The brush-off? He was giving her, his wife of twenty-plus years, the brush-off? She flew to her feet and stepped into her husband's precious personal space. "And who exactly is this team? You and who else? The town council? Your friend LeClerk? Your buddy *Kingston*?"

Gibson froze, his eyes wide.

Mary Ann kept going. "And where do I fit in all this? I thought we were a team. After all, isn't team-work what being a husband and wife is all about?"

"Of . . . of course it is. We are a team." Gibson dropped back into his chair, his deer-in-headlights look replaced with a knot of confusion. He gestured for her to sit. "Sweetheart, what's going on here?"

Refusing his invitation, she crossed her arms and planted her feet. "What's going on is that I don't know you anymore. This job, this team of yours, has become more important than our marriage."

"You knew—"

"I'm not finished."

Gibson held up his hands in surrender.

"The man I married would never have been as condescending as you've been to me here. He would never have brushed me off like you did. He would have listened and taken my concerns seriously, even if he didn't agree with them. He wouldn't have been the manipulative mansplainer sitting in that chair right now."

The door to Gibson's office slid open. Peter LeClerk peered around the edge. "I'm sorry to interrupt, Mr. Mayor, but your next appointment is here. Shall I tell them you're running late?"

Mary Ann grabbed her purse and swung it over her shoulder. "That's okay. We're done."

LeClerk disappeared back behind the door. Mary Ann gave her husband a steely gaze. "Don't bother coming home tonight, unless you're prepared to eat a full five-course meal of crow. And the dessert better be the repeal of that stupid executive order."

CHAPTER SIXTEEN

Tuck pulled open his office door and stepped inside. His foot hit something soft as he moved forward. *Oh, crap.* Much. He pulled his foot back and said a prayer of apology.

He grabbed the doorframe for support as stepped over Much's sleeping form. He tiptoed over the lumps of the other two Merry Men sprawled on the floor. When did sleeping at the shelter become sleeping in his office? Surely the beds in the dorms were more comfortable than the worn-out carpet on his office floor. At the very least, they could spread out their sleeping bags in the dining room.

Much's whimper and thrashing dismissed that question. Hood had suffered the same affliction. Maybe he still did. It had been a while since Tuck and Hood had slept in close quarters. A lifetime. Even tonight, Hood had opted to sleep outside, by the shelter's back door. But some memories don't fade. Even Tuck himself had a few that he couldn't let go, mini-movies that kept him up at night, flashes of the past that filled his gut with acid. Perhaps it was best that Much wasn't sleeping in the general population.

Tuck made it to his desk. Sitting down, he realized he'd forgotten to flip on the lights. He studied his slumbering friends and decided he could work with the little bit of light that came through the tiny industrial window high on the rear wall. That, and the glow from the computer screen.

He clicked the mouse, and the monitor sprang to life. Which icon to click first: e-mail or the bank register? Neither promised good news. He clicked open a web browser instead and checked the shelter's web traffic. Twelve people visited the site's donation page in the last twenty-four hours. Pretty good. Total donations: thirty dollars. Not great, but every penny helped. Thirty bucks could buy food for a day or two, maybe more with some haggling, definitely more if he handed over the funds to Cora the Coupon Queen.

A snuffle from one of the Merry Men elicited a murmur from another. Then one of them sighed and smacked his lips. Tuck bit his cheek. A better man wouldn't even be tempted to laugh.

With a quiet cough, Tuck returned his attention to the screen. He clicked open his e-mail and account register in rapid succession. Might as well rip the bandage off quickly.

A message from Mary Ann saying they'd fallen out of the running for a couple of grants. Disappointing but not surprising.

A message from Joe Huston over at the Universalist Unitarian about a joint service project. Tuck flagged that one to return to later.

A dozen spam messages dragged unopened into the trash. Maybe he should try being a Nigerian prince. See what funds that brought in.

Another message from Mary Ann, this one saying she'd be in late this morning. Tuck wished all his volunteers were so responsible.

He clicked over to the account register. Nothing

but red numbers. He rubbed the back of his neck. He added the thirty-dollar deposit from the donations, but it wasn't enough. The balance stayed stoplight red. Joe Huston had advised him ages ago to take out a line of credit for emergencies. Tuck had followed that advice, and it had saved his butt more than once. Now, even that line of credit was looking slim, and if Tuck didn't make a payment soon, he'd lose his good standing with the bank.

He dug into his pockets and pulled out some wadded bills and coins: a five, a ten, a couple of singles, and change. He grabbed a deposit envelope from the top drawer and slid the bills inside. He clicked back over to the register and added the seventeen dollars to the shelter's balance. The numbers still glowed bright red.

Tuck pressed his fingers to his forehead and kneaded his temples. Maybe he should take up Hood's panhandling spot along the interstate. Except that was illegal now. Tuck's sigh came from deep down in his toes.

"Are you okay?" John's voice came from the floor, somewhere between the desk and the door.

If anyone other than John had asked, Tuck would have brushed it off. "I don't know. We're in pretty bad shape, and I'm at a loss for what to do."

John scooted closer. "You've said that before, you know."

"And I meant it then just as much as I mean it now. But this is the worst it's ever been, John. By a long shot."

"You've said that, too. And every time, you've

found a way. I can't count how many times you've saved our butts." John thumbed toward the door. "I'm sure every single person out there would say the same thing."

A rock formed in Tuck's stomach. "It's different this time. I can feel it. I just can't explain it. It feels like . . . like the end."

"How apocalyptic."

Rojo sat up and yawned. Mid-stretch, he asked, "What about the apocalypse?"

The office door swung open and hit Much, who grunted and stirred awake. Patricia stood silhouetted in the doorway. "Sorry to interrupt, Reverend, but we have a situation?"

Something in Patricia's tone and expression suggested that *situation* was an understatement. Tuck blinked slowly and pushed himself to a standing position. "Animal, vegetable, or mineral?"

It was Patricia's turn to blink. "Reverend?"

Tuck waved his hand. "Bad joke. Sorry. Let's see this situation."

He followed Patricia out of the office, the Merry Men trailing behind him like ducklings. The ruckus brought Hood in from the back alley, and he brought up the rear. They wound their way through the flow of residents making their way to the breakfast room or the bathroom or just outside for a nip or a smoke. They passed more than one child clutching a hand-carved wooden toy. Every child's face lit up when they saw Much. The parade pushed its way through a crowd gathered outside the men's dormitory.

Stepping into the room, Patricia gestured to the

west wall. For the first time, Tuck noticed how pale she was. His gaze moved from Patricia to the wall. Two streams of water spilled down, forming a lake on the floor. He felt as ashen as Patricia looked.

John grabbed Tuck's shoulder, the weight of his hand providing reassurance. "I'm no plumber, but I'd say you've got a couple of burst pipes."

"Are you sure?" Tuck sounded like he was drowning. "Wouldn't we have heard the explosion?"

John didn't swallow his smile quickly enough. "No, Southern boy, that's not how it works. The pipes don't explode. More like fatigued metal that cracks."

Rojo whistled low. "That's a hell of a crack."

Tuck couldn't take his eyes off the flood-in-progress. "That apocalypse you were asking about, Red? This is it."

He put his head in his hands and fell against the nearest bunk. They needed a plumber, but where to find one? One they could afford, that is. That was the catch, wasn't it? How could a shelter with no money pay for emergency plumbing services? Extensive emergency plumbing services.

Worse, they were going to have to close the dorm. No way anyone could stay here with Lake Sherwood forming on the floor. The shelter that was supposed to help people get off the streets was now going to force men onto them in the coldest month of the year. Tuck's worries gathered in knots. He dropped his hands and looked helplessly at John.

John turned to Patricia. "Could you check with the shelter's . . . guests to see if any of them have plumbing experience?"

Patricia's shoulders relaxed ever so slightly, glad to have something to do. She headed out of the room, gently touching Tuck's arm as she went by.

"You boys," John said to Much and Rojo, "go back to the office and get online. Check out those home repair review sites. See if you can find a plumber suited for this sort of thing."

Rojo stopped in the doorway. "Um, Boss, wouldn't any plumber be suited for this sort of thing? I mean, fixing leaks is kind of their game, you know?"

"I know. Look for plumbers who promise quick service and low rates. Better yet, see if you can find plumbers with reviews from other charities, plumbers that advertise their charitable work, that sort of thing."

Rojo nodded and followed Much down the hall.

John waved at the remaining rubberneckers. "You all go get some breakfast. This room's off limits for a while."

When it was just John, Tuck, Hood, and the dripping water, Tuck mustered himself back to an upright position and held out his hand. "Thanks, man."

"No thanks necessary," Hood said, oblivious of John's side-eye. "That's what brothers are for."

"I don't suppose you've got a mop or a bunch of towels or something to clean up this mess," John said.

"In the janitorial closet. Down the hall, next to the family dorm."

Tuck watched John pull Hood out of the room. He didn't know how long he stared at the leak before Patricia returned. Calvin, one of the shelter regulars, loped in behind her.

"Tell him," she said to Calvin before turning on her heel and marching back toward the breakfast room.

Calvin shoved his hands deep in the pockets of his too-big jeans, his eyes focused on the floor. "I, um, I used to be a plumber's apprentice. Before."

Tuck heard Calvin's whole history in that last word. Before the accident. Before his workers comp ran out. Before he was denied Disability. Before he ran through his meager savings. Before he landed on the streets. Before he lost his pride and dignity and became dependent on the charity of others. Everyone who walked through these doors had a *before*. The question was, would they ever find an *after*?

"Tell me, Calvin," Tuck said as he stood up. "Did you ever deal with anything like this?"

Calvin leaned to see past Tuck. "All season long, sir. Burst pipes are a plumber's bread and butter come winter."

"About how much do repairs like this cost?"

Calvin pursed his lips. After a few moments of thought, he spoke, slowly and thoughtfully. "If this were an unfinished wall, 500, 600 dollars. But the wall's finished, so more—at least an even grand."

Shit. "Do you remember enough to fix it? Is it something you could do yourself?"

Hood pushed past the two of them, towels piled high in his arms. John followed him in, pushing the mop and wheeled bucket.

Calvin waited until they were past. Then he shrugged. "Maybe. You got insurance?"

Tuck nodded. Not much, but it was there.

"Then you're gonna hafta go through them. Get an estimate and all that. You'll need a licensed plumber, too, and that ain't me."

Tuck's sigh sounded dangerously like a whimper. *Pull it together, Tuck.* "You're right. I'll call the insurance and get the ball rolling. Once that's done, I'd like you to be project manager, if you don't mind. I need someone who knows what they're doing to find a reputable plumber and supervise the work. Make sure the work's done right, and we don't get ripped off. Of course, I'd pay you—not much, but something."

Calvin straightened and smoothed his hair. He hiked up his jeans before holding out his hand. "Yessir. Thank you, sir. I appreciate your confidence in me."

Tuck shook Calvin's hand. "Thank you for helping us through this jam. Much and Rojo are in my office looking for a plumber. Why don't you go down there and given them a hand?"

Calvin nodded. When he left the room, it was with his back a little straighter and more energy in his stride. Tuck couldn't help but smile at the transformation. This was why he did what he did.

Then he took one more look at the falling water and the smile fell from his face.

CHAPTER SEVENTEEN

It was the end of January and still frigid, but already, Valentine's Day was ceding shelf space to St. Patrick's Day. Christmas? New Year's? Long forgotten by retailers and consumers alike.

The Church of the Holy Light, however, still clung to the holiday spirit. Their solicitors guarded the entrances of every single one of Sherwood's upscale grocery stores, of which there were more than one might expect, given the demise of The Gourmet Grocer. More than John expected, at any rate. The Holy Light solicitors were relentless, too, and not just because of that impending February 1st deadline.

Even during the height of the holiday season, when everyone from the high school band to the VFW had their hands out, the Holy Lighters stood out with their relentlessness. They bore little resemblance to their sibling Salvation Army bellringers, who accepted rejection with polite holiday wishes. Nope, the Holy Lighters clung to customers like superglue, insisting on giving their whole pitch beginning to end whether the customer showed interest or not, following customers to their cars and not stopping until the customer's car began to move. And if the customer were wearing a hijab or a bindi or a Star of David or any other non-Christian symbol? Well, there was an entire "Don't You Want to Be Saved?" lecture for those occasions. The whole thing made John's skin crawl. Wasn't faith supposed to be personal?

Then there were all the Church of the Holy Light billboards, three or four along Yorkshire Road and half a dozen others scattered elsewhere in and around town. In every one, shining crosses, Reverend Hollis Zachary, his wife, and their pearly white teeth called on passersby to attend Sunday services and "walk with Christ." Whatever that meant.

Now John sat outside the church itself, wishing he could be anywhere else but committed to waiting for Tuck as he'd promised. John was the first to describe himself as old-school. He'd attended church growing up. His family belonged to his hometown Lutheran church, housed in a traditional white steepled building. *That* was a church. The Catholic St. Mary Margaret's, with its brick building and belltower, was a *church*.

This? This was an ostentatious glass castle that spoke of riches more than faith. The storefront rented by that Mexican evangelical group felt more like a house of worship than this one.

But Tuck needed money and the Church of the Holy Light had piles of it, so here they were: Tuck inside with his hand out, and John growing moss in the parking lot.

This was all Mayor Gibson's fault, too. That blasted order made Tuck's spring collection campaign illegal, pre-existing permit be damned, and Tuck's request for a pre-February 1st collection had been soundly rejected. Now Tuck had to get down on his knees and beg for donations from the rich and self-centered, of which Hollis Zachary was surely one. His photo graced every single Church bulletin, billboard, and television ad. His smiling portrait was plastered on a dozen books—surely ghostwritten—displayed face-out in every store. He hawked the airwaves for donations like an old-school used car salesman. He wore custom suits and a diamond encrusted watch and drove a Jaguar. His wife always wore diamonds or pearls, wrapped herself in furs in winter, and drove a Mercedes SUV. If that's what they considered "walking with Christ," then it was a very different Jesus than the one John had learned about as a child.

The slam of a door yanked John out of his spinning thoughts. Tuck stormed out of the building, two uniformed security guards close on his heels. He threw open the car door, dropped into the front seat, and slammed the door shut behind him. The sound echoed across the parking lot.

"What a self-righteous bastard!" Tuck sounded angrier than John had ever heard him. Looked it, too, with his red face and shaking hands.

"So it didn't go well?"

Tuck stared at John with an expression of utter amazement. A split second later, his shoulders relaxed and a half-hearted smile added a little light to his darkened manner. "You could say that."

Tuck's car became the confessional, the two men sitting side by side but each one's eyes focused straight ahead. Tuck spoke slowly, carefully. "I gave Zachary my pitch, explained how the shelter works, who we help, the challenges we face, how a donation would help us. Heavy on Christian duty but with some statistics thrown in for good measure. I might as well have been talking to a rock. A well-polished rock, but a rock nonetheless."

He picked up speed. "The 'reverend' gave me some rather rehearsed reasons for why his precious church couldn't help: hard times, everyone's struggling, that kind of sh—malarkey. All the while he's holding a sizable bottle of some fancy mineral water that I've never heard of. So I quoted Scripture at him. First, Timothy 6:18: 'Instruct them to do good, to be rich in good works, to be generous and ready to share.'

"Then I threw John 3:17 and Romans 15:1 at him: 'But whoever has the world's goods, and sees in his brother in need and closes his heart against him, how does the love of God abide in him?' 'Now we who are strong ought to bear the weaknesses of those without strength and not just please ourselves.'"

"That sounds about right to me," John said.

"Not to the right Reverend Zachary. He spewed that 'God helps those who help themselves' crap, suggested that maybe I shouldn't open the doors to the degenerate—"

"The degenerate?"

"I believe that's code for people who use drugs or alcohol."

"Which, except for one very stubborn, very ornery exception, you don't."

"Only because of the insurance. If I could, I would. You know that."

John gave a solemn nod. "But you didn't share that with the reverend."

"No, I did not. He wouldn't have believed me, anyway."

"So then?"

"He continued in that vein. Told me I should only help those who are serious about seeking the Lord. That's when I flew off the handle."

"And they threw you out of the building."

"Yup."

Much greeted them at the shelter's back door, his face falling as soon as he saw them. He turned back and shook his head, no doubt sharing the bad news with Rojo and Hood.

Tuck had one foot through his office door, John a step behind, when Hood growled, "Told ya so."

Tuck shrugged. "I had to try. It's my responsibility to take care of these people. I have to do everything in my power to look after them and this shelter."

Hood set his flask on the nearest bookshelf. "Everything?"

John rolled his eyes. Hood's tone suggested nothing but trouble, like it had when he suggested robbing the clothing donation bins. That had worked out for the better, but they were running out of close calls. Gibson or his lapdog were going to catch up with them eventually, and the more escapes they managed, the greater the chances they'd be caught the next time.

Tuck raised an eyebrow. "What did you have in mind?"

"Forget all that 'ask and you shall receive' bullshit. It's like my Pops said, better to seek forgiveness than ask permission. You want something; you take it."

Tuck shifted his feet. "Take it? You want to what? Rob a bank?"

Hood harrumphed. "Nah, man, I'm not stupid. You take it from that church. From their donation boxes."

"M-m-me? You want me, Reverend Michael Calhoun Tucker, to steal from a church?"

Hood shrugged. "Okay, not you. Us."

"US?" John and Much asked at the same time.

"Yeah," Hood said. "We're a team, ain't we?"

Rojo, uncharacteristically silent so far, spoke up. "I got a plan."

They chose Tulberry Farms because it was the store farthest from the shelter and in the "right"—meaning rich—end of town. It anchored a strip mall with a paint-and-sip place, a makeup store, and a beauty salon. A high-end steakhouse stood separately in the center. Every car in the parking lot seemed to be a Mercedes, BMW, or Land Rover. Tuck's old beater brought down the shopping center's property values just by being there.

With a forced casualness, the Merry Men mingled a fair distance from the Tulberry Farms entrance: Hood and Rojo on one side, John and Much on the other. The plan was simple and only required two players, but Hood was right, the Merry Men worked best together. So here they were. Tuck waited, anxiously no doubt, back at the shelter.

The Holy Lighters were easy to spot, and not just because of the giant donation baskets they carried. There were three of them today, all women, as bundled up as everyone else but a bit more scrubbed clean—and more insistent on contact. Eye contact, physical contact, whatever it took to cow someone into opening their wallet. One of the three held the basket; the other two corralled victims.

When the three were sufficiently close together, John nodded at Hood and Rojo. Operation Donation was a go.

John headed across the parking lot to warm up Tuck's car. Hood moved in the same direction. Much sauntered over to the Holy Lighters, who pounced on him like lions on prey. The boy had never been a conversationalist—that was how he got his name, after all—but his innocent questions were enough to keep the proselytizers busy. Rojo tensed, waiting for the right movement to make his move.

Rojo stared at the basket carrier's hands. She couldn't maintain that death-grip forever.

Sure enough, after minutes of engaging with Much, she began to relax. Rojo pulled the balaclava down over his face and took off.

He sped past the Holy Lighters, yanking the basket out of the woman's hands. She screamed.

"I'll get him!" Much shouted and launched himself in pursuit of Rojo.

They reached Tuck's car at the same time and dove into the backseat. John steered the car out of the parking lot and onto the road, merging with traffic as quickly and safely as possible. Behind them, the Holy Lighters yelled and shook their fists. One of them patted her pockets, in search of her cell phone. The Merry Men were gone before she was able to pull it out.

To be safe, John took a long, circuitous route back to the shelter, taking care to obey the speed limit and traffic lights while Hood tapped his foot in the passenger seat. Behind them, Rojo and Much poured the cash from the basket into a plastic shopping bag. Then Rojo tossed the basket out of the car window.

The boys burst into Tuck's office laughing. Rojo, holding the bag of money in one hand, clapped Much's shoulder with the other. "Dude! You shoulda seen it!"

John and Hood stepped in behind them. "Where's Tuck?" John asked.

A groan from behind the desk answered.

Much rushed over and found Tuck on the floor, bent over the waste basket, retching. "Rev! You okay?"

Another groan. Tuck rocked back on his knees. "I'm not built for this."

"For what?"

"For a life of crime. I'm a *reverend*, for Pete's sake." Tuck fell against the desk.

Rojo pushed forward, holding out the bag of money. "Maybe this will help you feel better."

Tuck pushed away the offering. "Son, I appreciate the sentiment, but I can't accept stolen property. It's not just against the law; it's against my conscience. And my innards just can't take it." He gestured at the waste basket.

"But . . ." Rojo turned to John and Hood, his eyes wide with confusion.

"It's a gift, Tuck," Hood said. "You telling me you can't take a gift from your oldest friends?"

Tuck sighed. "A gift of stolen property? No, Rob, I can't." He fingered a twenty-dollar bill poking out of the bag. "No matter how much I need it."

February

Tuck held the plumber's invoice with two fingers, as if it were covered in infectious sewer muck. When he thought about it, sewer muck didn't sound so bad. Not nearly as terrible as the word *deductible*. Why had he signed up for one of those high deductible plans in the first place? Blinded by the lower premiums, obviously. Confident that nothing bad would ever happen, that God would look out for him and his. Talk about hubris.

Calvin's initial thousand-dollar estimate had fallen woefully short. Opening the wall had been like opening Pandora's box, and the final costs totaled more than five times Calvin's guess. Thanks to Tuck's high deductible, the plumber's invoice had used the last pennies of the shelter's line of credit plus a chunk out of Tuck's personal bank account. Tuck had to put the last few cents of his own money toward the restoration company work. Then he'd finally hit that darn deductible. The rest of the restoration cost, thankfully, had been covered by insurance—until that cost showed up in next year's premiums. Assuming there was a next year.

Still, Tuck wanted to believe the worst was over, that things would only get better from here on out, but a nagging doubt wouldn't let him. He braced for the next crisis. Something worse than higher premiums waited for him around the corner. The knowledge sat deep in his bones. But the form that something worse might take? That escaped him.

He dropped the invoice in the to-be-filed pile, drawing some small comfort from the clomp of footsteps down the hall toward the newly-reopened men's dorm. Now if he could just figure out how to feed those mouths come morning—

"Penny for your thoughts?"

Tuck blinked. Mary Ann stood in the doorway, her coat on, her arms crossed, her purse hanging from her shoulder.

"If that's all you got, I'll take it. You headed out?"

"In, actually. I've spent the whole day on Gary's arm doing First Lady stuff."

"Your life is a complicated place."

Mary Ann rolled her eyes.

"You didn't have to come in, you know. You could have just gone home and put your feet up, wallowed in a nice cup of tea."

"I did have to come." She held up her hand to stop Tuck from interrupting. "For me. This place keeps me sane."

Tuck raised an eyebrow, drawing a chuckle from Sherwood's First Lady.

"I know, I know. What can I say? I'm a glutton for punishment." What she didn't need to say was that being First Lady was the punishment. Although she'd never said the words out loud, it had been clear from the beginning, in her body language and facial expressions, that she was not all that enthusiastic about her husband's career change. The political spotlight made her feel dirty; she needed the time at the shelter to cleanse herself.

"No," Tuck said quietly. "You're an angel and a saint. I'm the glutton for punishment around here. Or perhaps I'm the sacrificial lamb. Some days I'm not quite sure."

Mary Ann stepped into the office, closing the door behind her. She pulled a chair in front of Tuck's desk and sat, her purse landing on the floor with a soft *thud*. She put her hands on her knees, her posture straight as a schoolmarm's. "What's going on? Is there a problem with the insurance?"

"No. It's just . . . " Tuck looked to the ceiling for the right words, but the best he could come up with were "same shit, different day."

"Wow. You quoted Rob. And you didn't censor the curse word. Must be bad."

Tuck acknowledged Mary Ann's attempt at humor with a half-smile. He sighed and leaned forward. "In a good year, we survive on a shoestring. This year, the shoestring is fraying badly. It could snap at any time. And I don't have any more shoestrings socked away for a rainy day. I might even owe one or two."

The tell-tale lump formed in Tuck's throat. He tried to swallow it, but it wouldn't go away. Like his money woes. And then came the tears, still in his eyes but one kind word from Mary Ann and they would spill. He always had been the weakest of the Merry Men.

He took a deep breath and exhaled slowly. When he felt sure of his composure, he looked at Mary Ann. She licked her lips and fidgeted in her chair, signs she was contemplating something—probably ways to help.

Tuck cleared his throat. "Let me be clear. As dire as

our straits are, I do not want you bailing us out. You already go above and beyond."

Mary Ann shook her head. "You and your male pride. Fine, I won't give you money. But I will help you find it. You still need that new shoestring."

Tuck acknowledged that truth with a deep sigh. "You're right. What about those grants you were working on? Any joy there?"

"Not yet. We made the shortlist on a couple, but it will be weeks before the final decision is made. And, as exceptional as my grant writing skills are, there's no guarantee that decision will be in our favor. You need something more definite."

"Agreed. You know, I used to be able to count on our Boots and Buckets campaign to help us through times like this, but the city hasn't overturned that damned—darned—executive order yet." A glimmer of hope lit Tuck's eyes. "Unless you know something I don't?"

Mary Ann grimaced. "Nope. I know what you know."

Tuck banished the retort about the benefits of being First Lady. Mary Ann's dark expression made it clear that such sarcasm would not be welcome. "Any bright ideas, then?"

Mary Ann's gaze wandered around the room and settled on the window. She stared at it a good while before turning to Tuck with her eyes bright. "What about crowdfunding?"

"Crowdfunding?"

"Sure, marshal the power of the internet. There's a ton of sites out there that people and organizations use to solicit donations, sites that get more traffic than the shelter website. We find one and broadcast the campaign on social media—"

A knock on the door stopped Mary Ann mid-sentence. At Tuck's invitation, the door swung open, but Calvin wouldn't come in. "Sir, there's someone here to see you. Says he's an inspector."

Tuck shot Mary Ann a confused glance. They both stood and followed Calvin to the shelter's main dining room, where Calvin pointed to a middle-aged man in jeans and a blue button-down shirt then disappeared. Tuck whispered a prayer before approaching the man.

"Hello, I'm Reverend Michael Tucker. How may I help you?"

When the man turned, Tuck could see the laminated badge clipped to his shirt pocket. A city insignia. And a clipboard cradled in his arm. Yup, not just an inspector, a city inspector. Chicken Little was right. Or was it Henny Penny? Whoever it was, the sky really was falling.

"Don Harris," the inspector said, shaking Tuck's hand. "I'm sorry to spring this on you, and I don't want to cause a hassle. But we got a report that you had some significant work done on the building."

Was that a question or a statement? "We had a couple of burst pipes repaired . . ."

Harris checked his clipboard. "Yup, that was the report we got. Mind if I take a look? Just want to be sure everything's still kosher, code-wise."

"This way." Tuck guided Harris out of the room. As he passed Mary Ann, he flashed her a wide-eyed, worried look.

She gave him a thumbs-up.

Tuck led the inspector down the hall to the dorms. "Wait here, please."

Harris nodded as Tuck went into the men's dorm and dismissed the room's residents. One by one, they filed out, giving the inspector glances that varied from questioning to hostile as they passed. Once the room was empty, Tuck invited Harris in and pointed out the location of the repairs.

The inspector examined the wall, studying it with a flashlight, running his hands along the sheetrock. "You used a licensed plumber, yes?" he asked without turning away from the wall.

"Yes, I have the invoice back in my office. It's got the number on it."

"And the restoration company?"

"Also licensed. That's on their invoice, too."

"I'll need to see those before I go."

"No problem."

Harris made some notes on his clipboard. He started to say something but stopped, turning left to right, taking in the rest of the room. "How many beds you got in here?"

Tuck did a quick count. "Twenty-seven bunks. That's fifty-two beds."

Harris slipped a tape measure out of his back pocket and measured the wall. He walked across the room and measured the perpendicular wall. Tuck watched the inspector mentally calculate the size of the room, the butterflies in his own stomach starting to do a little dance.

"Is this the only sleeping area?"

"No." Tuck spoke slowly, his brain racing to keep

up with the inspector's. "We also have a women's dorm and a family dorm."

Harris raised his arm. "Lead the way."

Crap, crap, crap. Tuck guided Harris to the two other dorms, where once again, residents left with mixed reactions, beds were counted, walls were measured, and square feet were calculated.

Harris's pen raced across the clipboard. "Are these rooms always full?"

"This time of year? Yes. Once the weather thaws, though, our numbers will drop." Best not to mention the cots they rolled in here each night. Or the sleeping bags they rolled out in the dining room.

Harris made a noncommittal sound that bore a striking resemblance to a death toll and pushed past Tuck.

Tuck raced after him. "Inspector? Is there something else I can show you?"

Harris continued down the hall, stopping to peer in any door he passed. The farther he went down the hall, the more his footsteps sounded like a funeral march. So far, he'd only found the janitorial closet and linen storage. Did building inspectors have a patron saint? Father Timothy would know. Tuck sent up a small prayer that Patricia and the girls had finished cleaning the bathrooms. "Inspector?"

Harris breezed past the bathrooms, though, instead disappearing around the corner that led to the kitchen.

The kitchen! Where dirty dishes and pots and pans rose from the sink like the Leaning Tower of Pisa, because no one had time to wash them yet. Did that count as a building violation?

Tuck turned after Harris, snapshots of the kitchen

flashing in his mind. The kitchen was the most used and abused room in the shelter, and it was always at its worst right about now, at the end of the breakfast service. What were the chances that Harris wouldn't find something wrong?

Tuck entered the kitchen and found Harris at the butcher's block scribbling on his clipboard. Mary Ann stood at the sink, up to her elbows in sudsy water. She really was an angel and a saint. She shot him a questioning glance that he waved off with a shake of his head.

Harris whipped around. He waved a flimsy piece of yellow paper. "Reverend Tucker, your building is in violation."

"Violation? Was there something wrong with the plumbing work?" Tuck's head spun.

Harris continued as if Tuck hadn't said a word. "You have thirty days to become compliant. The necessary repairs and remedies are detailed on this citation. You have a good day, sir." He dropped the page in Tuck's hand and strode out without another word, his footsteps clipping and clopping on the shelter floor.

The inspector wasn't out of the building before Calvin and Patricia peered into the kitchen, where Tuck stood frozen. The citation weighed on his palm, far heavier than a simple piece of paper should be. The energy drained from him like air out of a balloon. The next thing he felt was his backside hitting the floor.

CHAPTER NINETEEN

Hood settled into his usual spot at the Route 46/Yorkshire Road on-ramp to the interstate. Borrowed motel down comforter under his ass, back supported by the signpost, cardboard sign propped against his knees. He could sit like that for hours and would, if that's what it took to make his daily bread. The triangular island was the perfect size and shape. Cars entered the interstate here from both directions, doubling his chances for sympathy.

Winter was on his side, too. A few exaggerated shivers as a fancy-pants car inched up the ramp and more likely than not a hand would pop out a quickly-rolled-down window waving a bill, usually a five-spot. Once someone handed him a Ben Franklin. That was one night Hood slept well. Not a single dream, thanks to his good buddy Jack Daniels.

Any Ben Franklins that came his way today, though, went straight to Tuck. Guilt was eating Tuck alive like a cancer. Hood couldn't stand by and do nothing. That's not what brothers did. Tuck wouldn't let him steal, and Hood was in no position to borrow, but he sure as hell could beg. Better than most.

"Suckers," Hood muttered as he folded himself into position. The boys thought working was better than this? What were they doing today? Shoveling driveways and clearing roofs, probably. How was that better than sitting back and letting it rain money? Naw, he wouldn't trade places with them for the world.

He wouldn't even trade with John, who had the luxury of doing indoor work, thanks to his deal with the motel manager for odd jobs in exchange for a room. Because they all worried about Tuck, the Merry Men had decided unanimously to vacate the shelter. It wouldn't do a whole heck of a lot, but at least Tuck would have four fewer mouths to feed.

Not that the Merry Men had much, either. They'd given away the loot liberated from the Holy Lighters. Bernie, unable to pay his fine, was behind bars. The stolen cash hadn't been enough to liberate him. Instead, the Merry Men distributed handfuls of bills to Sadie and some of the families at the shelter—the latter on the down-low so the good Reverend Tucker wouldn't know. They kept only a couple of the smaller bills for themselves, which was why the boys were out hustling for work and Hood was camped here. John, thumb finally freed from its prison of gauze, had taken on the task of negotiating for a place to stay. There was no better egg than John Lydell, a truth Hood knew all too well. If not for John, Hood would have been dead ages ago. Now, thanks to John's deal, Hood and the boys only had to earn a few bucks for food— and booze.

A beat-up pickup truck flying a giant American flag slowed down. Hood heard a mouse-like squeak as the window rolled down. A weathered working-man's hand hung a greenback out the window.

Hood grabbed it. "Thank you, sir."

"No, thank *you*, soldier." The driver gunned the engine, and the truck sped onto the highway.

"Marine!" Hood shouted to the taillights.

A fancy SUV roared past. Then another. And another. Did they even see Hood? Probably not. He could be just as invisible here as he was at The Moors or any other sidewalk in Sherwood.

More than a dozen vehicles later one of those upscale SUVs—a silver one dulled by dirt and road salt—finally slowed. The window lowered with a hum. This time, the hand holding the bill was female, with well-manicured nails but no wedding ring.

"Thank you, ma'am," Hood said with a nod.

The window buzzed closed, and the car continued up the ramp.

To keep himself awake, Hood played a game of license plates. Illinois, Illinois, Illinois, Illinois, Missouri, Illinois, Wisconsin, Wisconsin, Illinois . . .

The Illinois plate—a tan Honda—stopped. The back window rolled down this time, and a child's hand waved a bill at him. Hood smiled.

"Thank you, young man! That's very kind of you," Hood said with a bow.

He was answered with a shy giggle from the back seat. He turned to the woman in the driver's seat. "And God bless you, ma'am."

The car drove off, the giggle echoing in Hood's ears. He looked at the bill in his hand. It was only a dollar, but it would be Hood's favorite dollar of the day. Maybe even the week. *Kids, man.*

The parade of cars continued past him, and Hood returned to his game of license plates. Illinois, Illinois, Michigan, Illinois, Illinois, Illinois, Florida, Illinois . . .

BOOM!

Hood's mind flung him into hypervigilance. His body tensed. His heart raced. His eyes darted. He studied the landscape, looking for the source of the explosion, bracing for the next one, searching for Charlie and the attack that was bound to follow.

"Get down!" John yelled.

Frankie screamed, "AMBUSH!"

Then bursts of gunfire, in front of him, behind him, next to him on both sides.

Hood hit the deck, his belly to the ground, his face buried in the jungle mud.

The cold jungle mud.

Wait. That wasn't right.

Jungle mud wasn't cold. Cool, maybe, but not cold enough to sting.

Hood planted his hands on the ground and lifted his head, just enough to survey the horizon but not enough to make himself a target. The cold that stung his face now stung his palms.

Not again.

Five things you can see, he heard his old shrink tell him. Hood looked around. Asphalt, snow, road signs, cars, guard rail.

Four things you can hear. Hood closed his eyes and listened. His heart pounding out of his chest. Helos. No, not helos. Car engines, loud enough to drown out almost everything else. Underneath, he could hear a squishing sound. No, not feet in mud. Tires going through slush. The squeal of brakes. The whoosh of passing traffic. Okay, so that was five things.

Three things you can feel. Cold. Sharp, stinging cold,

pricking him like needles. Wet. Wet ground, wet cardboard stuck to his front. Not jungle steamy hot wet, though. Winter bone-chilling cold wet. Wind, as cars blew past.

Two things you can smell. Hood inhaled, held the breath, and then exhaled in a fit of coughs. Exhaust. No mistaking that noxious odor. Hood sniffed. Was that . . . ? He checked his pants. Yup. He'd wet himself. Well, with the wet from the snow, maybe no one would notice.

One thing you can taste. Hood licked his lips and grimaced. Bitter. Dirt? Road salt? Whatever he'd picked up when he hit the ground. He wiped his mouth with his sleeve, for whatever good it would do.

Hood wobbled to his feet and dusted himself off as best he could. Damn flashbacks. Damn broken noodle, mistaking a backfiring car for exploding ordinance, mistaking a frozen cement island for a steamy Vietnam jungle. Damn, damn, DAMN.

Grumbling, Hood picked up his sign, now damp and heavy. The letters were smeared from the wet but at least they were still readable. Maybe its extra-pathetic condition would work in his favor. Instead of crouching against the signpost, though, he stayed upright. Leaning against the pole, the chill of the metal leaching through his coat, he closed his eyes. He listened to his heartbeat slow to normal, felt his breathing become more even, and gave unspoken thanks that Red and Much hadn't been around to see that little display of weakness. It wasn't much to be thankful for, but it was something.

A car door slammed. Hood opened his eyes.

"Well, well, well. What have we here?" Officer

Dubrowski stood at the curb, thumbs hooked in his belt. "Looks like our old freeloading friend from the alley."

Dubrowski gave Hood a once-over while his stocky, dark-haired partner walked around the car to join him.

"What happened to your boy?" Hood asked. "You know, the one with the manners."

"Young Freed? He's still with the sheriff's office. I, on the other hand, have found another assignment and a new partner. This here's Benjamin."

Benjamin took a position next to Dubrowski and assumed the same stance as his partner.

Hood looked Dubrowski up and down. The deputy—no, cop—was indeed wearing a different uniform. Still that dark almost-black blue, but this one bore the insignia of the Sherwood Police Department. Once Gibson's crony, always Gibson's crony. Hood stood straight, leaning his sign against his legs and clenching his fists. "Well, look at you, two peas in a pod."

Dubrowski stepped closer. Grabbing Hood's sign, he read, "Homeless vet. Anything helps." He turned to his partner. "Sounds like panhandling to me. What do ya think, Benjamin? Does that sound like panhandling to you?"

Benjamin nodded. "Sure does, Dub."

"And panhandling is against the law." Dubrowski threw the sign to the ground.

Hood snapped to. Something fluttered in his belly. "Says who?"

"What? You don't get the news in that back alley

you call home? Oh, that's right. You don't live there anymore. What about your good friend that runs the shelter? He didn't tell you, either? Maybe he's not such a good friend, after all."

Benjamin chuckled. Hood narrowed his eyes.

"The new mayor outlawed it. Was in all the papers. On the internet too. He's cleaning up the city, getting rid of vermin like you. You shoulda moved to White Oak. Hell, you shoulda moved anywhere. That would have been the *smart* thing to do."

Hood should have known that Gibson would be behind this, the bastard. He held out his arms. "So arrest me, Officer. Take me to jail and throw away the key."

"Nah. That's too easy. You, sir, have a habit of resisting arrest—as do your boys, especially that beaner. Real temper on that one. He must take after you, eh? Too bad he isn't here to save your ass this time."

"You seem to be taking this awful personally. I mean, I know why the Lord High Sheriff hates me, but what did I ever do to you?"

Dubrowski pulled his nightstick from his belt. Benjamin did the same. "You? You *exist*. You're an embarrassment, a failure. You could raise yourself up, show respect for the uniform that you claim to have worn, for the flag you claim to have defended, but instead you choose to live like a feral animal, encouraging others to do the same. You pollute our streets, and it's my job to clean them up."

Hood tensed. Adrenaline rolled through his veins like roaring rapids. He heard John telling him to play it cool, but Hood, for once, wasn't the one looking for a fight. It was two against one, and no way was Hood going down easy. Not a scrapper like him.

Movement on his left caught his eye. A mom-mobile slowing down on its way up the entrance ramp.

Benjamin saw it, too. He nudged Dubrowski and motioned with a jut of his very square chin.

Dubrowski waved at the vehicle. "Move along! Nothing to see here. It's all under control."

Like a good law-abiding citizen, the mom-mobile accelerated and disappeared around the corner.

Dubrowski and Benjamin turned back to their prey.

Hood held up his hands. "I don't want trouble, Officer. If you don't want to arrest me, maybe you could just let me off with—"

Dubrowski's first blow stung Hood's hands. The next one slammed into Hood's raised forearms, knocking him back two steps, right into the signpost.

The blows kept coming, Dubrowski on one side, Benjamin on the other. Hood couldn't move fast enough to fend them off. Each strike left a painful throb—on his arms, his shoulders, his back, his calves, his knees.

The officers pounded Hood until he fell to the ground and curled into fetal position. Then they kicked him, stomped him, their heavy boots landing like anvils. All Hood could feel, all he could see, was pain. Deep, dark, searing pain. Pain that shrieked in Hood's ears like an air raid siren. Still the blows rained down on him, a hurricane that would not end.

Until it did.

It took an eternal moment for Hood to realize the beating had stopped, that the throbs in his body were echoes not impacts. He opened his eyes but couldn't see. Somewhere beyond the ringing in his ears there were voices. Far away, at the end of a tunnel. The words weren't clear, but the tone was angry. Hood's jumbled brain struggled to make sense of it— something about a phone and a free country.

The last thing Hood heard was a voice from the other end of the tunnel. "Dude, you okay?"

Then all went silent and black.

CHAPTER TWENTY

The first thing Hood noticed was the warmth. He didn't remember when he stopped being cold. The cold just wasn't there anymore. In its place, soft warmth. A bed?

It was quiet, too. Maybe not quiet, exactly. More like, the street noise was gone—no car engines, no whoosh of passing vehicles, no horns, no brakes— replaced instead by a pounding in his head. The voices were still there, though, at the edge of his darkness, but they'd lost their belligerence.

"Was she there? What'd she say?" a worried someone asked.

"She's on her way. She said to clean him up as best we can in the meantime." That voice was lower pitched, more assured. *John.* That was John's voice. The tension in Hood's body loosened a tiny bit.

His eyes felt weighted, but he managed to open them a crack. His whole body felt too heavy to move. Without turning his head, he glanced right. John and Rojo stood by the phone. A glance to the left revealed Much sitting at Hood's side.

"Where—?" Hood croaked.

His brain provided the answer at the same time Much did. "The motel. Our room at the motel."

"How?" With that one word, Hood's throat felt scraped raw.

"John found you," Much said.

John and Rojo appeared on the other side of Hood's bed. John spoke for the both of them. "When you weren't back by dark last night, we got worried."

Hood managed a wan smile. "Thanks, Ma."

John's voice was calm, but his eyes were filled with concern. "Much waited for you here. Red went to the alley. Tuck called hospitals. I—"

"Drew the short straw?"

John snorted. "More like, saved your ass again. It's getting to be a habit."

Hood strained to give a half-nod. With a grunt, he forced his arm off the bed and his hand into a fist. John acknowledged the gesture of gratitude with a fist bump, but the look he and Rojo exchanged didn't escape Hood's notice.

"What?"

Much cleared his throat. "It's just . . . you're not acting like yourself, Boss."

"Yeah? See what you're like after a beat down."

John turned back to Hood. "Speaking of which, buddy, you want to tell us what happened?"

Hood's response was part moan, part grunt. He closed his eyes again, hoping for relief from the relentless ache that filled his body.

"C'mon, Boss, we can't get 'em back if we don't know who they are." Rojo—raring for a fight, as always.

John's voice was stern, insistent. "We're not getting anyone back, Red. You got that?"

Rojo snorted.

"Red?"

"Fine."

John turned back to Hood. "Now, you. We've got a nurse on the way, and she said to get you cleaned up."

Much took the hint and retreated to the bathroom.

"You ain't giving me no sponge bath." Hood struggled to sit up, but his body betrayed him. He fell back against the pillows with a groan that became a series of coughs that cracked Hood's ribs.

Much returned with a pile of towels and washcloths, but it was Rojo who spoke. "No worries, Boss. Even we have our standards."

Hood managed to squint his dissatisfaction. A knock on the door spared him the chance to reply further.

Much hurried to open the door. A rush of air brought sharp cold and a faint flowery scent into the room.

Hood shivered, sparking which sparked another coughing fit. His chest felt like it was being squeezed in a vise. He let out an unintended whimper. With eyes closed, he wished the pain away. Instead, his pain grew, something he hadn't thought possible.

"So, do you feel worse or better than you look?" a familiar female voice asked with a hint of playfulness.

Mary Ann?

Hood opened his eyes. It *was* Mary Ann. Standing by his side, a tote bag slung on her shoulder. Her blue eyes, an ocean in which he once got lost, were haunted by worry. God dammit. All he ever wanted was to see her eyes shine with happiness. So why was it that all he ever did was make them cloud with pain?

"Go away." He tried to roll over, but his body was

too leaden to move. Forced to lie there, achy and sore, saturated with anger and helplessness, he resorted to clenching his teeth and squeezing his eyes shut. Mary Ann was smart. She'd take the hint.

Mary Ann's response was sharp, impatient. "So that's how it's going to be. I thought you boys were going to clean him up?"

"We never got the chance," Rojo answered.

Hood heard rustling fabric and felt something weigh on his mattress. Mary Ann's tote, probably.

"Okay, everyone back off." Hood imagined Mary Ann shooing the Merry Men away with a wave of her hands. "Let me get to work."

Three sets of footsteps tromped across the room, toward the door. Another, lighter set moved toward the bathroom. Seconds later, water ran in the bathroom sink. With a squeak, the faucet was turned off, and the light footsteps came back toward Hood's bed.

"This might hurt," Mary Ann said softly. "I'm sorry."

Hood stiffened, braced for a new layer of pain. With the touch of the cool, damp cloth on his forehead, though, he found himself exhaling and relaxing almost against his will. Damn, that woman had fine hands. He'd forgotten how fine. Eyes still closed, he surrendered to her ministrations, let her wipe away the evidence of his humiliation, let her cleanse him of his sins. His mind floated back into the fuzzy dark.

With Hood's face and neck wiped clean, Mary Ann called for John. "Help me get this coat off."

As fine as Mary Ann's touch had been, John's was

pure agony. The big man pulled, then pushed, his friend into a semi-upright position. Mary Ann gently slid Hood's jacket off his shoulders. She tugged at his sleeve, trying to get it off. It was stubborn, so she yanked harder.

Hood yelped. His eyes flew open and filled with tears. Pain seared his shoulder, knocking the air out of his lungs. "Jesus!"

"I'm sorry, Rob," Mary Ann said. "God, I'm so sorry. I know it hurts, but we've got to get this coat off."

"Maybe you could give us a hand, buddy," John added. "This would be easier if you didn't keep fighting us."

"I'm not fighting you." Hood punctuated each word with a breath. "It's not my fault I can't move."

Mary Ann gave John a warning glance. "We're not saying it is." One more tug and the sleeve came off.

As gingerly as she could manage, Mary Ann rolled up Hood's shirtsleeve. She gasped and slapped her hand over her mouth. "My God."

Rojo and Much rushed over. The three Merry Men grimaced.

"What?" Hood asked. "Ain't you never seen a bruise before?"

"Rob, that's not a bruise." Mary Ann held up Hood's arm so he could see it. "That's a boot print." She put down his arm gently, and she herself dropped onto the other bed. "Who did this to you?"

Hood stared at the ceiling. "No idea. Never saw 'em before."

"Let me call Gary then." Mary Ann grabbed

her tote and dug for her phone. "Get the police department—"

"NO." Hood put everything he had into that one syllable.

"Rob—"

"NO!" the other Merry Men shouted in chorus.

"I know the two of you have had your differences, but he could help—"

John put his hand on Mary Ann's. His voice was quiet but firm. "No."

Mary Ann sighed. "Okay. If you insist. But somebody should be made to pay for this."

"Don't worry, ma'am. They will. We'll make sure of it." Rojo stared at John, the dare clear in his eyes.

Mary Ann frowned but returned to her examination of Hood without further comment. Further audible comment, that was. Hood could see her lips moving. She was mumbling to herself, and he'd bet his life the words *stubborn* and *proud* were in there somewhere. A few moments later, she pulled a fancy cell phone—one of the newfangled ones with a built-in camera—from her bag and turned to John. "At least let me take pictures of the bruises. For evidence, before they fade."

John gestured to Hood. "I'm not the one to ask."

Mary Ann bent over and looked Hood in the eyes. He met her eyes, studied them, tried to peel the layers he saw there. Not just the question—but her smarts, her heart, her strength, her worry, her fear. And with all that, could he trust her?

Of course he could. She wasn't the one who left. She hadn't been the one who ended it. The opposite, in fact. Even after his Dear Jane letter, she kept writing.

When he came home, she called and called and knocked down his door. No matter how hard he tried to push her away, no matter how many *times* he pushed her away, somehow she always ended up back at his side. Like a damn bungee cord. Or maybe a life-line. With a grimace, he nodded.

He winced at every camera flash, and he was grateful when she put down the phone. His gratitude shrank when she picked up his bruised arm and began exploring it with her fingers. He knew she was trying to be gentle, but his screaming nerves didn't. He clenched his teeth and blinked away the tears that rushed to his eyes.

"I know it hurts," she said. "Use your breathing to manage it, like the doctor taught you. Remember?"

Hood did. He inhaled deeply, trying to count to five but only making it to three. His wheeze was loud enough to be heard across the room.

Mary Ann let go of his arm and put her hand and head on his chest. "Again."

Hood closed his eyes, and it was decades earlier, before the war, before the ambush, before the Dear Jane letter. They'd gone to California back then, in the Before. They wanted the sun and the surf. He was get-ting ready to deploy, and they wanted one last hurrah. They'd thought about going to the Gulf, but Hood had family in the Golden State. He wanted to see them one more time, just in case.

So, California it was. They'd gone to the beach, spread their hotel towels on the sand, and watched the waves roll in. He stretched out, and Mary Ann snuggled next to him, her head on his chest. They'd dozed like that on and off most of the afternoon. By sunset, Mary Ann's skin had turned the color of raw meat. The only place he could touch her without causing her to whimper was the callous her flip-flops had left on her toe. Come to think of it, the only place he didn't hurt right now was his—

"Toe," Hood croaked.

"We've got to get him to the hospital." Mary Ann sounded far away, hollow. "I don't like the sound of his lungs, and I wouldn't be surprised if he had a concussion or a fracture somewhere too. He needs a doctor, not a retired nurse."

Even in the distant dark, Hood could hear the catch in her voice. The mumbling, too, that happened somewhere else in the room. Talking about him like he wasn't even there. Exchanging words over the idea of the hospital. The very bad, very wrong idea of the hospital.

"We'll take him in my car," Mary Ann finally said. "I'll call ahead, see who's on duty. I still know people. I'll make sure he's taken good care of. I promise."

Then with strength that could only belong to John, Hood was lifted off the bed and carried into the cold night air.

CHAPTER TWENTY-ONE

Mary Ann's friend—a portly short-haired nurse in lavender scrubs under a heavy bubble coat—greeted them at the curb. Mary Ann skipped the social niceties, detailing in calm, clinical terms what she knew of Hood's condition. Her words came in a measured rhythm. Nothing in her voice gave away the depth of her worry. Only her eyes betrayed her feelings.

As she talked, the two women maneuvered Hood as gently as they could out of the car and onto a gurney, but even their experienced hands couldn't spare him some uncomfortable jostling, to which Hood responded with grunts and groans of protest. Once the patient was secure on the rolling bed, the women rushed him inside. John, Rojo, and Much followed behind.

Rojo kept his eyes on Hood, everything else around him fading into a blur. Then they stepped through the sliding glass doors. The emergency department assaulted Rojo's senses: blinding, buzzing fluorescent lights; constant movement; moaning, crying, and shouting; the metallic scent of blood; the nauseating odor of vomit.

He froze. Surveying the scene, he sought order in the turmoil. He found it: a doctor giving orders, a nurse deploying her troop of orderlies, another nurse deescalating an agitated patient—familiar scenes dressed in medical garb.

This was just another battlefield. He turned to Much, eager to share his realization, except Much wasn't there.

Rojo turned a circle. "Much? Much! Hey, Mitchell! Where you at?"

John had disappeared, presumably down the hall and into whatever exam room the women had taken Hood. Rojo studied the waiting room one more time. Not finding a sign of Much anywhere in the chaos, he backtracked outside.

Movement in his peripheral vision caught his attention. Much. Seated on the edge of a planter, hands on top of his head, rocking.

Rojo kneeled in front of his friend. "Hey, buddy, you okay?"

No answer. Rojo shook Much's knee. No response.

With both hands on Much's knees, Rojo said, "It'll be okay. You stay here and wait for me. I'll go check on Hood, and I'll come back for you. Deal?"

Again, Much failed to respond.

Rojo moved his hands to Much's shoulders. "C'mon, buddy, look at me."

Much made eye contact but barely. His eyes were glazed over with that thousand-yard stare.

"I'm coming back. Stay here, and you'll be safe. Okay?"

Much's head twitched; maybe a nod. Rojo headed back inside. Out of the corner of his eye, he saw Much rocking again.

Rojo found John and Mary Ann conferring outside an exam room halfway down the hall, past the mayhem of the emergency room. Maybe conferring wasn't the right word. The conversation, held in tones too quiet to hear clearly, appeared quite animated. Both were talking with their hands as much as their mouths.

"Goddamn it!" Mary Ann's voice was as close to a shout as Rojo had ever heard it. He increased his pace.

"What's wrong?" Rojo kept his voice soft, but he couldn't hide his worry.

Mary Ann waved for him to be quiet. "What is wrong with you? You . . . you *men* and your stupid pride." Her voice broke on the last word.

Rojo lowered his tone. "Is Hood—? Is he—?" He couldn't say the word. He couldn't even think it.

"We don't know anything yet." Mary Ann's words carried a clear undercurrent of impatience. "He's still being examined."

Rojo clicked his tongue. "Then what's with the fireworks?"

John snorted. "I was just explaining to Mrs. Gibson that we don't accept charity." He paused, searching over Rojo's shoulder. "Where's—"

Rojo shook his head.

Mary Ann, meanwhile, picked up the argument again. "I told you, it's not charity. Rob is family, John. My family. Since before you ever met him, and family takes care of each other. So don't tell me I can't—"

Rojo placed his hand on her arm. With a jut of his chin, he directed their attention to Hood's door and the doctor and nurse exiting it. The nurse was the same one who'd rushed Hood into the E.R., now without her hefty winter coat. The doctor could have been Rojo's kid brother Gabe, who would, if all went according to plan, graduate high school in the spring: same youthful complexion, same gait, same sharp intelligence in his features.

The duo approached at a steady, almost normal pace. Rojo took that as a good sign. If it were trouble, they'd be moving faster. And if it were over . . . well, if it were over, they . . . wouldn't.

The young doctor held out his hand. "I'm Doctor Araya. You already know Beverly."

"So what's the verdict?" Rojo asked.

"We're admitting your friend," Araya said. "I don't know that I can tell you more than that. There are privacy laws—"

John and Rojo started to argue, but Mary Ann got in the first words. "Please, Doctor. I'm his nurse. Tell me."

Araya nodded and directed his answer to her. "We'll need to do some more tests, but a cursory examination suggests he has bronchitis, maybe pneumonia, a variety of hematomas, a concussion, and fractured ribs."

"What's the prognosis?" Mary Ann asked, her voice all nursely and businesslike.

Araya shrugged. "The bruises will heal. The rest depends on the patient, how well he responds to treatment, how well he follows directions."

"Crap." Rojo had only known Hood for about a year, but that was enough time to know following directions was not something the old man was good at.

John and Mary Ann smiled.

"Not a good patient, huh?" Beverly asked.

John chuckled. "Not by a long shot. But we'll do our best to make sure he cooperates."

"Can we see him?" Rojo asked.

"We're transferring him upstairs. We don't normally allow visitors at this hour." Beverly gave Mary Ann a look born of years of silent communication. "But these aren't normal circumstances. If you'll just take seats in the waiting area, I'll bring you up to him once he's settled."

John exhaled.

So did Rojo. "I'll grab Much," he said. Turning to the portly nurse, he asked, "Is there another way to get up to Hood's room without going through the E.R.? Our friend is outside, and he can't handle all that." He waved at the chaos behind him.

"Not a problem. We're taking him up to the fourth floor." She turned to Mary Ann. "Could you bring these boys around through the visitor entrance?"

Mary Ann pushed her hair behind her ears and flipped it loose again. Rojo could see the tug of war in her eyes. Give in to Beverly's request or stay by Hood's side? Maybe he could spare her that decision. "It's gonna take some coaxing to get Much to come inside. Maybe you could go upstairs with the Boss and then, once he's settled, come back down for us?"

John gave a shrug of endorsement, as did Beverly.

Mary Ann sighed and took Rojo's hand. "Thank you." Then followed Beverly and Dr. Araya back into Hood's room. John and Rojo went in the opposite direction, back through the gauntlet of the emergency room, to find Much.

The Merry Men sat gathered around Hood's bed-side. The crisp night sky hung black outside the window. They'd made sure the curtains were wide open. Hood always felt safest sleeping under the stars. Given what had happened, Rojo couldn't help wondering if that was still true.

The television hung from the top corner of the room like a sentinel, playing the news but with the sound muted. John occupied the one chair in the room, elbows on his knees and gaze steadfastly on Hood. Rojo and Much found seats on the floor, leaning against the wall so they could see both the door and Hood. No one wanted to use the second bed in the room, not even to lean against. Hospital beds carried bad juju.

Hood had not yet regained consciousness. The Merry Men wore their worry like winter coats, but none spoke of it. Giving voice to their fears would only give life to the jinx.

The squeak of wheels broke the silence. Rojo looked up to find Beverly pushing a cot into the room. Behind her, an orderly pushed another one.

"Figured you boys would be staying here. Thought you'd like something more comfortable than the floor to crash on." Beverly pointed her finger at each man one by one. "But you better be quieter than mice. You staying here isn't exactly kosher, so you don't want to be drawing any attention to yourselves. For your sake and mine. Understood?"

One by one, each of the Merry Men nodded. Much hopped to his feet and helped fold out the cots. Another orderly came in carrying an armload of blankets and pillows. Much got those arranged the cots, too.

Rojo's attention was split between watching Much play housemaid and watching the late news dance across the television screen. Then a headline grabbed him by the throat and shook. Bright white capital letters against a blue banner screamed HOMELESS MAN BEATEN BY POLICE.

Rojo pawed for the remote before realizing it was sitting on the arm of John's chair. He pointed at the screen. "Turn it up!"

John followed Rojo's finger and shot up straight. He wasted no time cranking up the volume.

A video of the attack on Hood played while the perky news reader spoke. ". . . in the suburban town of Sherwood. The video, posted on YouTube earlier today, shows two Sherwood police officers beating a man at an on-ramp to Interstate 80. The victim is believed to be a homeless veteran. His whereabouts are unknown. The man who filmed the video was arrested and later released. No word on the condition of the victim. The Sherwood Police Department has declined to comment, as has the Sherwood mayor's office.

"Meanwhile, in Washington, D.C., demonstrators gathered on the steps of Congress to protest . . ."

Beverly and the orderlies looked from the television to Hood and back again. Pale and frowning, they quietly exited the room. John shut the TV off.

Rojo uttered a low whistle. "Holy shit."

Much, ashen, looked to John. "What do we do? Should we tell them where Hood is?"

John shook his head, bowed it, ran his fingers through his hair. He exhaled deeply and leaned back in his chair. He looked at his best friend, lying immobile and unconscious on the bed next to him. Softly he said, "I have no idea."

The scent of bacon tickled Much's nose. He smiled, sighed, and settled deeper into his pillow. Bacon made dreams better. Hell, bacon made everything better. That was one of the undisputed laws of the universe.

Then came a faint scent of coffee—not as enticing as bacon in Much's book, but he never turned down a free cup. Rojo and Hood probably had coffee running through their veins, but given a choice, Much would rather chug a cold pop. Still, pop wasn't a breakfast drink. He admitted that much. Chocolate milk, on the other hand, especially when the milk came from his own cows . . .

Much's stomach rumbled, and he opened his eyes. Why was the wall white? His bedroom walls were tan, the color of wheat at harvest time. The drawings were gone, too. He'd hung dozens of drawings around his room—some his, some Grandpa's—most of them sketches made in preparation for carving. "Draw first, then cut," Grandpa used to say. "Get the picture clear in your head, and your hands will know what to do."

Much heard raspy breathing behind him and snoring. The hum of machinery, too, and a repeating *beep*. He rolled over.

Hood.

The hospital.

Crap.

"Looks like someone's awake." Tuck's voice came from the direction of the television in the corner. Much twisted around to see the reverend sitting cross-legged in a chair.

Much surveyed the rest of the room. Hood still lay unconscious, an IV sprouting from his left arm and a heart rate sensor clipped to his finger. The monitor attached to the sensor beeped. Hood's heart still beat. Much had never been so grateful for such an annoying sound.

Rojo and John were asleep, The tangle of their blankets said their slumber was not a restful one. Much turned his sleepy gaze back to Tuck.

The reverend pointed at a wheeled cart at the foot of Much's cot that held three greasy fast-food bags. He raised his coffee cup in a toast and took a sip. "Might as well help yourself. Get it while it's warm."

Hot breakfast sounded good. Hot breakfast in bed sounded better. Much spider-crawled to the end of this bed. After grabbing the greasiest bag he could find, he settled back on the bed. His face was buried in a bacon-and-egg sandwich when Rojo and John finally stirred.

Much thumbed toward Tuck and the cart. Rojo pounced. John, always the gentleman, offered Tuck a handshake. "Thanks for the grub."

"The least I could do, man. What's the news on our buddy here?"

John's expression lacked even a hint of hope. "We're not sure. The doctors should be running some tests today."

"He looks so old."

John sniffed. "Don't we all?"

Tuck shook his head. "No, this is different. I could always see the miles Hood wore. You, too. But now . . . Geez, John, he looks like he's a hundred fifty."

"You're no spring chicken yourself." Hood's voice was no more than a scratchy whisper, but it was the finest music Much had ever heard. With his next breath, Hood was overcome by a series of phlegmy coughs, snapping the others to attention.

"Morning, all. How about giving me some room?" The nurse's question sounded more like a command. Tuck backed up, almost falling into John's lap.

Much studied the nurse as she checked Hood's vitals. She was taller and younger than Beverly. Sharper, too. Edgier. She didn't give off the same caretaker vibe that Beverly and Mary Ann did. This one was all business. Much didn't like her one bit.

She reached for Hood's IV bag. "You all shouldn't be here, you know."

Rojo tried to tell her they had permission. "Beverly said—"

"Beverly has a habit of bending the rules." The nurse finished swapping out Hood's bag and then turned. With her arms crossed, she said, "We're taking your friend up for x-rays and a CT scan. I expect you all to be gone by the time we bring him back."

She waved in an orderly, and together they maneuvered Hood into a wheelchair. Hood played rag doll, letting them manipulate his body without so much as a harrumph. He'd put up more of a fight getting out of the car last night. Much had never imagined Hood could be so cooperative. Whatever comfort and hope he'd found melted away.

John and Tuck stared at each other, carrying on a silent conversation that Much couldn't quite follow. All he could get was the worry that radiated from them, a worry he and Rojo shared. They all watched Nurse Not-Beverly and her orderly roll Hood out of the room, each praying for their friend in his own way.

An hour and a half later, the Merry Men, Tuck included, huddled around a wobbly plastic table in the hospital cafeteria, hiding from Not-Beverly and waiting for Hood's tests to be completed. The fare on their trays was sparse, and their collected funds—piled on the table's center—even more so.

"This isn't good." Much couldn't tell if John was talking about the money situation or Hood.

What he could tell was that his cookie tasted funny. It's not like he had high expectations—it could never taste as good as his sister's homemade cookies—but his worry made this one taste like sand. He dropped it back on the tray and shoved it aside. Even a gulp of chocolate milk couldn't wash the taste out of his mouth. Much forced himself to swallow.

John fingered the meager change on the table. "She's right, you know. We can't stay here. We're in the way, and we need money. We're not going to earn a damn thing sitting around here moping over Hood."

Rojo slapped his hand on the table, rattling everyone's trays. "It's not moping. We can't just leave him here, with these strangers, not in the condition he's in. He needs us."

"Son, these strangers can do more for him than you can right now," Tuck said.

"Just once, Rev, could you not be so reverend-like?"

"Maybe I could, once, if you let me finish my thought."

Rojo gestured for Tuck to continue.

"The best thing you can do is take care of yourselves. Get back to work and sock away some money. Make sure Hood has a place to go when he's discharged."

That made sense to Much. "You got anything for us to do at the shelter?"

Tuck shook his head. "Wish I did. But you're welcome to stay there. You built the beds. You might as well use them. And I charge far less than that motel you're all so fond of."

Rojo clamped a hand on Much's shoulder. "Looks like we're heading back to the House & Home parking lot."

"I'll get our stuff from the motel," John said. He turned to Tuck. "Think you can give me a ride?"

The reverend nodded. "Of course. You can stash everything in my office."

"Thanks. Then you'll have to bring me back here."

Rojo and Much couldn't have looked more betrayed.

John waggled his thumb. "This thing may look better, but it's still far from healed. I can't do a whole heck of a lot with it. Besides, someone's got to make sure Hood follows the doctor's orders."

That elicited smiles and a few chuckles.

"Hey, Much, you gonna finish that cookie?" Rojo asked, reaching across the table.

Dr. Araya found the Merry Men in the fourth floor waiting room collaborating on a "How Many Errors Can You Find?" exercise in a discarded children's magazine. Much and Rojo sat on either side of John, looking over his arms at the magazine on his lap. Tuck had returned to the shelter, with John's sworn promise to notify him when they learned something and with Much and Rojo's promise that they'd get to work once Hood's test results were in.

"Look!" Rojo pointed at a tree in the picture. "It has a shoe hanging on it in this one, but not in that one."

John dutifully circled the dangling shoe.

Dr. Araya stopped a few feet away and slid his hands into the pockets of his lab coat. "Gentlemen, good to see you keeping your spirits up."

The three men shot to their feet, the magazine spilling onto the floor. They each shook the doctor's hand. Much noticed a tattoo peeking out from Araya's rolled up sleeve—two snakes wound around a staff topped with eagle wings. The doc was a veteran. An Army doc. Much suddenly felt better about Hood's chances.

"How is he?" John asked.

"I'm sorry," Araya said, regret on his face and in his voice. "I can only share that information with his family. I was hoping you could put me in touch with them."

"With all due respect, Doctor, we *are* his family," John answered. "His parents are dead. He might have some cousins out in California somewhere, but that's just DNA. We're his brothers, in every sense of the word except genetics."

"Could you get a notarized document to that effect? Maybe a power of attorney? Something legal that identifies you as his next of kin?"

John nodded. "Absolutely. But that'll take a few days. Is there anything you can tell us now?"

Araya leaned back to check the hall. "I shouldn't but . . ." He waved the men back into their seats and took a chair facing them. Speaking low, he explained that Hood's situation was serious, approaching critical. "The bruises look bad, and they're deep, but they're healing. He also has a couple of fractured ribs and a fractured radius in his right arm. Those, too, will heal. I'm more concerned about his lungs. He has an advanced case of pneumonia. From the scarring, I'm guessing it's not the first time."

With a frown, John nodded. "Not the second or third, either."

Much heard the resignation in Araya's sigh. "I've got him on antibiotics and painkillers," the doc explained. "I want to keep him under observation for a few days to make sure the meds are working."

"So he's not going to die?" Much asked.

Araya breathed deeply. "I can't promise that. Your friend's in bad shape. In addition to his injuries, he's malnourished. He has reduced liver function. My guess is cirrhosis from years of heavy drinking?"

Without hesitation, the men nodded. There was no point in denying the obvious.

"His body is weakened. He'll need all his strength to fight this, and even that might not be enough."

Rojo asked the question Much was thinking. "What can we do?"

"For now, let us take care of him. When he's strong enough to be discharged, make sure he has a warm, dry, comfortable place to stay." Araya pulled a card out of his pocket and handed it to John. "In the meantime, here's my card. You're welcome to call and check on your friend any time, day or night."

It was just like Tuck said, only worse. The Merry Men were headed back to the streets, the weight of Hood's life on their shoulders.

March

The overnight snow dusted the ground, giving a sheen to the gray slush that accumulated this time of year. It almost looked pretty. Even the bite in the air felt welcoming, simply by virtue of being one of the last cold snaps in the stutter-start of spring. But it was the swarm at the shelter door that held Mary Ann's attention.

She'd seen them from the street, before ever turning into the lot. The county sheriff should have been her first clue. She'd had to stop and wait for the two sedans to pull out of the driveway before she could make her turn in. She saw the Nottingham County seal and black "SHERIFF" on the doors as the cars pulled past her. They barely registered. She was too preoccupied with the crowd to wonder why the sheriff had dispatched deputies to the shelter in the first place, let alone so early in the morning.

Now that she'd parked, she recognized faces in the group milling about the entrance. Calvin the plumber. Patricia the volunteer. Rose the young mother, clutching her blanket-swaddled toddler. Young Jenny—but without the teddy bear usually glued to her hands. Jimmy. Eddie. Margie. All regulars. Plus dozens of others.

The clock on her dash said it was after 9 a.m. Rose should be at work. So should Eddie. The older children should be in school. So what were they all doing here? Why were they outside instead of inside? Surely they—all but Patricia—had slept there.

Mary Ann slipped on her gloves, grabbed her purse, and slammed her car door, drawing the crowd's attention. Calvin jogged over, Patricia trotting at his heels.

"Miz Mary Ann! Miz Mary Ann!" Calvin waved, a gesture that spoke more of want than welcome. "Do you know what's going on? Did you talk to the reverend? Did he tell you?"

Patricia arrived panting, her hand on her chest. She gave Mary Ann a look of warning and a slight shake of her head. She knew what was happening. Why was she keeping it to herself?

Mary Ann took the hint. With a barely perceptible nod to Patricia, she looped her arm through Calvin's and turned him back toward the shelter. "I just got here, Calvin. You know more than I do. Why don't you catch me up?"

It had started early, before the usual 6:30 a.m. wake-up call. Tuck turned on the dorm lights, woke everyone up, and shoo'd them out the door. No breakfast. No explanation. Not so much as a "wash your face before you go." Just "grab your things and wait outside." Tuck escorted them to the sidewalk, watched everyone leave, and then shut the door behind them. The sun was just peeking above the horizon. Then the sheriff's deputies slid chains through the front doors.

Now, almost three hours later, everyone still stood outside, shivering and stamping their feet, waiting for

Tuck or the deputies or *someone* to unlock the door and let them back in. Waiting for an explanation. Or a direction. Or . . . something.

Mary Ann frowned. None of that sounded right. That simply wasn't the Reverend Michael Tucker that she knew. Even the Marine that Tucker had once been wouldn't do such a thing.

She dropped Calvin's arm to rummage through her purse. She slid a card out of her wallet and offered it to Calvin, who only blinked at her. "Tell you what. I'll track down the reverend and find out what's going on. In the meantime, we can't leave these people freezing outside. Take them across the street, buy them all a coffee or tea or hot chocolate—something warm. And breakfast. Everyone eats and drinks, got it? It's on me."

Mary Ann pressed the card into his hand. Gary could come and arrest her himself, if feeding the homeless was really that bothersome.

Calvin stared at the credit card in his open palm, eyes wide with awe.

Mary Ann rested her hand on his shoulder. "Reverend Tucker trusts you. So do I."

The tears in Calvin's eyes when he lifted his gaze sent a web of cracks through Mary Ann's heart. How long must it have been since anyone entrusted this man with anything? She swallowed her own tears and gave a nod.

Sniffing, Calvin nodded back, then he approached the crowd. Mary Ann watched as he led them toward the donut shop across the street. When they were safely out of earshot, she spun to face Patricia. "What the hell is going on?"

It was Patricia's turn to blink. "Did you just say—?"

"Hell? Yes. I think this qualifies. Is everything okay? Did something happen to Tu—Reverend Tucker?"

With a sigh, Patricia shook her head. "Yes. No. I don't know." She inhaled deeply and collected herself. "Something's happened, something with the sheriff, but what exactly, I'm not entirely sure. They put a padlock on the doors so it's got to be bad, but the reverend isn't talking. Not to me, anyway."

Mary Ann resisted the urge to roll her eyes at Patricia's hopeful look. Why did it always come down to her? Didn't anyone else know how to do *anything*? "All right. Go join the gang, get yourself a latte. I'll put on my Nancy Drew hat and see what I can find out."

With a relieved smile, Patricia threw her arms around Mary Ann. "You're a dear. I don't know what we'd do without you."

Mary Ann shoved her hands in her pockets and kicked at a pile of slush. She walked away muttering, "I'm beginning to wonder that myself."

A tug on the front door and a knock on the window brought nothing. Mary Ann peeked through the glass. Nothing. Just an empty dining room. She tugged the door again, this time noticing a jangle that shouldn't be there. Sure enough, Calvin and Patricia were right: chains and a padlock hung from the door handles.

Mary Ann pounded on the door. "TUCK! Michael Tucker, are you in there?"

She trudged around to the back of the building, stomping slush under her boots.

Mary Ann turned the corner. The back door was propped open.

Tuck wouldn't keep that door open in weather like this, not when every cent meant another minute of warmth. He'd never be so reckless. Creepy crawlies danced up and down Mary Ann's spine. She shook her head but couldn't shake the feeling that something was very wrong.

Her first concrete clue was the stack of boxes propping the door open. She lifted the cover of the top one. File folders. Lots of them, each one stuffed with papers, but no clear labels. Typical Tuck.

Mary Ann knocked on the doorframe. "Hello? Anybody home? Tuck?"

No answer.

She knocked again. This time she heard the scritching of moving furniture. She headed toward the sound: Tuck's office.

Mary Ann froze in the office doorway. Tuck had never been fastidious, but he had been orderly. The scene before her bordered on natural disaster. A tangled pile of blankets sat pushed into the far corner of the room. The computer monitor was tipped over on the desk. Chairs were upended. Books scattered on the floor. Papers everywhere. Except one—a single white page next to the overturned monitor on Tuck's desk, the one neat thing in the midst of the chaos.

She tiptoed over the obstacle course on the floor to get a closer look. The words at the top of the page were unmistakable: NOTICE OF EVICTION.

Mary Ann gasped, her hand instinctively flying to her mouth.

"Eviction?" she whispered. She should have forced her money into his palms, whether he wanted it or not. Then maybe he wouldn't be in this mess.

She picked up the notice. Angry red letters announced that by order of the court, the occupants of the building had been evicted and the property now belonged to the plaintiff. The plaintiff? Who could that be? Tuck didn't have a landlord or a mortgage. He owned the building outright, having bought it in a foreclosure auction years before. What the hell was going on?

She turned a circle, surveying the destruction one more time. Only one person could have done this. Where the hell was Tuck?

Mary Ann's feet planted roots. Her mind spun. She dug in her back pants pocket for her phone. What was the point in being First Lady if she couldn't pull a string or two in a crisis?

A crash echoed from the kitchen, and Mary Ann whirled around, stuffing her phone away, She sprinted toward the sound.

She saw the baskets first. Swept off the butcher's block, they were scattered across the floor. She stepped into the room with a *crunch*. Broken glass littered the floor under and around the baskets.

"What do we do with all this food?" Tuck asked.

Mary Ann turned in the direction of his voice. He stood at the refrigerator, holding the French doors open, staring blankly at the appliance's contents: a jug of juice, a couple trays of eggs, a dozen or so single-serve milk cartons, some butter and cream cheese, damaged produce from the market castoffs.

With another crunch of Mary Ann's footsteps, he turned to face her. "You shouldn't be here. You can't be here."

She pushed the refrigerator doors closed and led Tuck across to a clear part of the room. They sat against the wall, side-by-side.

"It's all my fault. I just . . . I couldn't get it all done." A shadow passed across Tuck's face.

"All of what? Tuck, what the hell happened?"

"I just couldn't find a way to make all the repairs. So we've been shut down. Evicted. The city took possession of the building." Then, with a great sigh that heaved his chest, "I have until noon to clear out what I need."

"What? *Noon?* Couldn't you reach some sort of compromise?"

"That *is* the compromise." Tuck's voice sounded heavier than Mary Ann had ever heard it. Worse than when he bemoaned the shelter's chronic financial struggles. Worse than when he wrestled with his conscience, when he flirted with suicide, after coming home. Worse than when he parted ways with Rob and John to attend seminary. Worse than when he'd found that homeless girl dead and frozen on his church's doorstep all those years ago.

"She wanted sanctuary, a warm safe place to sleep," Tuck had said through tears. "She found a locked door and an icy death. *I* locked that door. I *killed* her. After I'd sworn to never again take a life."

This shelter was born in the next moment, when Tuck pledged that he would never again lock another door. Now that someone had locked these doors for him, Mary Ann feared Tuck would be the one it killed.

She took a deep breath and did the only thing she knew how. "How can I help?"

CHAPTER TWENTY-FOUR

The hustle and bustle of the hospital faded to white noise as Hood's thoughts twisted into tighter and tighter knots. He'd been here too long. The damn walls were creeping closer every day. Hell, every hour. The air, tainted with the odor of antiseptic, burned his nostrils. As for the food . . . Well, he'd found better tasting grub in dumpsters. And the bed! Sure, it was comfortable, but it was making him soft. He was losing his edge—the very edge he relied on to keep himself alive. Everyone kept telling him how much he needed to be here, to get better. But he knew different.

This hospital wasn't going to save him; it was going to kill him. He saw how the doctors and nurses looked at each other when they talked about him, the doubt and disappointment in their faces. He even heard tinges of it in their voices, the way they talked to him, as if he were a damn child. It was the same look, the same tone, he got from those docs at the VA before they kicked him out. The same one the social worker had, right before she called him "incorrigible"—which was apparently high falutin' for "stubborn bastard." At least, that's what John had said and John, unlike these medical types, never lied to him or used fancy words to dance around the truth.

Now the doctors wanted to extend his stay. This wasn't a hospital; it was the Hotel California.

No, that wasn't true. It was worse than that. The damn doctors wanted to send him to one of those "rehabilitation centers." And Hood knew damn well that was code for "nursing home." A nursing home—where old people went to die. Robert Hood in one of those places?

"Over my dead body," he vowed to the empty room. The only response was the routine beep of his oxygen monitor. He listened to the quiet a moment more.

Beep.

"Fuck that." He had a family, responsibilities. His boys would never survive without him. And there was Sadie. Who was keeping track of her? Looking out for her? The longer he stayed here, the worse off they'd all be.

He slid the sensor off his finger and yanked the oxygen tube out of his nose. The beeps sounded loud and fast, an alarm calling in the cavalry.

Hood swung his legs over the side of the bed. He gasped for breath. How could such a simple act rip the air out of his lungs like that? A punch in the gut would have felt better. When did he become such a fucking weakling?

He took a deep, wobbly breath that ended with a cough. Grasping the bed for balance, he slid until his feet hit the floor. Then he stood—again with a wobble—and pulled the IV from his arm. He shuffled to the cabinet they called a closet. Hunched, Hood closed his eyes against the pain. Damn, he needed a drink.

He stole a glance at the wall clock. Less than ten minutes before the next nanny came to poke and prod him. *Get it in gear, Hood.* His clothes sat neatly folded on the shelf. They looked clean, as if they were almost new instead of a decade old. If the colors hadn't been so faded, he'd think someone had been on a shopping spree. He raised his shirt to his face and sniffed. He sniffed again, detecting a faint scent of vanilla and something flowery. Mary Ann's scent. It figured. He started to smile but bit it back. See? Going soft.

Hood wrestled his clothes on and moved to the doorway. He watched the traffic in the hall, plastering himself against the cabinet when a group in lab coats approached. Lab coats were like police uniforms: they were best avoided.

He waited for the voices to pass and peeked out again. A small family moved in his direction. He fell in line with them and followed them toward the elevators, hanging back while the matriarch of the group pushed the Down button. When the doors dinged and slid open, he stepped forward—and into John.

"Going somewhere?" the big man asked.

How had Hood missed seeing his friend, this mountain of a man? He really was losing his touch. He grabbed John's elbow. "C'mon, man, get me outta here."

He pushed past John as the elevator doors started to close. Taking full advantage of his long arms, John reached out and grabbed Hood, pulling his leader back from the elevator with a solid yank. Sharp pain shot deep into Hood's shoulder. He yelped.

"Are you fucking crazy?" John hissed. He pulled Hood aside, out of the flow of traffic.

Hood seethed, his breaths quick and shallow.

"You almost died," John continued in a stage whisper. "You're not even close to ready to leave. Look at you! You stand like the hunchback of Notre Dame. Your breathing sounds like a diesel engine with a dirty fuel line. The last place you belong is out there."

Bent over, Hood couldn't see John's face, but he heard the worry in the big man's voice loud and clear. Worrying like an old lady. After all these years, surely John knew him better than that. Hood struggled to take a deep breath. "The *last* place I belong is in here." He gasped for air. "In this prison."

John waited until the next group of passersby moved on. "This may feel like a prison, but you've got three hots and a cot, and that's a hell of a lot more than the rest of us got right now."

Hood narrowed his eyes. "Why? What's going on?"

John waited a fraction of a second before answering. "Same old, same old."

"Bullshit." Hood forced himself upright, squinting against the pain but swallowing the grunt.

John slipped his hand around Hood's arm. "We're going through a rough patch, and that's all you need to know. Now let's get you back to bed."

Hood pulled his arm free and planted his feet. "Not til you tell me what's going on out there."

Again, John hesitated. "It's bad, but it's nothing you can fix."

"Not if I'm stuck here, I can't."

"You can't, no matter where you are. It's out of our hands."

"Something at the motel?"

"We're not at the motel anymore."

"Tuck's place, then."

John's face lost color. "Nope."

Hood stood in front of John, arms crossed. "Liar. What happened?"

Shaking his head, John swallowed hard and grabbed Hood's arm again. This time, Hood let John guide him down the hall. Especially now that his room seemed so much farther from the elevator. If he didn't know any better, he'd swear they'd moved it.

They were two steps outside Hood's room when Hood spoke again. "When did you start throwing around the *f* word?"

"When did you become plumb stupid?"

Hood harrumphed.

"Well, well, well, look who's back." The duty nurse stood next to Hood's bed, a cat-ate-the-canary-grin on her face, Hood's IV line dangling from her fingers. She was petite, with short dark hair and brown eyes that now gleamed with a mix of humor and scolding. Hood could tell just by looking at her that she was a scrappy one, not like the Mary Poppins who'd checked on him earlier or his usual Nurse Ratched.

An orderly—a young man who looked to be twenty-five going on sixteen—stood behind her, phone in hand. "Never mind," the young man said into the receiver. "We found him."

Hood growled a curse as the orderly slid past him and out of the room.

"I get it," the nurse said. "You're here under protest." She patted the bed pillows. "Now get your ass back in this bed before I have to wrestle you into it."

Hood stared her down.

"I can wrestle you into that backless gown, too, if you'd like."

Like a sullen teenager, Hood obeyed—bed, not gown—and not least because John blocked his escape. Little John made a very effective door.

The nurse turned Hood's arm to slide his IV back in. He gave her the bird. She didn't miss a beat. "Nice finger. Bet you got a matching one on the other side."

She taped down the IV line and flicked the medicine bag to get the drug flowing into Hood's vein. In two smooth movements, she replaced Hood's oxygen line and heart rate sensor. She gave her patient the once over with a nod of satisfaction. Proper order had been restored. She moved toward the door and stopped. The nurse turned to Hood, giving him a pointed finger and pointier tone. "You stay put." Then she was out in the hallway and gone.

Hood grinned. "I like her." A moment later, he turned flat serious. "Now, what the hell is going on out there?" he said with a cough. "Where are Tuck and my boys?"

John tossed Hood his hospital gown. "Put this on, and maybe I'll tell you."

CHAPTER TWENTY-FIVE

Much checked his reflection in the library window and cringed. Was that really what he looked like? Keeping one eye on his mirror image, he spit on his hands, wiped his cheeks, and smoothed his hair. He still looked a mess, but at least now he was a neater mess. He adjusted the overstuffed pack on his back and stepped into the library. Past the foyer, he stopped, pausing just long enough to inhale deeply. Libraries always took his breath away.

Mama had led the family to church every Sunday, led grace before every meal, hung a cross in every bedroom and around every child's neck. She taught them to fear God and respect His church. Much was nothing if not obedient. He went through the motions, minded his p's and q's. But his only honest awe and worship happened in foxholes and libraries. Mama would spin in her grave if she ever found out. Grandpa, though, seemed to understand. Libraries were the keepers of mysteries, especially the one mystery Much had always struggled to solve—reading.

He lugged his bag to his favorite table, wedged in a corner behind the magazine racks. It was one of the few tables without a power strip, which meant it was almost always empty. After sliding the backpack across the table, Much peeled off his jacket, hung it on the back of a chair, and dropped into the chair himself.

Crossing his arms, he settled into the bag like it was a pillow. Somehow it felt softer in here than it did when he slept rough.

The smell of coffee roused him. A small Styrofoam cup filled with steaming black liquid sat at his elbow.

"Nice nap, Sleeping Beauty?" Rojo sat in the chair opposite, a smart-ass grin on his face.

"Shut up." Much downed the coffee like a shot. God, it was awful. But it was hot, and that was what mattered most. Maybe with another cup he'd be able to feel his toes again. The days were getting warmer, but the nights weren't quite keeping up. Every single Merry Man—including their new companion Tuck— woke up cold and stiff now that they were sleeping outside again. As if October was replaying itself. Much pushed himself to his feet. "I'm getting a refill."

Rojo rocked back in his chair and raised his cup. "God be with you."

Rojo's words were meant as a throwaway, but Much couldn't let them go. God should be with them: Hood, Rojo, John, Much, Tuck. Everything he'd learned in Mama's church told him that. So where the hell was He? Hood was in the fast lane on the expressway to the afterlife. Tuck had been living in Purgatory since the shelter closed. Bernie sat in jail, nearing the end of his sentence but behind bars none- theless—and with no job to go back to when he got out. The Merry Men barely escaped freezing to death on the streets at night. For now, they were surviving, if you could call it that, thanks to the library's free coffee and open tables. Lord knows what happened to the truly innocent—the families who'd depended on the shelter, those kids who clutched Much's hand-carved toys as if they were their most precious possessions. Where were they sleeping? How were they eating? Who was taking care of them? Who was on *their* side?

Much traded his scowl for a forced smile as he approached the coffee counter. No point scaring the librarians who were kind enough to provide the java and the shelter. They, at least, were on the right side of things.

Cup refilled, Much lingered to watch the staff set up an easel. AUTHOR VISIT, the sign read.

Come meet Peabody- and Pulitzer-Prize Winning
Journalist
Allan A. Dale,
reading from his memoir Warco
1 p.m., Saturday, April 12th
Bradbury Meeting Room.

Much approached the librarian at the reference desk. Something about her reminded Much of his favorite grandmother, even though this woman was clearly much younger. "Excuse me? Do you have a copy of that book?" he asked, pointing at the sign.

"We certainly do." She directed him to the New Books shelf. Dale's book stood in the middle, three copies lined up one behind the other.

Much thanked her, shoved two copies under his arm, and speed-walked back to the table. Coffee safely placed, he tossed one of the books at Rojo. "Remember him?"

Rojo flipped open the cover and studied the author's photo on the flap. "That journo guy. Yeah, I remember him. Guy was completely nuts." Rojo threw the book on the table. "But don't tell him I said that."

"He's coming here."

"Yeah? When?" Rojo picked up the book again.

Much returned to his chair. "April 12th. What's today?"

"Beats me. The Rev will know." Rojo scanned the blurb on the front flap and started flipping through the pages.

Leaning forward, Much spoke in low conspiratorial tones. "You remember what he was like? How he always called things like they were? Well, I was thinking—"

"Don't tell me. You boys won the lottery, and you're plotting how to spend your millions." John stood with his arms crossed, the tease in his words accompanied by a hopeful expression in his eyes.

Tuck stepped up next to John."Naw, that's not it. They're planning their escape. Gonna run away and join the circus."

Rojo snorted. "Well, at least with the circus we'd have a roof over our heads."

Much watched the hurt flit across John and Tuck's faces, feeling a stab of cold in his own gut. "That's not fair, man."

Rojo leaped out of his seat, the book landing on the table with a loud *thud* and his chair tumbling to the floor behind him. "Need more coffee," he mumbled before stomping away.

A couple of young men at a nearby table threw sharp, angry glances in his direction and then Much's. Much gave an apologetic shrug, and they returned to their laptops.

"Sorry," Much said to Tuck. "He's not really mad at you. He's just—"

Tuck held up his hand. "No need. We know the circumstances are, shall we say, trying?"

"Besides," John added as he straddled the chair next to Much, "Red's temper is his best quality."

Much chuckled. John had a knack for understatement.

"Look, son, nobody's in a good mood," Tuck said. "We're all just muddling through the best we can."

Much studied Tuck's face. Was he talking to Much, or to himself? Did he even know?

"How's the boss?" Much asked.

John answered. "Same as ever. Tried to escape—again. I thought about tying him to his hospital bed, but that wouldn't be fair to the bed. He'll be out soon enough, though. Doc says he'll be released one way or another within a week or two, either to our care or a nursing home."

Much rolled his eyes. Hood in a nursing home? A snowball had a better chance in Hell.

John grabbed a copy of Dale's book and scanned the jacket. Flipping through the pages, he asked, "You boys reliving the good ol' days?"

Rojo handed John and Tuck cups of coffee before sliding back into his seat, his tantrum apparently over. "We knew him. He embedded with us in Iraq a couple times. He did some time in Afghanistan, too. I think he did more tours than the two of us did, combined."

"Yeah? Are you in here?" John paged through the index.

Much traded a look with Rojo. "Not by name."

It was John and Tuck's turn to trade glances. "What does that mean?"

Rojo pointed at the book. "It means things went pear-shaped on an op. He was there. And it's all in here."

Much pulled his jacket back on, but it didn't do much to warm the cold that seized his bones or to calm the twitch that seized his hands.

"You think it's his fault things went FUBAR?" Tuck asked.

Rojo shook his head. "Naw. He wasn't the one in the way."

Much pushed himself away from the table. He couldn't get out the front door fast enough. Maybe outside he could get some air into his lungs. Maybe outside his heart would stop doing the hundred-yard dash. Maybe outside he wouldn't feel like throwing up.

He made it to the planter that lined the stairs in front of the building but couldn't stop the dry heaves.

Or the hyperventilating.

Or the tears.

He sat on the steps and buried his head in his arms. He felt people pass by him, sensed they were giving him a wide berth. He was grateful they left him alone. At the same time, it hurt. But what kind of stranger would put an arm around his dirty stinking shoulders and tell him he was going to be okay?

He startled at a hand on his back.

"You okay, kid?" The old man's baseball cap announced him as a Korean War veteran. Just like Gramps.

By instinct, Much raised his hand in a salute. "I'm fine, sir. I just needed some fresh air."

The old man pursed his lips and nodded. Giving Much a pat on the shoulders, he continued up the steps. At the top, he stopped and turned. "The bad memories fade, kid. They don't go away completely or forever, but they do fade. At some point, you will be able to live with them." With a wave, he disappeared into the library.

Much let the old man's words settle on him. Grandpa had said something similar in those first weeks after Much came home, when the nightmares were at their worst. Gramps was the only reason he'd made it through that time, the one thing that anchored him, the one family member who understood. But then Gramps died. . . .

Much shook his head. That wasn't a place he wanted to go. He took a deep breath, pushed himself up off the step, and went to rejoin the Merry Men at their corner table. When he got there, Rojo was leaning on the table singing Allan A. Dale's praises.

"He had better intel than the h'ups," Rojo was saying. "If it weren't for him, I don't wanna think about what woulda happened. He saved our asses more than once."

"Maybe he can save them again," Much said.

The three men stared at him. John patted Much's chair. "Do tell."

"Well, the guy's always ad...ad..." Much turned to Tuck. "What's the word?"

"Advocated?"

"That's it. *Advocated*. Dale's always advocated for us. Soldiers. Grunts. Veterans."

"That's right!" Rojo jumped in. "He's the one that wrote all those articles about how messed up the VA is. That's what got him all those awards.

"It would probably piss him off to find out how the mayor and his flunkies are treating us. Those laws making us criminals just for existing. The beating they gave Hood. What happened with the shelter. I bet if we told him what's going on, he'd write about it. And people would listen. Then they'd have to do something about it."

Much nodded. That was exactly what he'd been thinking.

John grabbed a newspaper from the top of one of the magazine racks. He tapped a headline located just below the fold: LEGIONNAIRE'S FOUND AT SECOND VA FACILITY. "Do what exactly? It's not like the VA has changed a heck of a lot."

"I don't know." Much's stage whisper reeked of exasperation. "Something."

"Yeah, *something*," Rojo said.

John looked at Tuck and the boys and back at Tuck again.

"You never know. It just might work. It's not like we have a whole lot of other options." Tuck put his hand on Much's shoulder. "When do we get to meet the Great and Powerful Oz?"

April

Allan Dale stepped out of the rental coffin and stretched his cramped limbs. The chilly air shocked him to alertness but did nothing to relieve the knots in his neck, shoulders, and back. The perils of being a tall man in a small car. The glamorous life of an author on a self-funded promotional tour. Dale's back finally cracked, and he groaned with relief.

He surveyed his surroundings. Recon—a habit he picked up overseas and couldn't put down now that he was "home." The library building itself was average size, not much different in size, shape, or design than the other brick-facade Midwestern municipal libraries he'd been frequenting. This one sat on top of a hillock, so it had wide steps leading from the parking lot to the front doors. Terraced planters filled with flora getting ready to bloom framed the steps. A ramp for handicap access rose behind the planters on the right.

About half of the sixty or so spaces in the parking lot were occupied, and nearly half of *those* spaces were held by minivans and family-size SUVs. More likely here for story time than the signing. Still, the book talk wasn't scheduled to begin for another thirty minutes, leaving plenty of time for more to arrive. It didn't seem all that unreasonable to anticipate a respectably-sized crowd. Feeling optimistic, Dale decided to lug both boxes of books inside for the sale table.

Another look at the stairs leading to the library doors gave him pause. Maybe just one box.

No, both boxes. That's what ibuprofen was for.

Dale's gaze landed on a group of five men as they made their way across the parking lot and trudged up the ramp. Three were clearly older and two, younger, but they all looked like they'd seen better days. All five of the men were homeless, Dale guessed, and judging by the ease with which they bore their burdens, they had been for some time. One of the older men towered over the others. He walked in the middle of the group, supporting the shortest of the men, the one who shuffled more than walked. Injured, perhaps, or ill? Or maybe his age and lifestyle were catching up with him. No one who lived on the streets ever looked young. Even children looked older than their years. The fifth man in the procession, the one bringing up the rear, looked to be about the same age as the really tall man. His posture was hunched, as if he carried the heaviest burden of all of them, even though he carried no bags.

Dale turned his attention back to the two younger men at the head of the group. Both carried overstuffed bags on their backs and shoulders and moved with more spring in their step than the others. One of the young men was white; the other, Latino—maybe.

The Latino man bounced as he walked, clearly worked up about something. He turned around and shot a verbal volley at the men behind. The short man mustered some vinegar and shot back.

Something tickled in the back of Dale's memory. Did he know that young man?

Dale stared with more focus, squinting to make up for the glasses he refused to wear. The young Caucasian man looked familiar, too—something about his tousled blond hair and farm-boy looks—but Dale couldn't concretely place either face.

Oh, well. He'd find out soon enough. A group like that shouldn't be too hard to find in such a small building. Dale kicked the car door shut and started to push the alarm button on the key fob, pulling his thumb back at the last minute. *You still have to get the books out of the back, dummy.*

Gripping the box with white knuckles, Dale gave a prayer of thanks for the library's automatic doors and the duct tape holding the box bottom together. Then another small prayer for patience when he noticed the librarian barreling down on him, parting the crowd like Moses and the Red Sea. She was of average height, middle-aged, with her hair in a ponytail at the base of her neck. She was dressed in a floral skirt and sweater, but she could have been in military uniform, the way she moved with the posture and bearing of a four-star general. There was no question. This was *her* library.

The general held out her hand, her expression polite but friendly. "Mr. Dale! I'm Hilda Kiernan, head librarian. Welcome to Sherwood."

Dale shifted the box so he could accept the handshake. A few books tumbled out and skidded across the carpet. In trying to catch them, he almost dropped the whole box. The wobble didn't escape Hilda Kiernan's notice.

With a nod and a wave, she summoned one of her

minions, a young woman not long out of college. "Let's get Mr. Dale a rolling cart for his books." She picked up the fallen copies and handed them to her young colleague. Then she turned to Dale and gestured at the box. "Is that it? Or do you have more in your car?"

Before he could answer, she continued directing the poor junior librarian. "Get whatever he has in his car, too. Bring it all to the large meeting room downstairs." She pulled the box out of Dale's hands and laid it on the floor before guiding him to the stairwell. "You don't mind if we take the stairs, do you?"

Dale watched in wonder. The woman must have been a logistics officer in a previous life. He couldn't help but imagine how much more successful his book tour would be if she were running it. Meanwhile, Kiernan chattered on as she led Dale down the carpeted steps. "I can't tell you how pleased we are to have you here. A war hero in our little town!"

Dale grimaced. "Ma'am, with all due respect, I'm not a hero. The young men and women in uniform are the heroes. I'm sure your town has its fair share. I just have the privilege of telling a few of their stories."

"Of course, of course. Well, you know what I mean." With a flourish, she pulled open a set of double doors. "Here we are."

About twenty-five chairs lined up in rows filled the space. A single folding chair behind two long white tables graced the front of the room. A barstool and microphone stood off to the side. The institutional gray walls were spared of any decoration. Just inside the doorway, an easel announced Dale's visit. In one smooth motion, Kiernan lifted the easel and placed it outside the room, facing the stairwell they'd just descended.

"What do you think?" she asked.

Dale surveyed the room. "It's perfect. Thank you."

With a *ding* of the elevator, the junior librarian arrived with the rolling cart and the box of books. Dale hauled the box off the cart and carried it to the front tables. Returning to the women, he said with a practiced smile, "Would it be possible to get some water too? My voice doesn't hold up as well as it used to."

"Of course," Hilda Kiernan said, an expression of self-chastisement washing over her face.

Dale turned to the woman's younger colleague. "Let's get the rest of the loot from my car."

Thirty minutes later, the room was fully staged—books stacked, thin-tipped markers laid out, cashbox set up—and the first guests trickled in. By the time Kiernan stepped up to the microphone to introduce Allan Dale, the room was almost half full. Not the biggest crowd Dale had ever drawn, but not the smallest either. He estimated he'd sell five or six books at most. So much for needing that second box.

Dale thanked Kiernan for the introduction and turned to the crowd. The five men he'd seen outside slipped into the back row. The pieces of Dale's memory slid into place.

Fallujah. The firefight. The dead boy. In a flash, the memory sprung to life. The shouting of orders. The flashes of muzzle fire. The relentless *rat-a-tat-tat* of the guns. The explosions. The smoke. The screaming.

Dear God, the screaming.

The echoes after the shooting stopped. Then the silence. The heavy silence born of shock. The boy—no more than eight or nine—lying on the ground like a discarded rag doll. His mother, tearing from her hiding place and throwing herself on her son's body, screaming curses in a language Dale didn't speak. At that moment, though, Dale understood her perfectly. The blood drained from the face of the young blond Marine beside him, his eyes wide with guilt.

The young blond Marine who now sat with his buddies in the back of this room in Sherwood, Illinois.

Sherwood, Illinois.

Dale blinked. How long had he spaced out? Long enough for the audience to stare at him blankly. Damn it.

Dale cleared his throat and gave the crowd an embarrassed smile. "Sorry about that. Where was I? Oh, yes. I fell into war correspondence by accident. In college, I dreamed of becoming a muckraker, following in the footsteps of Lincoln Steffens and Ida B. Wells, becoming the next Woodward and Bernstein. How that got me to the mountains of Afghanistan and the deserts of Iraq, I'm still not entirely sure. But it changed my life forever."

Dale continued with his rote autobiography, not taking his eyes off the men in the last row. He flipped open his book, the spine broken from so much use that the pages always fell open to this spot, and recited from memory the excerpt he always shared at these readings.

The signings went by in a blur: *Who do I make this out to? Best wishes, Allan A. Dale. Yes, of course I was scared. Thank you for coming.* Again and again. Ten books later, the room was empty except for Dale, Hilda Kiernan, and the men who still sat in the back row.

Dale dismissed Hilda with a handshake. "If you don't mind, I need a minute with these gentlemen. Then you can have your room back."

The librarian pursed her lips but nodded before making a hasty exit.

Once she was gone, Dale wiped his hands on his pants and approached the men, going to the young blond first. "Mitchell . . . No, Much, isn't it? Good to see you, son."

Much, in his usual quiet fashion, nodded but said nothing. Dale could see tears in the young man's eyes. It seemed he hadn't forgotten the dead boy, either.

Dale turned to Much's companion. "And Rojo. How are you, man?"

Rojo greeted Dale with a bro-hug and a slap on the back. "Good to see ya. Making millions off our exploits, are ya?"

Dale grinned. "Pennies, my friend, mere pennies. And every cent goes to veterans' charities."

"See? What'd we tell you?" Rojo said to the rest of the group. "Allan Dale always puts the men first."

"Speaking of men . . .?" Dale prompted.

Rojo made the introductions, and Dale shook each man's hand. "Good to meet you all. Tell you what. Is there a donut shop or a coffee place around here? I'd like to buy you all a cup."

The men exchanged glances. "Funny you should ask," Rojo said. "I never took you for a lawbreaker."

Dale raised his eyebrow. "Coffee's a crime in Sherwood?"

"Only if you buy it for the homeless," Much mumbled.

"What? What kind of town is this?"

"The town council passed a law making it a crime to provide food or drink to the homeless. Our friend Bernie was arrested and lost his job because of it," Rojo explained. "That's actually why we came to see you. We were hoping you could help."

A spark lit in Dale's mind, one he hadn't felt since his VA investigation ended. Same for the energy that rushed into his muscles. He smiled. "Let's live dangerously. Why don't I buy you that coffee and you can tell me all about it?"

CHAPTER TWENTY-SEVEN

Dale held his coffee cup aloft. "To your health!"

"To your health!" The Merry Men responded in chorus, lifting their own cups.

Everyone took long a swig and sighed with contentment.

"So," Dale said, "who's going to give me the grand tour?"

"Reverend Tucker," Much answered first, without hesitation or a glance at his comrades. "He knows the community better than anyone."

Instead of taking the expected offense, Hood approved the suggestion. "I been living rough the longest, but Much is right. Tuck's the man with the connections."

Tuck blinked. Those words were the most praise Hood had ever given him, and they were practically effusive by Hood's standards. "Thanks, man," he said in soft wonder.

Rojo slapped Tuck's knee. "C'mon, Rev, don't be modest. No one does more to help us than you. If it weren't for you, Sherwood wouldn't have a shelter—"

"Sherwood *doesn't* have a shelter, Red. Not anymore. If it did, I wouldn't be living on the streets with you."

It was hard to miss the surprise on Dale's face.

"The shelter hit a rough patch," Tuck explained. "I

gave up my apartment and moved into my office. Used my rent money to try to get the shelter through. Only it wasn't enough." Tuck spoke the last words to the floor. No matter how much he wanted or willed it, he couldn't look his mates in the eye. Not after he failed them and their community like he had.

It was everyone else's turn to look surprised. They all spoke at once.

"When did that happen?" John asked.

"So *that's* why you've been bunking with us," Rojo said.

"Why didn't you say anything?" Much asked.

Tuck started with John. "About a month ago, when that building inspector cited us, I couldn't afford the repairs he wanted otherwise—even with insurance."

Next, he addressed Rojo. "Why'd you *think* I'd been bunking with you? For my health?"

Rojo pointed his thumb at Much. "We thought you felt guilty about having a roof when your shelter residents didn't."

Tuck pursed his lips. "You're not entirely wrong, but I wish that's all it was."

He turned to Much. "And what would I say? There was nothing you could do. Turns out, there was nothing I could do, either."

Hood's dam broke. He slapped his leg and stood. "What is wrong with you, man? We're brothers. We got each other's backs. Or have you forgotten?"

Tuck flew to his feet. "This from the man who does everything he can to avoid setting foot in my shelter. The man who would rather barter his dignity than consider sleeping under my roof. The man who views my every invitation as an insult. How is that brotherly, my *brother*?"

Dale looked to Much and Rojo for an explanation, but both men bowed their heads and bit their lips. He looked to John, who shook his head.

Tuck agreed. It was time to have this out. His stare dared Hood to respond.

Hood stepped up, into Tuck's space. "You made it very clear that my kind wasn't welcome under your roof."

"Your *kind*?"

"Drinkers. Dopers. Smokers. Tokers."

Tuck threw up his hands. "That had nothing to do with you. That's an insurance rule. One I happily broke whenever you deigned to cross my threshold."

"How magnanimous of you. But if everyone ain't welcome, I ain't welcome." He softened his posture just a bit. "Besides, you know I'm not cut out for life under a roof."

"How do I know it?" Even as Tuck spoke the words, he knew Hood was right. That's why, when he did come to the shelter, he slept by the back door. He just wasn't built for life inside four walls, hadn't been for years. He'd spent a decade cycling through mechanic jobs and rented rooms and firings and evictions until no one was willing to give him another chance—not even Hood himself. Now the walls of a motel room were enough to drive him to drink to beyond-normal excesses. But Tuck couldn't take his words back.

For a split second, Hood's bravado cracked, something like pain or guilt filling his eyes, then Tuck watched the fissures seal over again.

"Naw, I'm not doing this." With a wave, Hood dismissed Tuck and stomped away, the stares of his men and Dale following him out the door.

Tuck fell back into his seat. "Stubborn bastard."

John grunted in agreement.

Dale took another swig of coffee. "Is there always this much drama with you lot?"

Rojo took a long gulp from his cup. "What drama? This is just an ordinary Saturday."

Much chuckled and soon the other Merry Men followed suit. Dale shook his head, but Tuck interpreted the gesture as one of appreciation rather than disapproval.

Dale leaned forward. "So about your friend, I noticed a rather large bruise on his arm, near the crease of his elbow. What was that about?"

The four Merry Men traded looks before John finally said, "That's from the IV. He was in the hospital for a while."

"Anything serious?"

"If it wasn't serious, he wouldn't have been in the hospital." Rojo's words overflowed with snark.

"Point taken. But he's okay now?"

John answered. "He's as okay as he'll ever get."

Dale nodded and the group sat in companionable silence while they finished their drinks.

With the paperboard cups tossed in the trash, Dale placed his hand on Tuck's shoulder. "Now, how about that tour?"

John took one look at Dale's car and begged off, refusing to fold his gargantuan self into such a tiny vehicle. So while Not-So-Little John went off in search of Hood, the other Merry Men clambered into the clown car and led Allan Dale on a tour of homelessness in Sherwood, Illinois.

Their first stop was the House & Home parking lot, where Much and Rojo tripped on their seat belts and tumbled out of the car. With the boys sprawled on the ground, Tuck slammed the car door shut. "Sometimes I wonder how you boys ever made it home."

With both boys standing and brushed off, Tuck explained that many homeless families—those with cars, at least—often slept here in this parking lot. The store let them park their cars overnight and had a security guard on the premises in case of emergency.

Meanwhile, a House & Home employee—a young man in the standard purple apron uniform—sauntered over. Offering his hand to Rojo and then Much, he said that he'd seen them among the day laborers and asked if they were looking for work.

"What'd you have in mind?" Rojo asked.

"My girlfriend and I are moving. We could use some extra hands."

Something didn't feel right to Tuck, but he couldn't pinpoint what. Hiding in the shelter for so long had dulled his radar. Too bad Hood wasn't here. He'd have known lickety split. Tuck shifted his weight and cleared his throat.

Rojo must have heard alarm bells, too. His voice took on a sharp edge. "What? You don't have friends to do that for you?"

"What can I say?" The young man shrugged and flashed a shallow smile. "We have a lot of shit."

Rojo grimaced and shook his head. "Sorry, man. Can't do it. Good luck, though." He reached for a handshake, but the young man walked off with nothing more than a "whatever" and something about being grateful.

"That happen a lot?" Dale asked.

"Not this time of year," Much explained. "I mean, yeah, we pick up work here. Day labor stuff. Usually seasonal work. Moving jobs are normally summer work. This time of year, we generally get asked to help folks get ready for spring. Removing storm windows, laying mulch—that sort of thing. In the fall, it's raking leaves, resealing windows, hanging storm windows. We don't get as much work in winter, but occasionally someone will hire us to do some shoveling."

Dale looked impressed. "I think that's the most I ever heard you say in one go," he said with a smile. "Thanks."

Instead of acknowledging Dale's comment, Much turned to Tuck. "We should take him to the shelter."

The shelter. The debris of Tuck's life. The monument to his failure. Tuck closed his eyes and sighed. He let his shoulders fall. Maybe he could just send the boys over there with Dale. Then he wouldn't have to face it.

No, that wouldn't be fair. The boys couldn't explain the shelter, make Dale see that it was a living, breathing being just like the people who depended on it. That was up to him. He dug in his pocket and found the one key he'd saved.

"Let's go."

The four of them piled into Dale's rental. Dale

drove, Tuck navigated, Much and Rojo provided color commentary. They pointed out the alley that the Merry Men once called home and the padlock that still barred them from their sleeping quarters. They pointed out the Chicken Shack and told the story of Bernie's arrest. They described Sadie and pointed out her bus stop. They explained how the wide flat benches that Sadie and others used to sleep on had been removed and replaced with the uncomfortable narrow angled ones. They pointed out the thrift shop where they—and many others in the community— bought the blankets and jackets that kept them warm. They pointed out the motel where they holed up during the blizzard. That story led to the story of Hood's beating at the highway on-ramp, of being rescued by John, of being forced into the hospital— almost restrained to his bed—so he could get proper treatment. By the time Rojo finished his Hood impression, everyone was convulsed with laughter.

Dale wiped the tears from his eyes, his serious expression returning. "So that IV bruise? That's what it's from?"

"Yup," Rojo answered.

"You said the attack was caught on video?"

"Yeah," Rojo said. "They even showed it on the news. Not that it made a difference. That bastard cop is still on the job. Hell, they just made him acting chief."

Tuck knew by the way Dale squared his jaw that their new friend would be watching the video. Not only watching it, but writing about it, reporting on it.

"Here," Tuck said, pointing to the driveway of the abandoned shelter parking lot. Maybe it was his imagination, but the place looked more desolate than he'd ever seen it. Those weeds sprouting in pavement cracks—had they always been there? And when did the building get so dingy? Had it always looked that gray? Tuck's stomach fell farther with each noticed detail.

Dale stopped catty-corner across two spaces.

"No," Tuck said. "Pull around back. It's better if we're not seen."

Without so much as a questioning glance, Dale put the car back in gear and drove to the rear of the building, stopping near the shelter's back door. Much and Rojo tumbled out from the back seat after him. This time they landed on their feet.

Tuck clicked his seatbelt loose. With his hand on the door, he closed his eyes and took a deep breath. *Pull it together, Tucker. You can do this.* Tuck blew out another deep breath and stepped out of the car.

Avoiding eye contact with his companions, he shuffled to the shelter entrance, turned the key in the lock, and popped open the door. Only after the door swung open did he wonder why the rear entrance had never been padlocked like the front. Well, thank goodness for the ineptitude of local law enforcement.

He stood aside as Dale and the boys slipped past him.

"What the hell happened here?" Rojo's voice carried from the office. "They couldn't just lock up the place, the *pendejos* had to trash it first."

With a sigh, Tuck joined them. His voice was soft and meek. "Actually, that was me."

Rojo whistled and slapped him on the shoulder.

"Wow, Rev, I didn't know you had that in you. Color me impressed."

Leave it to Rojo to be impressed with an outburst of anger. Not much of a surprise, though, given Rojo's own affinity for the emotion.

Tuck followed them to the kitchen, where Much made a beeline for the refrigerator and Rojo headed straight for the pantry. Both were disappointed at the emptiness. "I gave it away," Tuck explained. "Distributed to those who slept in the parking lots that first night."

"What are we? Used tissues?" Rojo asked.

"Of course not. You—the four of you—are the most self-reliant people I've ever met. You know how to feed yourselves. The families sleeping in cars, the ones who depend on me and this shelter for warmth and a meal, not so much."

"He's right," Much admitted. He turned to Dale. "C'mon," he said with a wave. "We'll show you the rest."

Much led them on the tour. Tuck narrated—the hundreds of men, women, and children who'd walked these halls; the annual financial struggles and recent crisis; the unflagging work of Mary Ann, Patricia, and the other volunteers . . .

Dale stopped him. "The mayor's *wife* works here?"

"More than that," Rojo said, with a skip in his step. "She's Hood's ex-girlfriend. I think she still has a thing for him."

"No one asked you," Tuck snapped.

Much entered the family dormitory. A moment later, he returned to the hall, dangling a well-worn teddy bear from his fingers.

Tuck couldn't stop the whimper from escaping his lips. He reached for the toy. "That's little Jenny's. She could never sleep without it."

Dale pulled a spiral notebook and pen from his back pocket. "Where is she now?"

"I have no idea."

CHAPTER TWENTY-EIGHT

The men regrouped in the kitchen. Much leaned against the counter, cradling Jenny's teddy bear, while Rojo dug through the shelves, his voice echoing as he called, "There's got to be *something* to eat in here."

Tuck rolled his eyes and shook his head. "Trust me, Red. The cupboards are bare. And if they aren't, whatever you find wouldn't be fit for human consumption."

"Maybe I'm not human," came the answer from deep in the pantry.

Much snuggled his face into the teddy bear's belly, his voice muffled by the toy's plush fur. "None of us are. We're like animals." He sniffed before dropping the bear on the countertop. "No, worse. People actually care about animals."

Tuck swallowed a lump. "I know it doesn't always seem like it, kid, but people do care."

Much shook his head.

"Mary Ann Gibson isn't a person? She doesn't count? What about Bernie? Do you think he gave you all that Chicken Shack food because he hated you?"

Much looked at the floor, rubbing his shoe against the worn linoleum.

Dale put a hand on Much's shoulder. "I care too. And it's my job to make other people care. So, tell me what I need to know."

Rojo danced backward a few steps as he extricated himself from a bottom cupboard. "What's left to tell? The mayor hates us and is doing everything he can to get rid of us."

"Not just us," Much added. "Our friends and everyone we try to help, too."

Dale set his notebook on the butcher block, his pen poised above it. "So let's start at the beginning. How did you two end up on the street? How'd you meet the reverend?"

Rojo and Much tag-teamed their stories. Rojo had gone home to Chicago; Much, to his family farm in western Illinois. Both struggled to adjust to civilian life. They met regularly here in Sherwood, the halfway point between their family homes, to drink, reminisce, and commiserate. Rojo grew tired of the anguish on his mother's face, her worry over him and his struggles to adapt. Much, after his grandfather died, felt snowed under by his sister's expectations and frustrations. One night after drinks, the boys just didn't go home. Rojo had reached here by train, so they slept in Much's truck for a time, until they ran out of gas money. They abandoned it on the road where it died, pushing it onto the shoulder and walking away with their meager possessions on their backs. A few weeks later, they found their way to Tuck and the shelter. Tuck introduced them to Hood and John. "The rest, as they say," Rojo said with a bow, "is history."

Dale turned his focus to Tuck. "Your turn. Tell me again about the shelter—how it started, why you started it. Then work your way forward to where things are today."

Tuck started a bit earlier in his story, explaining how his postwar crisis of faith led him to the church and his vows. Eventually, he got to the story of the girl who froze to death on the church steps. Much and Rojo stood with wide eyes and slack jaws. It was clear this story was new to them.

"What was her name?" Much asked.

Tuck blinked back tears. "Not a clue."

Dale scribbled something along the edge of his notes.

No one interrupted as Tuck told the rest of the story, not even to add two more cents about recent events.

"So what have you done to get the shelter back?" Dale asked when Tuck had finished.

Tuck pulled a folded yellow page out of his back pocket and slid it toward Dale. "Until I can afford the remainder of these repairs and renovations, and this place can pass a city inspection, there's nothing I can do."

Rojo perked up. "City inspection? Rev, did it ever occur to you that you might have been set up?"

Dale and Tuck turned to face Rojo.

"C'mon. A *city* inspection?" Rojo paced, waving his arms as he talked. "In a city run by a mayor with a grudge against Hood and that fat cat Kingston's hand up his ass? In a city with a town council determined to criminalize homelessness? That never struck you as the least bit fishy?"

"No." Tuck sounded as baffled as he looked. "Harris—the inspector—was totally legit. There's nothing on that list that he made up or imagined. I mean, yes, Mayor Gibson carries some sort of grudge against Rob and yes, that animosity is heated and mutual. But you've never seen Gibson and Mary Ann together; I have. He loves her, and he knows how much she loves this place. He would never hurt her by taking it away from her."

Rojo stopped, his lips pursed as he considered Tuck's point. A moment later, he snorted. "You sure?"

Tuck let out a long breath. "Honestly, Red, I'm not sure of anything these days."

Dale, meanwhile, flipped the page in his notebook and scribbled more notes. He flipped to another page and put down his pen. "All right, tell me what you know about how foreclosures work."

Tuck shrugged. "You stop paying your mortgage. The bank sends you letters and notices, and then they take your house. It's how a good portion of the shelter's residents—former residents—ended up here.

"You do know this isn't a foreclosure, right? This is an eviction. They're not the same thing."

Dale blew out his breath. "My point is, there's a legal process that must be followed. It's not simply here's-a-notice-goodbye. It's —"

"But that's what happened." Tuck dropped his arms, his voice at once disbelieving and insistent. "Two Nottingham County sheriff's deputies showed up with the notice, chains, and padlocks and told us to get the heck out."

Dale knitted his brow and shook his head. "No, that's not how it's supposed to work. There's a whole legal process that's supposed to be followed—summonses and complaints and other legal notices. You have rights, Reverend."

Rojo punched the air. "See? I knew this didn't smell right."

Dale flipped his notebook shut and fastened his pen onto its cover. "Let me get my laptop. We can look up the details. Start searching for a lawyer."

Much grinned, his grin dissolving into a giggle. Looking at Rojo, he gasped, in his best Hood impression, "Lah-yer."

Rojo and Tuck chuckled, the latter slapping Much on the back. "That's not bad, kid."

On the outside of what was clearly an in-joke, Dale shook his head and started for the back door, freezing at the squeak of brakes in the back alley. Glancing over his shoulder, he saw the others just as stiff and silent and looking at him for direction.

A car door slammed shut.

Motioning for them to stay put, he tiptoed down the hall. Pushing the door open a crack, he saw a police car and a uniformed officer standing behind Dale's rental, seemingly writing the plate number in his notebook.

Dale glanced back down the hall, saw the three men peering at him around the kitchen doorjamb, and inhaled deeply. He pushed the door open. "Can I help you, Officer?"

"This your car?" The officer stared at Dale through dark-tinted sunglasses, a bigger cliché than Dale had seen in . . . longer than he could remember.

"It's my rental, yes. Is there something wrong, Officer—" Dale squinted at the officer's name tag. "Dubrowski?"

Behind him, one of the Merry Men cursed.

"You're trespassing, Mister—?"

"Dale. Allan Dale. I'm a reporter. Maybe you've heard of me?"

Dubrowski grimaced. "I'll need to see some ID."

Dale dug his wallet out of his back pocket and slid out his driver's license.

Dubrowski snapped it up. He studied the license, comparing the card with Dale's face, and scribbled in his notebook before handing the license back. "As I said, Mr. Dale, you're trespassing."

"I don't see how. I have Reverend Tucker's permission to be here." He felt a small bump against his foot. Jenny's teddy bear, slid down the hall by Much. Dale picked it up and showed Dubrowski. "Collecting some possessions that were accidentally left behind."

"You're trespassing. Your friend the reverend and his riffraff have been evicted. This building belongs to the city. At least, it does until next month's auction."

Auction? Nothing about that sounded right, but Dale bit his tongue. "That's too bad. Reverend Tucker did good work." He held up the bear. "At any rate, I got what I came for, so I'll be on my way." He stepped forward and waved at Dubrowski's car. "If you don't mind."

Dubrowski didn't move. As far as Dale could tell, he didn't even blink. He just stared through those darkened sunglasses. A civilian might be cowed by Dubrowski. Hell, Dubrowski himself probably thought he was the epitome of intimidation. He certainly fit the stereotype. But this suburban police officer was nothing compared to the warlords and military men Dale had faced down in war zones.

Dale stepped closer, his height giving him a couple of inches on Dubrowski—enough that he had to look down to make eye contact. "Excuse me, Officer. I'd like to obey your order and vacate the premises, but to do that, I need you to get out of my way."

Dubrowski stood stock still for a ten-count before stepping out of the way, gesturing at Dale's rental with exaggerated magnanimity. What a prick.

Dale forced himself to smile. "Thank you, Officer."

With Dubrowski watching, Dale unlocked the car, threw the teddy bear onto the front passenger seat, and folded himself into the driver's seat. Behind the officer, the shelter door slowly opened. Tuck, Rojo, and Much slid out, pressing themselves against the wall.

Dale flooded the engine and shook his head as the car sputtered and coughed. The three Merry Men moved along the far end of the building while Dale turned the ignition again. Again, the car sputtered. He rolled down the window. "Sorry, Officer. They don't make these babies like they used to. I'll be out of here as soon as I get her going."

Dubrowski leaned against his own car and crossed his arms. "I'll wait."

Behind him, the Merry Men ducked around the corner of the building.

"It's your funeral." Dale shrugged. He turned the key again and the engine groaned to life. With a wave, Dale steered the car toward the street. In the rearview mirror, he saw Dubrowski grab his radio. By the time Dale disappeared around the building to pick up the others, the cop's car had roared to life.

CHAPTER TWENTY-NINE

Tuck, Rojo, and Much were crowded in the back of Dale's rental coffin, traveling north on Yorkshire Road, one more vehicle migrating with the evening commute. Out the windows on the left, the sun slid toward the horizon. Much—squeezed between the other two—kept glancing over his shoulder, unable to stop himself from looking for Dubrowski's car. Rojo's fingers danced on his knees, tapping out an anxious rhythm. Tuck sat still and stoic, but whether he was in shock or simply lost in thought, Much couldn't tell.

The reverend's cell phone rang, a snippet of that Hallelujah song. Maneuvering to get the phone out of his pocket, Tuck banged his head on the roof—and cursed. He managed to slide the phone out using two fingers but then bobbled it.

Much pursed his lips, but that wasn't enough to stop a giggle from escaping. Rojo tried to resist. He really did. But between the clumsy reverend and Much's giggle, he couldn't help himself. It wasn't long before he and Much were doubled over with laughter. Tears in his eyes, Rojo caught Dale's expression in the mirror. Even the journo was smiling.

Tuck seemed immune to the fun. With exaggerated concentration, he studied the display and shook his head. He pushed the answer button. "Hello? This is Reverend Tucker."

Whoever had called sounded like a male version of Charlie Brown's teacher. Rojo couldn't make out a single word, but the tone seemed friendly enough.

"We're just leaving the shelter. Where are you? Whose phone are you using?" Tuck paused to listen and then his voice rose at least two octaves. "What?! Where?"

Rojo and Much snapped to attention.

"We're on our way." Tuck, his self-assurance restored, turned to Dale. "That was John. He's at the House & Home. Something's going down."

Dale fed the accelerator. Rojo and Much leaned forward as Dale weaved through traffic.

"What is it, Rev?" Much asked.

"Don't know. John just said to get there lickety split."

Rojo coughed. "Lickety split?"

"PDQ, Red. PDQ."

Rojo rolled his eyes. "I know what it means, Rev. I just can't picture John saying it."

Tuck's eyes narrowed. "I was paraphrasing."

Rojo held up his hands in surrender—apparently, it was not a time for jokes—and sat back in his seat.

"What's going on?" Much asked.

Tuck shook his head. "He only said something was going down and that we needed to get over there." Tuck gave Dale's seat a gentle punch. "He said for you bring your camera."

Dale, his attention on the road, nodded. He took one hand off the wheel and patted the cell phone in his jacket's ticket pocket. "Right here."

The foursome were silent the rest of the drive, but not comfortable. The hair on Rojo's arms stood up.

Adrenaline rolled through his limbs, arms first, then legs. He tapped his feet to let a little bit of it out.

He glanced over at Much. The farm boy fidgeted with his fingers, touching them to his thumbs one at time, index to pinky, pinky to index. His lips moved, but Rojo couldn't make out the words. was gearing himself up for battle.

Rojo looked out his window, watching Sherwood pass by as they made their way up Yorkshire Road.

It had to be Hood. He should still be at the hospital. Everyone knew it, but no one wanted to say it. Brick walls were more receptive than their fearless leader.

By the time Dale steered onto the frontage road that led to House & Home, Rojo knew exactly what they were going to find: Hood collapsed on the pavement, John standing guard over him.

So what was with all the cop cars?

It looked like the entire City of Sherwood Police Department had been called out. Rojo counted four— no, five—cars. Much spotted two more. Then, as if on cue, Officer Dubrowski roared past them with lights flashing.

Where the hell were John and Hood?

Dale flipped on the car's turn signal, ready to make the left that would bring them to the line of parked police cars.

"Maybe we should go the back way," Tuck said. "Just in case."

"Good idea." Dale swung out of the turn lane and drove up and around the block. He eased the car into the service driveway, angling the car to a stop behind the mammoth House & Home building.

They exited the vehicle in silence, closing the car doors as softly as possible. A tangle of voices and car doors and banging on metal carried from the front parking lot. With Rojo in the lead and Dale bringing up the rear, the four men crept along the side of the building, stopping when Rojo held up his fist.

The others waited, pressed against the concrete wall, while Rojo surveyed the situation. Police officers walked up and down the parking lot, pounding on cars. Rojo recognized a few of them. The brown station wagon. The blue Explorer. The gray Honda. They belonged to former residents of Tuck's shelter.

Something to Rojo's right moved. The security guard. He stood close to the building, in the light by the now-locked entrance, shifting from foot to foot despite being bundled up against the cold. Ordinarily, his job consisted of unlocking the front doors so that those sleeping in the parking lot could use the bathroom. Tonight, he seemed completely out of his element. With a wave and a low whistle, Rojo called him over.

"What's going on?" Rojo kept his voice soft, just above a whisper.

The guard, Rick according to his name tag, pulled a folded piece of paper from his pocket. A child's wail echoed across the parking lot as he handed it over.

Rojo unfolded the page and angled it toward the light. He read it three times, but the words still didn't make sense. Why couldn't they write these things in simple English? It was an order, the legal kind. That much he could tell. The rest sounded like gibberish. Where the hell was John to translate?

Rojo studied it again. Lots of *herebys* and *therefores,*

as if lawyers got paid by the syllable instead of the hour. "Shall be prohibited"—he understood that. The mayor and his cronies had made something else illegal in Sherwood. Big surprise.

Rojo handed the paper to Tuck. The Rev had more schooling than anyone else he knew. If anyone could decipher the words, Reverend Tucker could. "What does this mean?"

Tuck scanned it, a crease forming on his forehead as his eyes moved down the page. He handed the paper back and shrugged. "I have no idea. They didn't teach Legalese at seminary. But whatever it says, it means these people can't park here overnight anymore."

Security Guard Rick nodded. "That's what the cops said."

Rojo surveyed the parking lot scene. Uniforms going door to door—how often had he done that in the Corps? All those times: were they as wrong as this one felt? Funny how he never questioned it back then.

"Where are we supposed to go?" a woman asked, her voice breaking with desperation.

Focus, Red.

"A couple of our friends called us here." Rojo scanned the scene again as he spoke. "One tall; one short, angry, and sick. You seen them?"

Rick shook his head. "I'll find them for you."

Rojo patted the guard's shoulder and slunk back to the others. He handed the paper to Dale. "What the hell does this say?"

Dale skimmed it, the creases in his brow deepening the farther he got down the page. "It's an executive order from the mayor of Sherwood. Makes it illegal to sleep in non-residential zoned areas. Like commercial parking lots."

"Or back alleys of strip malls," Rojo said, his hands forming fists.

"Or bus stops," Tuck added.

Dale handed back the paper. "Yep."

"So?" Much's voice was heavy with confusion and worry.

Dale put his hand on Much's shoulder. "This is an evacuation, son. A forced evacuation."

Much's eyes filled with panic. He turned to Tuck. "We have to do something."

"Damn straight." Tuck zipped his jacket to his neck and marched toward the fray.

Rojo and Much shared a stunned look and then chased after him. "Rev!" Rojo called. "Wait up!"

Rojo heard Dale's footsteps behind him, catching up. None of them were fast enough to stop Tuck.

"What do you think you're doing?" Tuck stood inches in front of a police officer, barely enough room between them for the Holy Ghost. "Where's your heart? Have you no compassion?"

"I'm going to have to ask you to step back, sir." The cop's voice was calm but far from casual. It set Rojo's nerves on fire. Dubrowski, the mayor's lapdog. Again.

Tuck started forward. Dale yanked him back and slid in front of the officer, holding out his hand. "Officer Dubrowski. Allan Dale, remember? We met earlier today."

The officer hooked his thumbs in his belt and rocked back on his heels. Smug bastard.

Dale dropped his hand, but kept his voice

conversational. "As you may recall, I'm a reporter. Care to fill me on the evening's events?"

"Just doing our job." Dubrowski matched Dale's tone.

"And what job is that?"

"The department press officer will be able to give you any information you need. Now, I need to get back to work, and you need to step back."

Dale grabbed the executive order from Rojo and waved it at Dubrowski. "What can you tell me about this order? Does it have anything to do with what you're doing here?"

"I said, you need to speak with the department press officer." Dubroswki turned away.

Dale stayed on the cop's heels, holding his phone in front of him. Rojo hoped he was recording every word of his encounter with Sherwood's Finest.

A loud *thud* made the three men spin around. Tuck, Rojo, and Much followed the sound to an old Dodge Challenger.

"You can't make me go anywhere. I got rights." A man—not young, but probably younger than he looked—stood squared off with an officer. This cop was younger, shorter, and slimmer than Dubrowski but exuded the same authority, an authority the man didn't have any hesitation challenging.

"I know him," Tuck whispered. "That's Jake. He's a regular."

"Try that again," the cop said, "and I'll arrest you for assaulting a police officer."

Jake stepped closer. "I dare you." With a growl, he pushed the cop.

"That's it." The officer grabbed Jake's arm and spun him around. "You have—"

"Officer!" Tuck stepped forward. "Surely we can solve this without an arrest. Isn't that right, Jake?"

Jake hesitated.

Tuck narrowed his eyes.

Jake grimaced. "Sure Rev. Anything you say."

"Sorry, sir." The officer almost sounded apologetic. "Once the cuffs are on, there's nothing I can do."

"Surely that's not true. Handcuffs can be unlocked as easily as they're locked. It's not like you've started any paperwork."

"Get out of my way, sir, or I'll arrest you too."

"For what? We're just having a conversation."

"For obstructing justice. Now get out of my way." The officer pushed Tuck.

Rojo launched himself at the officer, knocking the cop and Jake to the ground. He heard shouts, recognized Tuck's and Much's voices, but all he saw was red. No one touched Reverend Tucker. No better man walked the earth. No one did more to help his fellow man. Lay a hand on the good reverend, and a beat-down was in order.

The cop landed a punch. Rojo flinched and punched back. More punches. More wrestling. Rojo saw fists, not faces. He heard voices but couldn't make out the words. Then someone grabbed Rojo's collar and yanked him to his feet.

"That's enough, Red. We don't need any more trouble." John. When did he get here? Where was Hood?

Rojo blinked. Cops ran toward them from almost every direction.

Much tugged Rojo's sleeve. "C'mon, let's go!"

Rojo looked at Jake, still on the ground and wrestling with the officer who had cuffed him. He nodded. Rojo took off, following the others to Dale's car. He heard someone say something about living to fight another day. The way Rojo's hands itched, that day better come soon.

May

The Merry Men crowded into Allan Dale's motel room, a slightly more upscale version of the no-tell motel where they had spent much of the winter. One and a half stars compared to, say, half a star. Empty pizza boxes and soda cans littered the room, with one narrow path from the double bed to the bathroom the only clean place on the floor. The single bedside lamp cast a yellowish-orange light that made everyone look slightly jaundiced.

Dale sat cross-legged at the head of the bed, laptop perched on his knees, the Merry Men scattered on the bed and floor around him. Dale hit one final key on his keyboard and shut the computer. "That's it. I pitched your story to three of my favorite editors. I'm sure at least one of them will bite. For now, we wait."

"You really think that'll help?" Much asked.

Dale's nod exuded confidence. "I do. It's like I told you back the shelter, kid. People care. They'll read about what's going on in Sherwood, and they'll want to do something about it."

"Nobody did nuthin' about the VA," Hood shot back.

Dale conceded the point. "There was an outcry, but the wheels of government move slowly."

Hood grumbled.

Rojo balled his hands into fists. As he spoke, he

stared at the well-loved teddy bear in Much's hands. "That's all well and good. But in the meantime, we can't just sit here and do nothing."

It had been a week since the evacuation of the House & Home parking lot, and Sherwood police still patrolled local parking lots nightly, rousting homeless families with nowhere else to sleep but their cars. Some had left town already, but many were determined to stay until the school year finished, a small bit of stability for their kids. But no one had any illusions of sticking around once that last school bell rang.

The Merry Men did what they could to help friends like Sadie find safe harbor. They scouted locations, searching for hotel and apartment complex parking areas and church pop-up shelters where at least one night's undisturbed sleep might be grabbed. It was like trying to stop an avalanche with a skateboard. So many of Sherwood's homeless didn't have the luxury of a car to sleep in. Many didn't meet admission requirements for the church shelters. They didn't have a guardian angel like Allan Dale, either. How many of them now slept behind bars in the city jail?

"I'm with Red." Hood punctuated his comment with a swig from his flask—the flask Dale had refilled twice tonight. The swig was followed by a cough, something else that hadn't improved during the last couple of weeks. "Sitting on our asses isn't going to reopen the shelter." Another swig. Another cough. "Or get that bastard Gibson out of office."

"Gibson?" John called from his corner spot by the door. "What does he have to do with this?"

Hood swung around. "You think it's an accident this all happened on his watch? Who do you think signed that evacuation order? He and his executive orders stirred up this shit. He should be forced to lick the spoon."

"You think it's personal?" Dale asked.

"Naw, he'd have to see us people for it to be personal." Despite the hoarseness of his voice, there was power behind Hood's words.

"What about Mary Ann?" Tuck asked. "You go after Gibson, what's it going to do to her? Like it or not, she's his wife. You want to put her in the middle?"

Hood bowed his head. A slow blush creeped along his cheeks. Much shifted uncomfortably. So did Rojo. Mary Ann was a touchy subject.

It was John who answered. "With all due respect, Tuck, she already *is* in the middle, whether we want her to be or not."

Dale cleared his throat. "Taking down a politician, even one with a proven history of corruption—which this Gibson is not—is no easy task. Let's start small. Focus on one thing."

"What thing?" Rojo challenged.

"That's for you to decide."

Much held up the teddy bear. "The shelter," he said, in usual soft voice.

Rojo nodded vigorously. John nodded, too, but more slowly.

Tuck reached for the bear. He stroked the toy's head, ran his thumb along the seam on its back. He blinked back tears and nodded.

Hood looked up, at Much, at Rojo, at John, watched Tuck. "Yeah."

Dale flipped open his laptop again and started typing. "Okay. Let's see what I can find out."

He stopped talking and squinted at the screen. "What's today?"

"Sunday," Much answered.

"The eleventh," Tuck said at the same time. "Why?"

Dale slid his computer around so Tuck could see the screen. "Because the shelter building is being auctioned off in four days."

The color bled from Tuck's face as he read. "Kingston Enterprises is the likely buyer, who hopes to use the location for a new high-end condo development."

Rojo punched the wall, denting the sheetrock but not quite breaking through.

Hood hopped to his feet. He wobbled and reached for the wall to steady himself. "That's crap. They got no right to do that."

"I don't think so, either." Dale spun the computer back around and tapped some keys. "This hasn't felt kosher to me from the beginning. Rev, did you ever get in contact with a lawyer?"

Tuck shook his head. "I know I should have, but—"

Hood coughed and spat in the nearest pizza box. "Bullshit. Ain't no lawyer gonna stop this. The courts ain't on our side. Never have been. They take fucking forever, anyway. The shelter will be long gone by the time some judge decides it's worth saving. We gotta take care of this now, and we gotta do it ourselves."

Rojo jumped to his feet. "The boss is right."

"What did you have in mind?" John was standing

now, too, arms crossed, his frame blocking the door. Dale was tall, but John was taller—and bigger. Dale made a mental note to never get on the big man's bad side.

The room fell silent, everyone's eyes on Hood. Dale could hear the seconds ticking by. The numbers on the digital clock changed twice before Hood finally spoke.

"We take it back." His voice was calm and sure. Matter of fact. He might as well have been saying, "It's dark outside."

"Yeah." Rojo's voice begged for a fight.

John, Tuck, and Much, on the other hand, were more practical. "How?"

"What?" Hood said with familiar sarcasm. "I gotta come up with all the ideas around here?" He pushed Much aside and dropped onto the bed between the boy and Tuck. His raised eyebrows challenged his men to answer his question.

"The article say anything about the auction?" Rojo stepped away from the wall.

"Just date, time, and location," Dale answered. "And Kingston as the likely buyer."

Rojo's face lit up. "We blow up Kingston Enterprises."

Much rolled his eyes.

"Okay, genius." John stepped closer to the group. "Where are we going to get the explosives? How do you plan on paying for them? More importantly, how does that help the shelter? Kingston doesn't own it yet—the city does. You want to blow up that too?"

Tuck shook his head. "The problem with that is, you'd probably end up in jail."

Rojo shrugged. "So there are kinks in my plan. But it's a plan. And if we did end up in jail, we'd have a roof over our heads, three meals a day, and a pillow to lay our heads on. You got anything better?"

John leaned against the bathroom doorframe. "I'm with Tuck, Red. I'd prefer not to spend my life behind bars."

Dale raised a finger. "If I may?"

Hood ceded the floor with an open palm. "Be my guest."

Dale gave Rojo a pointed look. "Explosions are not the way to win hearts and minds. You need something that attracts attention and wins public support."

"Like that video of Hood getting the shit beaten out of him," Rojo said, with perhaps a bit too much enthusiasm.

Hood held up his hand. "Oh, hell no, boy. That horse is dead and gone." Dropping his hand, he dropped his voice too. "Besides, I don't recall there being much of a fuss the first time around."

The air in the room felt heavy and awkward. Hood was right. The video had aired on the news multiple times on several channels, but there had been no consequences, no public outcry. No charges had been filed. Dubrowski and his partner Benjamin still drove the streets. No one had come forward to pay Hood's hospital bills.

Dragging out that footage again wasn't likely to generate anything new. What was that old chestnut? If you always do what you always did, you'll always get what you always got. The trick here was to get something new: not just attention, but action.

Hood sat straighter, the effort clearly causing him pain. "We're overthinking this, boys. What if we just do what I said? What if we just took back the shelter?"

Much perked up. "What do you mean?"

Hood turned. "I mean, we walk in and take it back. Tuck has the key, right?"

Tuck nodded.

"He lets us in. We keep them out."

Rojo bounced on his heels. "Yeah. Yeah. We shelter in place. Make them come to us."

"You're talking about a sit-in." John's voice stayed neutral, but the spark in his eyes betrayed his interest.

Tuck remained cautious. "No, he's talking about an occupation."

Hood nodded. "Damn straight."

"Um . . ." Dale scrolled through the auction announcement. "I don't mean to rain on anyone's parade, but there's only five of you and the shelter is thousands of square feet. How are you going to lock down and defend that building all by yourselves?"

The room fell silent again, but Dale could practically hear the whirring of the Merry Men's brains. Each one had pursed lips or creased brows or both.

John answered first. "We don't. The shelter is important to a lot of people. We find the people who stayed there, like Calvin. We get them to help us."

Hood pursed his lips. "That's not a bad idea."

Much looked down at Jenny's teddy bear with worry. "But they're civilians. We're supposed to protect them. We can't put them in danger like that."

The room fell silent, Much's point having hit its mark.

Dale closed his laptop. "I don't think they're talking about using your friends as human shields, kid. More like, asking for volunteers. Only those who want to be there and who understand the dangers. Okay?"

Much nodded. Soon the rest of the Merry Men were nodding too.

"All right, then," Hood said, "Tuck and Much, you visit the parking lots and recruit. Red, John, we need a battle plan. Tomorrow, gentlemen, the occupation begins."

CHAPTER THIRTY-ONE

Tuck turned the key in the lock and pulled open the shelter's back door. A stale, musty smell slapped him in the face, knocking him back a couple of steps, right into Much. They both watched cautiously as Hood, Rojo, and Dale slipped past them into the building, but the smell didn't seem to faze the others at all.

John brought up the rear, stopping to pull out the key and hand it to Tuck. "You'll need this."

Tuck accepted the key, wrapping his hand around it like a child clutching a favorite candy. "Be safe."

John put his hands on Much's and Tuck's shoulders. "You, too, my friends, you too." Then he ducked inside to join the others, Much's "See you soon" following him down the hall. A moment or two later, Dale's rental car rumbled back to life and back into the streets.

The sound of the car engine had barely faded when a giant scraping sound—not all that different from nails on a chalkboard—echoed through the empty shelter building. John followed the sound to the main hall, where Rojo pushed one of the bunkbeds toward the dining area. The big man grabbed the other end and pulled. "Where we taking this?"

"To blockade the front door."

"We'll need to block the windows, too."

Rojo waved toward the hallway behind him. "There's plenty more where this came from."

"A few more wouldn't hurt. Where's Hood?"

Rojo took a breath of hesitation.

John stopped pulling. "What?"

Rojo bit his lip.

John peered around the beds. "What?"

Rojo stepped around. "He's in the kitchen with Dale. 'Setting up HQ,' he said."

"And?"

"And he don't look good, John. His breathing isn't right. He's still got that cough. He can't stand straight for very long, and he looks . . . gray."

"Did you ask him about it?"

Rojo snorted. "He told me to mind my own business. It was like he wanted to start something."

"So he's feeling like himself?"

Rojo gave a reluctant smile. "Yeah, I guess he is. But there's no way he's strong enough for a fight—or moving furniture. As much as I hate to even think it, he really needs to be back in the hospital."

The two resumed dragging the bunkbed toward the shelter's front door, but Rojo's words planted themselves in John's mind. Hood put up a good front—he always had—but now his mask was webbed with cracks. It had been since before he ditched the hospital. Maybe even longer. Maybe that's why he left against doctor's orders in the first place—some kind of death wish. John wasn't the only one who saw Hood's fragility, either. The others were seeing it, too. The question was, did Hood see it? Did he care? Or would he stay in denial until his last breath?

John refused to answer his own questions, choosing instead his own denial. He and Rojo slid the bunkbed into place with a bang and started back for another, the sound of their footsteps filling the large empty front room. They moved beds in front of two shelter windows in thoughtful but companionable silence, while Hood and Dale remained in the kitchen headquarters, whatever that meant. What the hell could they be doing in there?

John shook off the thought as he and Rojo maneuvered the next bed through the doorway of the men's dorm and down the hall. They rounded the corner into the main room.

"Lemme give you a hand with that," said a vaguely familiar voice at John's back.

John turned to find Calvin the Plumber.

"Ran into your boy Much and the reverend. They told me what you was planning. I'm here to enlist," Calvin finished with a salute.

Rojo jogged around the bed and offered Calvin his hand. "Good to have you, man."

Calvin turned to John. "I got some bad news, too. About Sadie." He leaned forward, speaking so softly that John could barely make out the words.

John sighed. Just when he thought things couldn't get worse. He shook hands with Calvin, then left him with Rojo to finish maneuvering the bed into place, blocking the last of the shelter windows. Time to see what Hood and that reporter were up to and deliver the news about Sadie.

Dale turned up in Tuck's office, cell phone plastered to his ear. John listened at the door a few moments, long enough to deduce that Dale was calling in tips to various news outlets. Good. They needed the publicity. Without the attention, the police would be able to do whatever they wanted without any consequences whatsoever. It would be a bloodbath. The police in Sherwood generally did what they wanted anyway, but this time, there might be cameras to bear witness. Not that having a witness had helped when Dubrowski and his buddy beat Hood to a bloody pulp.

Assured of Dale's loyalty, John concentrated on Hood—the least solid variable in this equation, thanks to his questionable health and loose cannon nature. He found the loose cannon in the kitchen, as expected, and leaning into the bottom shelf of the pantry—which he did not expect.

"Whatcha looking for, Rob?"

"Where do ya think Tuck keeps the booze?" Hood's voice echoed in the empty pantry.

John pulled Hood up by the shirt. "There's no booze here, Rob. Besides, we need you sober if this has any chance of working. This was your idea, after all.

"And I need you to hear this." He put steadying hands on Hood's shoulders and took a deep breath. "It's Sadie. She was found in the park, under a bench. She's dead, Rob."

Hood stood stock still, hurt radiating out of every pore. "You're sure?"

John nodded.

Hood slammed the pantry door shut. "What the fuck was she doing in the park? We got her into that pop-up shelter at the Baptist church."

"They found her flask. They threw her out." John stepped back, waiting for the explosion.

Hood spit on the ground. "Those *bastards*. Sending an old lady to her death because she took a nip every now and then. As if they didn't ever take a tipple themselves. I bet they can't even watch a football game without a beer in their hands.

"But why was she in the park? Why didn't she go back to her bus stop? Or find a storefront?"

John broke the latest news, the gut punch that Calvin had whispered in confidence. The city had started laying spikes in storefronts at night, specifically to prevent people from seeking shelter there. The bus stops were no better. Not just Sadie's. All of them. Not only had the benches had been replaced, the bottom panels of the shelters had been removed too, leaving no protection for anyone sleeping on the ground. If John hadn't thought of Gibson's campaign as a war on homelessness before, he sure as hell did now.

Hood stared daggers, giving off waves of anger. John didn't blink. The men stared at each other in silence, the only sounds in John's ears his own heartbeat and Hood's wheezing, which grew increasingly labored. About the time John's eyes felt dry and shriveled, Hood stomped and spun around, right into a wobble. John reached to steady his friend.

Hood ran out of air. His whole body deflated. He managed a deep wheeze. "Help me find some aspirin, man. My head is killing me."

"Try my desk." Tuck stood in the doorway, silhouette after silhouette filing past behind him. "There might be one or two stuck in the back of a drawer."

Hood shuffled past John. As he pushed past Tuck, he muttered, "What? No AA meeting?"

"Not this time," Tuck shot back with a smile. He turned to John, stood straight, and clicked his heels. Behind him, the line of people continued to move. "The cavalry has arrived. Sir."

"Holy shit, Tuck." John couldn't believe what he was seeing. The line kept going: men, women, young, old. Over Tuck's head, he caught sight of Allan Dale in the office doorway. He, too, seemed mesmerized by the new arrivals. Where had they all come from? They couldn't all be Sherwood homeless.

Could they?

John made eye contact with Tuck. "Who are they? Where did they come from?"

Tears filled Tuck's eyes. "They didn't think twice. Not a one. They all wanted to come here. To come home. That's what they called it. *Home.*" Tuck sniffled and shook his head. "Home. This place. Can you believe it?"

John studied his friend. Saw Tuck as the young Marine who'd marched by his side in Basic. Saw the young comrade who'd slogged through mud and muck and gunfire with him. Saw the young man with the old eyes when they were sent home. Saw the broken man trying to reconcile his soldiering with his faith. Saw the pastor who pointed Rojo and Much in Hood's direction. Saw the friend who never gave up on him or Hood or the boys. Saw the closest thing to home he'd ever felt.

A lump in his throat, he pulled Tuck into a hug—a real one. "Yeah, man. All day long."

Released from John's hug, Tuck continued his answer, the voice no less incredulous than before.

"We found a group camped out at the House & Home. They got in their cars and went around to the pop-up shelters, the bus stops, the parks, anywhere they could think of, to round up the others. It was . . ." Tuck shook his head and shrugged. "I don't know the word. A miracle, I guess."

John kept his tone all business so he didn't fall into the same emotional abyss. "Let's get everyone up to speed." He waved Dale to join them, and the three men followed the last arrivals into the main room.

The sight of the crowded room knocked John back two steps. A quick headcount estimated nearly 200 people crammed into what usually felt like a large room. Now it seemed more like a closet—and smelled like a forgotten gym sock. The smell, John could shrug off. He was sure he didn't smell much better. But the size of the crowd—he would never get over that.

Everyone's attention was on the front of the room, where Rojo, Calvin, and Much stood framed by the bunkbed bunkers.

"Rev!" Calvin called. "This is your show. How about a few words?"

Tuck stepped through and over the crowd. Standing there next to the boys, he suddenly looked old. John saw wrinkles and gray hair he never noticed before, a tiredness in Tuck's eyes and posture. If they didn't save this shelter, they might not be able to save Tuck.

"I cannot thank y'all enough for coming." Tuck marched back and forth in front of his audience, hands clasped behind his back. "I can't deny it. It broke my heart when we were kicked out of this building. When I heard Kingston Enterprises wanted to buy it and turn it into expensive condos, it nearly broke my spirit. But these boys," he reached for Rojo and Much, "these boys insisted we fight. They restored my spirit with their fervor and determination.

"And you." Tuck swallowed hard. "Look at all of you. Your presence, your devotion, your belief in me and in this place—well, you are nothing short of a miracle. You've restored my faith, not just in God, but in my fellow man. They say God helps those who help themselves. If that is true, then God will surely be helping us as we take back what is ours, as we take back our home." Tuck choked on that last word, clearly still struggling with the idea that this temporary way place meant something permanent to so many.

The crowd's cheers, hoots, and hollers were deafening, their whistles sharp and shrill. The longer and louder the noise, the taller Tuck stood. John smiled and joined the applause. Tuck deserved every moment.

Hood appeared at John's side and gave a nod in Tuck's direction. Except it must have been directed at Much, because it was the younger man who reached into his backpack and pulled out two cans of spray paint—seemingly, the same cans they'd used to tag Kingston's offices and the Veterans' Walk. Much tossed one to Rojo, and the two boys stalked toward the back door.

Tuck looked at the boys and then at Hood.

"It's time to stake our claim," Hood announced. "It's time to declare war."

CHAPTER THIRTY-TWO

So this is what a war zone looks like, Mary Ann thought. The scene at the shelter looked like images she'd seen on television, but it felt so much worse. She stood behind the police lines, next to the RV that served as the command center, her arms wrapped around her midsection, her belly empty with fear, her body cold with worry.

Somewhere in the organized chaos surrounding her, her husband conferred with the Sherwood Police and Nottingham County Sheriff. Her attention, her focus, her worry remained on the shelter and the people inside. On one man, in particular.

Gary had told her to stay home, begged her not to get involved. But how could she possibly stay away? This shelter was her life as much as it was Tuck's. Gary had tried telling her there was nothing to worry about. "A minor incident," he called it. She looked around. What a bald-faced lie.

Then again, they'd hardly said three words to each other since her tongue-lashing in his office, months of polite small talk that barely covered the cracks in their marriage. Cracks that only widened when he told lies like this one.

She read the scrawled messages on the shelter windows over and over, repeating them like a mantra: HOME, SWEET HOME. THERE'S NO PLACE LIKE

HOME. WE WILL NOT BE MOVED. The writing was unfamiliar, but not the sentiments. Not the desperation they represented. It all seemed so obvious now. How had she missed it?

She felt someone standing at her shoulder, but her gaze didn't waver from the shelter. She couldn't make out the words of the voice behind her. She started at the touch of a hand on her arm.

"Honey?"

Mary Ann turned. Gary stood behind her, his brow creased with worry. Maybe his lie had been meant to comfort himself. His hand stayed on her arm, not gripping it but resting on it, as if he wanted to be sure of her. "I'm not leaving," she told him, her voice wobbly but firm.

"I know." He dropped his hand and sighed. "I'm not happy about it, but I know." Rocking back on his heels, he shoved his hands in his pockets—a gesture Mary Ann knew all too well. "And since you're here, maybe you could help us out."

Of course. "Help you out? What does that mean exactly?"

"You know the shelter—"

Mary Ann shook her head and took a step back. "No. I will not help you break in. I will not draw you a floor plan. I will not do anything that will help you hurt those people, help you hurt my friends. I will not put them in danger in any way. I won't."

Gary didn't blink, didn't react at all, except to say in a calm, professional tone, "We're not there yet. Right now, we just want to make contact. To talk. But we're not getting any answer."

"Talk? Like your officers 'talked' with Rob?"

"I told you, that was unsanctioned and the people responsible have been punished."

Mary Ann snorted her disbelief. "What exactly do you want from me?"

He waved over an officer. Mary Ann recognized him, one of Gary's cronies. His name escaped her, but she thought maybe it started with D. Duggan? Dunbar? Dub-something? Whatever he was called, he set her teeth on edge, plunged a steel rod down her spine, filled her bones with dread.

Gary held up a megaphone he'd gotten from the officer. "Help us make contact. Just get someone to pick up the phone inside. We'll do the rest."

The rest? Mary Ann's eyes widened. Her breath fell short.

"The rest, not the worst." He gestured toward the command center. "We have a trained negotiator standing by. Okay?"

Mary Ann sniffed back the worry that had been climbing up her throat. She put on a mask of neutrality. Acknowledging Gary with a nod, she took the megaphone. She made her way to the front line, weaving through cars and people, her way lit by the flashing lights of the emergency vehicles.

She stood between two police cars, leaning against the bumper of one for support. She stared at the megaphone in her hands, searching for words—any words—among the muddled worries that swirled through her mind.

She raised the megaphone to her mouth, squeezed the button, and released it. She raised the megaphone again and dropped it. She blew out her breath and brought up the megaphone one more time. She pressed the button on the handle.

"Tuck?" She jumped at the sound of her own voice. What she'd spoken as a whisper reverberated across the parking lot. "Tuck? It's Mary Ann. Can you hear me?"

Stupid woman. Of course, he can hear you. Every damn person in the whole of Nottingham County can hear you.

She squinted at the shelter windows, hoping for movement, a wave, a signal. "Tuck? Are you in there? Answer the phone. Please."

Mary Ann looked back over her shoulder, searching for Gary in the crowd. She found him next to the command center, watching her, a stern, willful look on his face. She held her hands in the universal "What now?" gesture. He waved her back.

Having returned the megaphone, she started back toward her original vantage spot when her cellphone vibrated in her pocket. She hunched over the screen. She didn't recognize the number, and the area code wasn't local. Telemarketers had the worst timing. With a muttered curse, she declined the call.

A moment later, her phone pinged with a text alert.

The message was short and sweet: REVEREND TUCKER SENT ME.

The phone rang again, the same long distance number as before. This time, she accepted the call. Plugging her right ear, she brought the phone to her left. "Hello?"

"Mary Ann Gibson?" The voice was faint but clearly male. Harder than Tuck's, softer than Rob's.

She looked over her shoulder before answering. "Yes. Who is this?"

"My name is Allan Dale. I'm a reporter. Can you talk?"

"Can I . . .?" Mary Ann spun around. She was surrounded by first responders, emergency vehicles, and a growing number of camera crews and gawkers. "No," she hissed. "I cannot talk. I'm kind of in the middle of something right now."

"The stand-off at the shelter."

"How do you know that?"

"I'm inside, in the shelter office. I heard you on the megaphone."

Mary Ann swiveled her head around one more time. "What in God's name is going on in there?"

Something slammed behind her. Gary's crony stormed out of the command center, followed quickly by Gary himself and a man Mary Ann assumed was the negotiator. That could not be a good sign.

She returned her attention to the phone. "Let me talk to Tu—Reverend Tucker." Gary and his companions huddled at the horizon of the chaos, joined by Bruce Kingston and his damn embroidered-crown scarf. The hairs on the back of Mary Ann's neck stood at attention. "NOW."

Unintelligible whispers and scratching and scrambling and then, finally, Tuck's voice. "Mary Ann?"

Her words tumbled out faster than she could control them. "Tuck? Are you all right? What the hell are you doing? For God's sake, have you lost your mind?"

"My mind? No. But I lost everything else.

Everything that mattered. I—we—couldn't let them take this, too." Tuck paused. "We just hadn't planned on the big guns."

"We? Who's *we*?" No sooner had she finished the question than it hit her. Who else would *we* be? She heard a familiar rough voice shouting in the background, something about the damn sheriff and hell, and then cheers. Lots of them. That explained Gary's mood—and tightened Mary Ann's already-knotted insides. *Damn it, Rob.*

"Tuck, you've got to answer the phone. You've got to talk to the negotiator. It has to be you." Mary Ann couldn't keep the pleading out of her voice. "You can't leave it to Rob. I love him, you know I do, but he's too angry. He doesn't know how to listen, how to give and take. He's all piss and vinegar, and this situation calls for honey. Lots of it."

Tuck huffed. "Rob's not the only one full of piss and vinegar, Mary Ann. We all are. I love you and all that you did for me, for us, for this place, but I am plumb out of honey. Besides . . . No, never mind."

"Never mind what? Besides what? Don't stop talking now."

"Please don't take this the wrong way, but this is at your husband's feet. All of it. He's the one who closed down the shelter. He's the one who issued the orders. He's the one in cahoots with Kingston."

Mary Ann's gaze flicked back to the edge of the parking lot, where Gibson and Kingston were conferring. The picture of cahoots if she ever saw it.

"I was stupid not to see it," Tuck continued. "I was stupid not to say anything. Your husband the mayor criminalized homelessness in this town, he tried to erase us and the people we serve, the people we *did* serve, and these are the consequences. We're not going down without a fight."

Tuck's speech echoed in Mary Ann's head. He had always been the dove to Rob's hawk, he and John both, and now that had changed. As much as she wanted to blame Kingston for bringing out Gary's worst, she knew Tuck was right. The blame sat squarely at Gary's feet. For the benches. For the panhandling law. For the shelter. For Hood's beating. For all of it.

And she hated herself for that.

A horn sounded; an engine rumbled. A SWAT van rolled into the scene.

No. That couldn't be.

Things were escalating way too fast. There hadn't been a single conversation with the negotiator. This couldn't be standing operating procedure. It couldn't.

"Tuck, I'm not joking. SWAT is here. Get on the damn phone with the negotiator before Rob gets you all killed." Mary Ann choked on the last word. She punched the End Call button and blinked up at the sky. The clear sky with its pristine stars. How could the sky be so clear when the ground was so murky?

Everything tilted. Mary Ann reached for the nearest stable object and found herself leaning against a Nottingham County Sheriff's cruiser. She bent over and clutched her stomach, gasping for air as she slid to the ground.

"Ma'am? Ma'am, are you all right?" A young man in a sheriff's uniform peered into her face, a concerned hand on her shoulder.

Mary Ann managed a nod, and he helped her to her

feet. "Let's get you some water." He guided her toward the rear of his vehicle. "My name's Freed, by the way."

"Mary Ann Gibson."

Freed lifted the trunk and yanked a bottled water out of a case of them. Nestled next to the case were folded blankets and a box of protein bars. "Any relation to the mayor?"

"His wife." Mary Ann gestured at the trunk. "What's all this?"

"Oh, that. For emergencies. I hand them out to the homeless."

"That's illegal, you know," she scoffed.

Freed smiled. "Not outside Sherwood, it's not."

Mary Ann's heart did a pirouette. She reached for Freed's arm. "Deputy Freed, may I ask you something?"

"Sure."

They watched Gary, Bruce Kingston, and the others hop up the steps into the command center.

She waved at the scene. "All this. Does this seem normal to you? Is this how these situations are supposed to go?"

Freed studied her face. She recognized the questioning look. "You can trust me. I work at that shelter. I helped set it up. Those are my friends in there. My . . . family." She realized the truth of her words as she spoke them. Tuck, Rob, John—they *were* her family. Even the boys, she'd begun thinking of as her own. They were more her family than Gary had been, especially in recent days. It just took her too long to see it.

Freed relaxed, but only slightly. He frowned and

shook his head. "No, ma'am. This is not at all how it should be. There are protocols for situations like this, and they're not following them."

"They? Not we?"

"Yes, ma'am. *They.* The Sherwood Police Department. This is their scene. They're the ones in charge. We're only here for backup."

No, they're not the ones in charge. They just think they are, Mary Ann realized, remembering Gary and Bruce Kingston with their heads bent in conversation. She opened her mouth to speak, and the world exploded.

CHAPTER THIRTY-THREE

The bang at the back door came a split second before the crash at the front, booms that sounded like IEDs. Then came the flash. Rojo hit the floor, finding not the warm sand of Iraq but cold hard linoleum. *What the hell?*

The screams—male, female, young, old, all jumbled together—pulled Rojo back into the moment, wrapping him in a king-sized quilt of panic. Bodies rushed around him, running, diving, dodging for cover. His heart pounded, his muscles tensed, his senses sharpened. This was a firefight. His body knew exactly what to do. His hand reached for his weapon— and found nothing.

Voices shouted orders. Lines of dark uniformed figures moved along the walls. More scurrying in the room's middle, people desperate for safety with no idea how or where to find it.

A young woman ran in front of Rojo and stopped short, her eyes wide and disoriented, a rabbit paralyzed with fear. He reached out, placing his hand on her arm. "Do what they say," he said. "You'll be fine." He let her go with a nod.

Rojo looked to his left to see Calvin the Plumber also frozen, another frightened rabbit. Beyond him stood Much, his body—like Rojo's—tensed and ready. But ready for what? The invaders had weapons—rifles, tear gas, flash bangs, who knew what else. Rojo and Much had . . . their hands.

They needed John. They needed Hood. They needed a plan.

Rojo signaled Much. *Move to the back.*

Much nodded, grabbed Calvin by the collar, and ducked. Crouching low, he moved into the crowd and started toward the office—the last known whereabouts of their leader. Rojo did the same.

The invaders' shouts carried over the cries of the frightened civilians. "Freeze!" "Get down!" "Don't move!" "Down! Down! Down!"

Rojo kept moving, winding through the chaos of the panicked crowd, avoiding the uniformed invaders on the crowd's edges. Much did the same, dragging a fearful Calvin behind him. Rojo sensed rather than saw the invaders communicating with their own hand signals. He felt them fall in line behind him and Much. Seemed everyone wanted to find Robert Hood.

They reached the back hall, lit only by the broken-in door at the rear of the shelter. They needed to find Hood and lose their tail. Best way to do that was to split up.

Rojo caught Much's eye, used his hands to signal his plan. He counted down with fingers: *three . . . two . . . one.* Much and Calvin dove right into the kitchen as he broke left into the office and slammed the door behind him. Seconds later, another slam echoed from the kitchen. Much and Calvin had landed in their bolt hole.

With the door shut and window boarded over, the office was pitch black. Sounds of heavy breathing—not just Rojo's—filled the darkness.

"Who's there?" Rojo whispered.

"Red? That you?" Hood's hoarse voice came from Rojo's right.

"Yeah, Boss."

"What's going on out there?"

"Hell's broken loose, sir. Infiltration from forward and the rear, converging on this position. Much and Calvin holed up in the kitchen. Panicked civilians scattering for cover. What's going on in here?"

John answered. "Not a damn thing. We're keeping our heads down, waiting for the cavalry."

"That would be you, by the way." Tuck's shaky voice came from across the room. "What about everyone else? Anyone hurt? Anyone—"

"Dead?" Rojo finished for him. "I don't think so, but I can't say for sure. I couldn't see much, Rev. Just a lot of scared people running in circles. Sorry."

Dale's baritone came from Tuck's direction. "The best way to help them is to end this. Peacefully. What set them off, anyway? This sure as hell wasn't SOP."

"Naw," Hood growled. "This is personal. Bet our friend the sheriff and his lapdog Dubrowski are behind the whole thing. Those bastards killed Sadie and now they're tryin' to kill us."

"Sheriff?" Dale asked.

Tuck clarified. "Mayor Gibson."

Boots stomped down the hallway, stopping outside the door. Muffled screams and cries filled the vacuum. The air in the room changed, charged with electric tension.

Rojo turned in Hood's direction. "What do we do now, Boss?"

Rojo's question hung thick in the air, propped up by the sounds of fear and panic outside.

"Boss?"

"Shhh. We keep jabbering, we're dead." Hood's voice was quiet but sharp. Then silence.

For a second, all Rojo heard was the breathing of the others in the room and the pounding of his own heart.

Then the door burst open.

The force knocked Rojo to the floor. The invaders swept the room, the lights on their weapons creating a strobe effect. One flash revealed Tuck and Dale standing with their hands up. Another, John backed against the bookcase, his arms also raised in surrender. Then movement from Rojo's right and a light in his eyes, blinding him to anything beyond.

"FREEZE!" The sturdy voice came from behind the light. What else was going on? Rojo couldn't see, but he could hear shuffling and movement. Then the unmistakable sound of someone falling or banging into furniture.

Rojo started in that direction.

"I SAID DON'T MOVE."

Rojo raised his hands. "My friend, is he hurt? John, are you okay?"

No answer from John's direction but a low groan. Rojo took another step.

The invader stepped closer, close enough that Rojo could see the weapon's muzzle, right at eye level. If the room had been brighter, he'd have a clear view right down the barrel. Two words filled Rojo's head: *Oh, shit*.

A silhouette launched from a crouched position

with a howl full of rage and pain. The figure tackled the invader facing down Rojo and knocked him to the floor.

The lights focused on the tussle: Hood pinning the intruder down, wrestling to get control of the gun. A chorus of shouts, ordering Hood to stand down, release the weapon, put his hands up. Hood did none of the above.

Rojo could see John, Tuck, and Dale in the shadows. They appeared to be shouting, too, but their voices were drowned out by the yelled commands of the SWAT team. The scuffle on the ground continued, neither Hood nor his prey gaining any advantage. The shouts grew louder. Rojo's ears rang from the tumult.

A whoosh of movement caught Rojo's attention. Much and Calvin stood in the doorway, mouths agape. Much grasped the situation first and added his shouts to the chaos, pausing only long enough to pull Rojo clear of the kerfuffle.

Rojo turned in time to see one of the invaders raise his weapon and bring its butt down on Hood's head. Light strobed as weapons moved, making the attack on Hood appear in slow motion. Rifle butts and heavy boots landed on the old man, who barely managed to hold up one arm in meager protection.

A lantern shined through the doorway, a large figure silhouetted behind it. "That's enough, boys." Dubrowski's voice boomed with authority. As the team stood back, he took stock of Hood's limp, lifeless body with smug satisfaction. "Mission accomplished."

June

Her last shirt stowed in the suitcase, Mary Ann stopped and let her head hang. She should be crying, shouldn't she? After all, the last twenty-six years of her life have boiled down to what fit in this one bag. That should provoke some reaction. So why did she feel . . . nothing? Numb. Empty. Where was her anger? Her grief? Her . . . anything?

Her gaze found the newspaper she'd thrown on the bed. SHERWOOD MAYOR UNDER INVESTIGATION, the headline proclaimed. She'd carried that paper with her for more than a week. A few days later, another headline had blared SHERWOOD CORRUPTION SCANDAL GROWS. She hadn't kept that one. Side-by-side portraits of Gary and Bruce Kingston accompanied the article.

In its own way, that first paper had served as both a prod and a security blanket. She hadn't spoken to Gary since that night at the shelter, when she saw Rob wheeled out on a gurney and turned on her husband with the fury of a wildcat. Whatever the investigation revealed about Gary's shenanigans as mayor, he would never face charges for murder. Attempted murder. Rob wasn't dead—yet—but it wasn't for lack of trying. And Gary Gibson was guilty as sin. Mary Ann knew that to the very core of her being. He may not have swung the gun that knocked Rob unconscious, but he orchestrated the events that led to it. That was the one thing she remained certain of in her world-turned-upside-down.

She kicked herself for not accepting that truth earlier. So many people she trusted had tried to tell her: Tuck, John, the boys. But she never listened. Maybe if she had . . .

No, she couldn't go there.

She clicked her suitcase shut, stuffed the newspaper into the bag's zippered pocket, and hauled the luggage off the bed. She glanced around the bedroom, a room that was once her sanctuary but now felt like a hotel. Her framed wedding photo poked out of the top of the trash bin. There was nothing left here that she wanted. Even her memories—happy, sad, and in between—felt tainted. Sure, there was a chance she would change her mind, but that chance was, as Beverly might say, somewhere between slim and none.

What she really needed, and had needed for a while but refused to see, was *out*. She could never share Gary's bed again. Never live under the same roof. Maybe someday she'd be able to look him in the eyes without wanting to stab him with a rusty serrated knife, but that day remained far beyond the horizon.

She dropped her keys on the kitchen counter and pulled the door shut with a satisfying *thud*. She hadn't so much kicked Gary out that night as refused him entry. She'd been so determined to keep the house and make him start anew, make *him* know what is was like to be homeless, but endless nights wandering the empty rooms changed her mind. He could have the damn house. It had been a bribe, anyway, one of those grand gestures he called love but were really meant to buy her loyalty and affection. Like her car. Like the mahogany dining set. Like the kitchen backsplash. God, she'd been so blind.

Now that she could see, she preferred to have her freedom. She needed her freedom. Pulling out of the driveway and onto the street, she resisted the urge to slow down and look back.

Mary Ann's turn into the shelter parking lot filled her with an odd sense of light and hope. Shadows still hung here, echoes of the chaos and trauma of the epic showdown that had filled even national news broadcasts. Those shadows, though, were fading in the hustle of movement that now filled the place. Everywhere Mary Ann looked, someone was doing something to restore the shelter.

Calvin and a workboot-clad man were prying plywood off the front windows. The boards had gone up within hours of the SWAT take-down, as if the powers that be wanted to hide the crime scene from the world. One of the boards popped loose, and Calvin and his partner lowered it carefully to the ground. Through the gap where there had once been glass, Mary Ann could see at least three different women with brooms, sweeping glass shards and other detritus from the floor of the main room.

Patricia stood at the corner of the building, her back to the parking lot, waving her arms as if directing traffic. Mary Ann couldn't suppress her grin.

Nurturing Patricia, who acted like everyone's mother, now acting like she was born to be Queen Bee. She greeted Mary Ann with a hug and stepped back to give her friend the once-over. "How are you, dear?"

Mary Ann shrugged. "Hanging in there. It feels better when I have something to do."

"Well, we've got plenty of that." Patricia smiled as she slid her arm around Mary Ann's waist.

A horn honked behind them. They turned and watched a beat-up blue pickup truck bounce across the parking lot then lurch to a stop in front of them. Mary Ann couldn't stop the lump from lodging in her throat when she saw Bernie step out of the cab. She clapped her hands in delight. She and Patricia rushed to give him welcoming hugs.

Bernie pulled away, a deep blush staining his cheeks. "Now, now, ladies. Enough of that."

Mary Ann wiped away a tear. "We're just overjoyed you're free."

"Yeah, well, with those town ordinances overturned, they didn't have any grounds to sustain the charges. My fines were dismissed, and I was freed with the deepest apologies of the people of the state of Illinois. Whatever that means." It was clear by the break in Bernie's voice that he knew exactly what that meant and was overcome at his good fortune.

Mary Ann gestured at the bags and boxes in the bed of the truck. "And you got your job back."

Bernie kicked at an imaginary pebble. "Not exactly. Chicken Shack wouldn't take me back. Said I'd tarnished their image. They offered their deepest apologies, too."

Mary Ann saw her own grimace reflected on Patricia's face. Patricia began to sputter, stopped only by Bernie's raised hand.

"Not to worry, though. Luciano's snapped me up.

Called me a folk hero, if you can believe it. Said they'd be 'honored to have me in their employ.' They're really good people, Mr. and Mrs. Luciano." Bernie thumbed at the piles of boxes and bags in the back of his cab. "Mr. Lu even sent me here with all this grub—pizzas, pastas, garlic bread, salad. The works. Got a place we can set it all up?"

Mary Ann threw her arms around Bernie and let out a whoop that became a small sob. She stepped back and, with a sniffle and an embarrassed smile, looped her arm through Bernie's and led him off with a skip in her step. "Let's go find out."

They left Patricia directing traffic once again and made their way past piles of rubble and into the shelter. Mary Ann directed Bernie to the kitchen, where the Armchair Angels were doing yeoman's work restoring order and restocking shelves. She followed the stacks of unopened boxes to Tuck's office. The books had been restored to their shelves, but the room still had an air of chaos about it. Remnants of crime scene tape hung from the doorframe. The chairs were upright but set at haphazard angles rather than their usual position parallel to the desk. The monitor of Tuck's computer sat at a right angle, facing the bookcases instead of Tuck, whose attention was on the mountain of envelopes that overwhelmed the top of his desk. His expression was one of disbelief and amazement, a relief to Mary Ann after seeing Tuck eaten away by worry the last few months. She'd expected to find ghosts in here, the place where it happened, but seeing Tuck like this was so much better.

"Good news?" she asked.

"Mary Ann!" Tuck sprang from his chair and leaped across the room to give Mary Ann a hug. "I wasn't expecting to see you. I thought you'd be—"

"In jail for killing my husband?"

Tuck gave her a scolding expression. "At the hospital. Looking for an apartment. Submitting job applications. Certainly not at the scene of the crime."

Mary Ann couldn't meet Tuck's eyes. Looking anywhere except at him, her gaze landed on the newspaper peeking out from under the pile of envelopes. SHERWOOD MAYOR INDICTED, the headline declared. A closer look revealed yesterday's date in the masthead. There was some justice left in the world, after all. Well, maybe not justice. Justice would mean punishment for Hood's condition. But this, this was at least accountability, and that was something.

With a nod at the big bold type, Mary Ann said, "That's the crime scene, not here. Here . . ." She stopped, looked over her shoulder at the hubbub around them. "Here, there's life. Purpose. I . . . " She couldn't complete the sentence. Not out loud.

Tuck turned one of the chairs toward his desk and guided Mary Ann toward it. She fell into the seat and set her purse on her knees.

Tuck resumed his seat behind the desk. He pushed aside the heap of envelopes as if he were Moses parting the Red Sea and folded his hands in the middle of the split pile. "Do you want to talk about it?"

Talk about it? Mary Ann could barely *think* about it. She shook her head. But then her mouth betrayed her. "I used to be so good at it."

Seeing Tuck's querying expression, she sighed. "Starting over. It used to be so easy. Now . . ."

"We're older. Change is harder when you're older."

"That's supposed to help?" Mary Ann scolded herself for being so sharp. Tuck was only trying to offer comfort.

"No? How about this?" He picked up a handful of envelopes and let them rain on his desk like confetti. "Every one of these envelopes has a donation. They're from all over the country. There's even one from Australia. I've only gotten through a couple of handfuls, and we're already in the black! If there's just ten dollars in each of the rest of these envelopes . . ." His voice cracked. They both knew many of the envelopes would contain far more than ten dollars.

A lump of tears formed in Mary Ann's throat. She reached into her purse and pulled out her own envelope. Her own voice breaking too, she said, "Let me add one more to that pile."

Tuck pushed away her offering. "No. You've done—do—more than enough already. You need that money. Starting over, remember?"

With a snort, Mary Ann flashed Tuck a look of exasperation. "It's not my money." She slid the envelope in front of him and tapped the return address. "Look who it's from."

"The Riis Foundation?" Mary Ann could practically hear the gears turning in Tuck's head. She knew the pieces clicked into place when his expression brightened. With a gasp, he tore open the envelope. He moved his lips as he skimmed the letter, and Mary Ann followed along by reading his lips—even though she already had the letter memorized.

"We got the grant?" Tuck looked to Mary Ann for confirmation.

She nodded.

"We got the grant!" Tuck laughed, a deep belly laugh, and threw the letter and his arms up in the air. Mary Ann couldn't stop herself from grinning widely.

Tuck slammed his hands on the desk. "You know what this means, don't you?"

"What?"

"You can start over right here. I can even afford to pay you something semi-decent."

Mary Ann laughed and cried at the same time, her body a tangle of relief, excitement, overwhelm, and a half dozen other emotions she couldn't name if her life depended on it. Maybe starting over wasn't so impossible after all.

The phone on Tuck's desk rang. Mary Ann watched his face pale and his shoulders tighten as he listened through the receiver.

Tuck stood and replaced the phone in one motion. "We have to get to the hospital," he said, grabbing his coat from the tree. "Now."

Mary Ann followed without question.

CHAPTER THIRTY-FIVE

Allan Dale stood in the corner of the hospital room, a silent sentinel watching the Merry Men attempt to lure their fearless leader back from the depths of his coma. This afternoon, it was John in the bedside chair, a newspaper spread open on Hood's blanket. Rojo and Much leaned against the wall on the other side of the bed. Their gaze stayed focused on Hood, watching for even the slightest sign of life. Occasionally, though, they glanced at John. Something in their eyes made Dale think they were wishing magic into John's words, willing his voice to be the miracle tonic that saved Hood—just as John had saved Hood a million times before.

John's gaze, however, never left the paper in front of him. "Rob, you're gonna love this one!" John said with a false chuckle. "*Sherwood Mayor Facing Recall.* Sherwood mayor Gary Gibson is likely to be recalled in the upcoming election, thanks to the overwhelming support that put the recall issue on the ballot. Gibson, who was elected in November, overstepped the limits of his mayoral authority and did so almost immediately upon assuming office. The mayor lost public support when it was revealed that he rushed legislation before the town council and pushed that legislation through, denying the public a voice in the very body that was meant to represent them. Criminal charges have also been filed against the mayor, but the grand jury indictment is sealed."

Dale slipped out of the room. He didn't need to hear more. He knew what the article said—he wrote it. And watching Hood in his hospital bed hooked up to those machines . . . A man can stand playing vulture for only so long.

Dale reflexively exhaled when he stepped into the hallway. The tension eased out of his back and shoulders and a craving for coffee took its place. An army marches on its stomach, especially armies on extended campaigns like the Merry Men. Dale fingered the cash in his pocket; he had enough to at least provide some snacks. He turned toward the elevators.

He hadn't taken two steps before he saw Tuck and Mary Ann barreling down the hall, weaving through the carts and nurses and personnel that clogged their path. Everything about them screamed panic. Dale braced himself.

Mary Ann flew past him with a mere nod of acknowledgement. Tuck stopped, watched Mary Ann enter Hood's room, and swallowed hard. "How bad is it?"

Dale shook his head.

Tuck responded with a single nod. He swallowed hard again, sighed, and shuffled toward Hood's door with his head bowed.

Dale watched for a second, looked back at the elevators, and turned to follow Tuck. Bowing his head, he unconsciously mimicked the reverend's posture.

The arrangement of Hood's room had changed in Dale's short absence, but not the mood. Worry and expectation hung in the air, creating a pocket where time did not move, would not move, until Hood awoke—or worsened. Mary Ann now sat in the bedside chair, John's newspaper carelessly cast to the floor. With one hand, she held Hood's hand. With her other, she stroked his forehead. She spoke to her former lover, but too softly for Dale or anyone else to make out the words.

John leaned against the window on the wall behind Mary Ann, his gaze never wavering from the scene at the bed. Still, his posture spoke of nothing but resignation. Dale met John's eyes and gave the big man a sympathetic frown. John mustered a small grateful smile before returning his gaze to Hood's bedside.

The boys looked like hell warmed over, a million times worse than they'd looked when Dale had left the room moments ago. How was that possible? What could possibly drain their hope that quickly?

Dale put a hand on Much's shoulder and beckoned Rojo with a nod. "C'mon, boys, let's rustle up some grub. My treat."

The boys looked to Hood. They looked at each other, frozen and mute. They shook their heads.

A firm hand pushed Dale aside, and a nurse slid past him and the boys. Without a word or even an acknowledging glance, the nurse checked Hood's vitals and IV drip. Dale watched her reflection in the window by John. She was all business, but there was something about her stoic expression that made Dale think she was less than thrilled to have an audience supervising her. She stepped to the end of the bed, marked Hood's chart, and marched out of the room as efficiently and stoically as she entered. Every other nurse who had checked on Hood in Dale's presence had offered at least a smile of comfort.

Dale told himself that it might mean nothing at all. Maybe she was having a bad day. Maybe her feet hurt.

"Hell."

Everyone—well, everyone except Hood—swiveled their heads to look at Dale.

He waved them off. "Sorry, just thinking out loud." He grimaced. *God, that sounded callous.* "Going to get coffee. Be right back." Dale decided to buy a round for everyone anyway and started out of the room.

The groan stopped him in the doorway.

Dale whipped around. Everyone stared at Hood. Another groan—from Hood. He was awake! Or getting there. Dale signaled a nurse.

By the time the nurse scurried into the room, Hood was trying to open his eyes. Even that little movement, though, required a taxing effort.

Dale stepped forward, studying Hood carefully, hoping he was wrong about what he was seeing. Sure, Hood was regaining some semblance of consciousness, but there was no life in him. His eyes seemed dull. His skin faded, almost gray. It was not the look of a man coming back to life, but rather one headed in the opposite at direction.

One glance at Mary Ann told Dale that he wasn't wrong. While the others looked hopeful at Hood's rousing, Mary Ann looked weary and despondent. By the time Hood opened his eyes, though, she had put on a mask of hope and comfort.

"There you are," she said with a smile, her hand still grasping Hood's.

Much grabbed Hood's other hand. "Boss!"

"Took ya long enough." Rojo plopped his hand on Much's shoulder and gave their leader a grin.

Hood answered with a groan.

"Shhhh, don't talk," Mary Ann told him as she brushed his brow.

Tuck and John stood straighter, each man taking a step closer to Hood's bed. Their expressions were a balance of optimism and caution, as if they wanted to believe but were afraid to let themselves do so.

The nurse pushed the boys back from the bed. She took Hood's hand. "Welcome back," she said, her voice chipper but not enthusiastic. How many times had she said those exact words?

Moments later, a doctor swooped in—the same doctor who'd treated Hood for pneumonia a matter of weeks ago. A modicum of relief filled Dale's heart. The Merry Men—the boys, specifically—trusted this Dr. Araya. The truth would be easier to accept coming from him.

"Could you give us a minute?" The doc asked, holding his hand toward the door. The Merry Men obeyed without question. "You, too, ma'am."

With a reluctant sigh, Mary Ann released Hood's hand. "I'll be right back," she told him and kissed his forehead. She didn't take her eyes off him until she'd joined Dale and the others in the hallway.

Dale could hear the doctor and nurse conferring in mumbled tones. He couldn't make out the exact words, but he inferred the gist. His eyes met Mary Ann's. Her closed-lip smile was betrayed by the tears in her eyes.

Tuck put his arm around Mary Ann's shoulders.

The rest of the Merry Men shuffled aimlessly in silence. If they were this lost now, how much worse would they be after?

Araya slipped his hands into his lab coat pockets as he stepped out of the room. It was a gesture Dale recognized. It must be something doctors learned in med school: Have bad news? Put your hands in your pockets!

"Well, Doc? How is he?" Rojo and Much rushed to Araya's side. The others stepped closer, too, to hear the answer.

Araya shook his head. "It won't be long now."

Mary Ann sniffled. Tuck tightened his grip on her shoulder. She pulled away and flew back to Hood. Tuck ducked in behind her.

Rojo watched them enter the room. "There's gotta be something you can do."

John answered first. "I'm sure if there were, the doc would be doing it. Besides, Hood wouldn't want us to go to any trouble to keep him alive, no 'extraordinary means' or whatever it's called."

"How do you know?"

With a frown, John said, "Because this isn't our first rodeo. We've had that conversation, he and I. He wanted a DNR, so he's got one."

"Shit." Rojo stomped his foot and turned away.

"I don't understand." Much spoke to Araya, but his eyes followed Rojo. "Boss—I mean, Hood—woke up. That's good, right?"

"In a way. It gives him, and you, a chance to say goodbye. But you need to understand, he's not going to get well. His organs are shutting down. There's no reversing what's happening to him. It's a matter of time. Frankly, in my experience, there's not a lot of that left, either."

"But he woke up." Rojo's voice was forceful, as if being stubborn would change the facts. "He woke up!"

"Yes, he did." Araya kept his voice calm. He must have had this conversation dozens of times before, to be so unflappable in the face of such resistance. "But he didn't wake up because his body was healing."

Araya shifted his weight. "Think of it as a last hurrah. Many terminal patients rally right before they succumb. That's what's happening here."

The doctor pulled his hand out of his pocket and stepped away from the doorway. "You need to go and say whatever it is you need to say while your friend is still awake to hear it." Then he left them with a heartfelt, "I'm sorry."

The Merry Men stared after him, paralyzed by the news. John recovered first, pulling the boys by the sleeve. "Let's go, boys."

Dale trailed behind them into the room.

They found Hood in bed, a pile of blankets and pillows holding him upright. Mary Ann once again sat his side, clutching his hand. Tuck stood next to her, his hand resting on the top of Hood's pillow pile.

Hood gave them a wan smile. "Took ya long enough," he croaked.

"See?" Rojo said to Much. "I knew that doc—"

John cut Rojo off with a pointed finger. His eyes stayed on Hood. "What do you need, Rob?"

"Tuck?"

The reverend pushed his way to Hood's bedside and took his friend's hand. "Right here."

Hood took a couple of rattly breaths. "The shelter?"

"Safe. It's safe, Rob."

Hood gave a weak nod. "Good. John?"

"Yeah, man." John spoke quietly from his position behind Tuck.

Hood lifted his arm, with great effort, and pointed at the window. "Out," was all he could muster.

"No, Rob," Mary Ann said. "You need to be in bed."

"No." Hood's voice was barely a whisper, his breathing becoming erratic even with the oxygen tube. "I need—"

John stepped up. "He needs to be outside. It's where he's lived most of his life, Mary Ann. It's where he belongs. His life shouldn't end here, not in this . . . prison."

Mary Ann looked to Tuck, who nodded.

Hood nodded. "Please."

"But the doctors . . . You can't leave the hospital. They won't let you."

"Watch them try and stop us." Rojo pushed his way to Hood's bedside and reached for a wire connecting Hood to one of his many machines.

Mary Ann grabbed his arm. "Don't." They stared at each other briefly. Then Mary Ann blinked. With a sigh, she released Rojo. "Let me do it."

Rojo nodded and stepped back. The Merry Men watched Mary Ann disconnect Hood from each wire and tube, one by one, and then his IV. Dale watched the Merry Men, studied the reverence on their faces. No one seemed to notice the alarms that blared after each disconnection.

John slid forward and crouched. The crack of his

knees carried across the room. He maneuvered his arms under Hood as gently as he could and lifted his friend into his arms.

John carried Hood out of the room. Rojo and Much followed close behind. Tuck returned his arm to Mary Ann's shoulders; she laid her head on his. Dale brought up the rear.

Surprisingly, Rojo was right. No one interfered— though a couple of nurses tried. Dr. Araya stopped them with a wave of his hand and a shake of his head. After that, those in the hallway and the elevator and the hospital lobby all cleared a path. Others took places behind Dale in the procession.

Once outside, he watched as Dr. Araya, the nurse from earlier, and assorted hospital staff gathered around the Merry Men. John sat Hood against a tree and folded himself beside him.

Hood took John's hand. "Thank you, my friend."

Mary Ann dropped to Hood's other side.

"Promise me," Hood whispered.

Mary Ann bit back her tears. "Anything."

Hood spoke in gasps, struggling for a deep breath between each short sentence. "Bury me in open ground. Lay me facing west. Toward home."

Mary Ann nodded with a sniffle.

Then Hood slouched against John, his raspy breathing slowing until it stopped.

The minutes ticked by in silence. Finally, Tuck spoke. "Long live Robert Hood."

HOW TO HELP

Homeless Veterans

National Coalition for Homeless Veterans
https://nchv.org/

U.S. Vets
https://usvets.org/

Veterans Community Project
https://www.veteranscommunityproject.org/

Midwest Shelter for Homeless Veterans
https://www.helpaveteran.org/

Suburban Homelessness

National Alliance to End Homelessness
https://endhomelessness.org/

Housing Forward
https://www.housingforward.org/

Sarah's Circle
https://sarahs-circle.org/

Plus state and local organizations near you

ACKNOWLEDGEMENTS

Robert Hood started yapping at me to tell his story in 2013. It has taken me a little more than ten years to get it right, and as with any book, it took a village to make it happen. So many thanks to everyone who read the manuscript, whole or in part, at one point or another and who shared their feedback, including (but not limited to) Heidi Hewett, Larry Konn, Alice Voith, Sue Wells, Jeanmarie Dwyer-Wrigley, Melissa Amateis, Leah Rhyne, and Amy BA. Deep thanks, too, to my accountability squad, for their support and encouragement along the way: Mars D. Gill, Debra Klein, Helene Dunne, and Olga Tararukhina. And, of course, my editor, Julie Hutchings—the only person who can call me a monster and have it be a *good* thing—and my cover designer, Hannah Linder, who took my vision of the cover out of my head and made it real—thank you for your time and your talent.

ABOUT THE AUTHOR

Ilene Goldman lives and works in northern Illinois, where she is closely supervised by her two canine editorial assistants. She is the author of the Stephen King-inspired novella *Greeks Bearing Gifts*, and she has short stories in the anthologies *A Wink and a Smile* (Smoking Pen Press, 2018) and *ProleSCARYet* (Rad Flesh Press, 2021). You can find her on Instagram @ilenegoldwrites and the World Wide Web at www.ilenegoldman.com.